PRICK of the NEEDLE

PRICK *of the* NEEDLE

Above the Rain Collective
2022

Above the Rain Collective

abovetheraincollective@gmail.com

North Georgia, USA

Contributing Editor:

J.A. Sexton

Publisher's note:

ISBN: 978-1-7377970-2-9

First Printing March 2022

julietrose.author@gmail.com

authorjulietrose.com

Cover photograph, graphics and interior formatting by J.A. Sexton
Above the Rain logo artwork by Bee Freitag, text by Jack Freitag

To my best friend, Justin. Thank you for encouraging me to push myself, and believing I could do this.

Prologue

I n order to reduce recidivism, the likelihood of a released prisoner returning to that which incarcerated them in the first place, the state of Arizona implemented a program to work with inmates, and those post-release, to learn how to fight wildfires and manage land through mitigation for future fires. The program had shown success for the state and offered a way for low-risk inmates to reclaim their lives, much like the land they recover and protect. A second chance.

While the program and its success were a gold star for the state financially, the question remained. Who among those inmates should've been incarcerated in the first place? Whose lives were put at risk for crimes, which were truly the need for better programs, to begin with? Youth programs to support at-risk kids before they get drawn into a system of despair and retaliation. Programs for addicts before they turn to petty crime to pay for their addiction. Programs to lift people out of poverty through transportation and skills training. Free childcare for working parents. The list goes on.

The problem of life after incarceration exists, but more so life before incarceration. No one wants to be in prison in the first place. They want to be heard. They want to be respected and appreciated. They want to be safe. They want to have food in their bellies and a roof over their head. They want the work they do to be fairly paid, with the ability to move up. They want to not have the only way they feel good to be from a substance coursing through their veins. They want the cycle to stop long before the doors close, locking them in.

Of course, programs won't eliminate the need for prisons, but they'll greatly reduce it. By the time a person has gone before the judge and sentenced, they've been locked up inside already for the most part. They've given up on life, either by believing the only way to survive was through crime or by shutting down and giving in to the cycle.

Not everyone who commits a crime does drugs, and not everyone who does drugs is a criminal. Yet in the eyes of the system, they're one and the same, placed behind the same walls. Those who turn to drugs do it for many different reasons. Abuse, connection, release, loneliness, frustration, hope, companionship, emptiness. Like before, the list goes on. No one wants to be an addict any more than they want to sit behind bars. We all want to be part of something, to have our lives matter.

All children are born pure, with the trust the world they take their first breath in will care for and value them. Some are given that trust, others quickly learn they need to survive on their own. They all deserve to be treated like the delicate, intricate beings they are. Even some who are loved and told they matter, fight

• • • •

demons inside they can't run from. On the outside, their life was perfect... on the inside, a nightmare. So, they run to whatever gives them some relief. It's always temporary. The relief. Eventually, it wears off and the darkness creeps back in. It takes more sacrifice every time to regain the feeling of ease, of freedom from constriction. From the deep, endless hole. More use, more money, more isolation, more risk. No matter what they believe, it's the only way to get out and away. Just another hit, just a little more this time. Anything to be able to take a breath.

The reality is, no one wants to be trapped inside with the monsters.

•   •   •   •

Chapter One

"**M**ove your asses, now!" Wren yelled down the line. It'd been a long, hot summer and she couldn't wait to take all the gear off. They'd been working on mitigation most of the time, but small wildfires were keeping them on their toes. They'd successfully extinguished the latest one and circled back to make sure no new baby fires had sprouted. Once they cleared the area, she could get back to the camp and take a shower. It'd been going on a week now and her sense of humor was more than shot.

Not that she didn't love what she did. It was a love-hate relationship. Probably the most healthy relationship she'd ever been in, she mused. She hauled her equipment down the hill, glad to see trucks were waiting in the clearing ahead to transport them back. Everyone was bone-tired and covered in dirt. She was the only female on this crew and had moved her way up to supervisor rapidly.

• • • •

If only she'd had this focus before she'd been incarcerated, she might have gone on to college or some type of career, instead of blasting her veins with heroin, disappointing her whole family. It'd begun harmless enough. A crush on a guy which moved at a breakneck pace. He'd seemed interested and she'd wanted to grab onto it. To shed the ugly-duckling phase she'd been in as long as she could remember. She'd been chubby with red, curly hair and pale skin, marked only by freckles. Man, how the other kids had teased her. It was relentless. She'd never dated or gone to dances. She kept her head down and her eyes on the ground. She wasn't even a star student. Just a chunky, pale, frizzy-haired nobody.

Fresh out of high school, she'd found a crowd who didn't seem to care what she looked like, instead, focused on how fucked up they could get on any given day. She took it. It was the acceptance she'd so desperately craved. Before long, she'd shed her baby fat and was more intent on staying outside of her head than in. Then he came along. He was funny, with dark brown hair which fell over his blue eyes. Thin, tall, and a smile that was both sweet and evil. She fell head over heels and when he reciprocated, she would've done almost anything for him.

The thing was he was like her. An outsider who found something which made him feel in. Movies make drug users seem less than. Selfish, conniving. He was none of that. He held her and told her she was beautiful. He spoke of his dreams to leave and go to the coast. He never talked about giving up heroin, but he always had plans for a life outside of it. Their life. The day she woke up and turned over to him to see his beautiful, soulful eyes staring back empty at her, no breath left in him, she knew it was over. She'd nothing to live for. He was gone and she was an empty shell.

11

• • • •

From that point on, heroin was it. She didn't care if it made her vomit or stopped her heart. As long as it stopped her pain. Sometimes she'd look up and not recognize anyone around her anymore. People came and went, on to the next place, the next fix. She didn't care. Nobody mattered. She didn't matter. When the house they were squatting in was raided and she was arrested, she was hoping they'd just shoot her. She was in her early twenties with nothing to live for. The raid resulted in criminal charges and she was sentenced to eight years in the state penitentiary. Eight years for being addicted. The amount of drugs in the house made it a felony, and she was locked up as a criminal.

The first few years were a blur. Shoving, yelling, sleeping, not sleeping. Getting over the addiction was hell and Wren didn't care about the light at the end of the tunnel. She didn't make friends or find herself. She merely existed. But she didn't cause trouble and kept to herself. When the offer of time off for good behavior was presented, working with a new program to fight fires, she shrugged and thought, *why not*? It was mostly men, the pay was shit, and they were watched closely, but getting away from the prison, doing something... anything, helped her see outside of herself.

At first, it was just labor. Cutting trees and vines, clearing forests floors. Mitigation they called it. But then there were the fires and suddenly the prisoners were doing serious work. They were heroes, working together as a team to make a difference. For the last two years of her sentence, Wren donned heavy firefighter gear, using every ounce of her energy to do something for someone else. When she was released, they'd asked her to stay on as a paid employee. Now, a year later, she was running her own crew.

· · · ·

It wasn't an inspiration. She still thought about heroin every day. About sticking the needle in her arm and letting go. She'd wake up from dreams, crying because he was in them and they were fucked up, naked, holding each other. She'd go back in a heartbeat if it meant seeing him again. Part of the job was making sure she didn't go back. If she stayed out and away from society, she didn't have access. She told her parole officer all of this.

He shrugged and said, "Whatever it takes."

The crew loaded on the cargo trucks and began to strip off their gear. They'd go back to basecamp for food and showers. Some, like Wren, were free to leave. Some stayed at the camp to complete their service. Wren stayed at the camp. It was easier than trying to assimilate into a society that'd spit on her since she was a child. She pulled off her helmet, using a cloth to wipe her face. She caught a glimpse of herself in the plexiglass window and grimaced.

She was no longer pudgy and her bright red, kinky curly hair had settled into a lighter, wavy mop she kept braided at her back. She appeared tired, not so different from the guys on her crew. She was muscular and dressed much the same. Most people didn't even know she was a woman when they saw the crew. Which was fine by her. No one gave her unwanted attention, even though now and then the guys teased her when she washed up. They never tried to make a move. Not that she wasn't womanly. Sometimes, after she showered and stepped out of the water, she'd catch a glimpse of her body in the mirror and think, *oh yeah, there you are.*

The trucks jerked, rumbling through the fields towards camp and a few of the guys dozed off. They were just ramping up for fire season and were already beat. Once they had food in them, and a few beers, they'd perk up and be ready to hit it again the next day. As the trucks slowed into the camp area, firefighters began

• • • •

jumping out, heading to their bunks and showers. Wren waited and climbed out last. The drawback of being the only female was they'd all shower around each other, so she'd wait until they were done. She saw her friend Rob coming her way with a beer and grinned.

"You read my mind," she said and gratefully took a swallow of the beer.

"How was it out there?" Rob asked, his gray eyes scanning the horizon. He was a crew supervisor like her but had his crew working on maintenance that day.

"Hot as fuck."

"You don't say? Arizona in June during fire season is hot?"

Wren chuckled. She and Rob had hit it off right away when they met, and she was glad for his company. He'd served time for petty crimes. Once he was locked up, he proposed to his high school sweetheart and never looked back. They had a couple of young boys and one would never know he'd ever been a wild one. As soon as his shift was over, he was home with his family and seemed like an All-American guy. Well, except for the tattoos which stretched from his hands all the way up to his neck. They leaned back against a signpost and watched the camp buzz with activity. It was never dull, for that Wren was grateful. She saw the last person exit the shower tent, gulping her final sip of beer.

"Alright, my turn." She stood up and cocked her head at Rob. "Are you here for a bit?"

"Yep, covering the night and tomorrow. If you're up for some food after your shower, I'd like to go over the forecast for the next couple of weeks. It's looking to be super dry."

Wren nodded, setting her mouth in a line. "It's going to be a brutal season."

• • • •

She headed to her tent for clean clothes. Once at the showers, she locked the door behind her. Dirt stained the water as she let it cascade down her back and relax her muscles. Had she seen outside herself, she'd have seen a lean, strong, curvy woman with golden-red hair down to the middle of her back in ringlets. But what she saw was another guy. Just another body moving through the world. She rinsed and turned the shower off, reveling in the silence of the space before dressing. She slipped on shorts and a tank top, already feeling sweat pooling at the small of her back. There was no relief from the heat. She wrung her hair out, leaving it loose to dry, and went to find food and Rob.

He was sitting at a table in the cafeteria tent with maps and charts spread out. He had his large hand wrapped around the back of his neck as he bent over, gazing at the map. He kept his light brown hair short like most of the guys to keep it out of the way. Wren grabbed a sandwich and chips along with another couple of beers for them. She sat across from him and peered at the map. He glanced up, watching her for a moment.

"I almost forget you're a woman most days. Under all the gear and filth. Is one of those beers for me or are you two-fisting it tonight?"

Wren laughed and slid a beer toward him. "Yes and yes. This probably won't be my last."

Unlike heroin, alcohol didn't do much for her. It was pleasant and cold, but that was about all. Rob cracked his beer, tapping his finger on one of the weather charts. He shook his head and slid it towards her.

"They're saying no rain for weeks. We only have the two crews for this area, everywhere else is maxed out, as well. We'll have assistance from the prisons, but so many of those guys are green

15

● ● ● ●

and won't be much help at first. One stupid hiker, one errant campfire, and this is going to go up like a match. How is mitigation going?"

"Good, we cleared a few acres today. But you know how it is. If the winds pick up, it can skip through the treeline," Wren replied, shoving a bite of sandwich in her mouth.

"Yeah." Rob sighed. "We need to be prepared and hope we get backup. Let me call Lindsay and say good night to the boys. Are you going to be up for a bit?"

"You know it. It takes me forever to wind down."

Rob left to call his wife as Wren propped her feet up on the chair beside her. Whether it was from age or always being outside, her freckles blended with the light gold her skin had become. She picked at a scab on her knee and peered around. The camp was winding down, only the few who were on night duty were milling around. She saw Rob instructing a group to clean the equipment to have it ready to go for the morning, then he headed back to where she was sitting.

"Lindsay says hello. Okay, so where were we? Oh yeah, the hellscape that is our job. I talked with the Forestry team today, they're hiring up for the season, as well. Predictions are this will be the worst fire season in decades. We have a seasoned crew which is good. Hopefully, the predictions are wrong and we have time to recoup between fires and restock supplies."

Wren nodded and stared at the map. Each area had crews responsible for it, but depending on how big a fire was or how fast it spread, it could quickly overtake a team. The whole state was on standby and they'd been working to prep the land. She leaned back in her seat, yawning.

• • • •

"I guess there is nothing left to do but wait and see. Pray for rain," she muttered.

"Mmm, I don't see you as a praying type," Rob teased.

Wren glanced up, meeting his eyes. "You have me dead to rights, there. Maybe a rain dance then?"

"Ooh, Wren, crossing into inappropriate territory there. You know cultural appropriation?"

Wren blushed. "Fair enough, I take that back. So, back to praying. Or maybe I'll just talk to the sky."

"I think that is like praying."

Wren shook her head at him and grinned. "I can't win."

They went over some different courses of action and Wren felt her eyes getting heavy. Rob would be there in the morning, and they needed to make some calls to other agencies to see who and how many crews would be available in the event of a major wildfire. Or a lot of minor ones. Either way, this is what they were there to do; Wren had nothing else in her life. Rob had his family and something to live for.

Wren was simply killing time.

• • • •

Chapter Two

B y the next week, their worst fears had come to fruition. Three different fires were raging around the state and the largest, triggered by a downed powerline, was consuming much of their region. All crews were fighting it full force, but the dry weather and winds weren't helping. Crews from around the state and other states were coming in to help. It made national news and while politicians pointed fingers, those on the ground were losing hope. The problem was larger fires were also burning in California, so much of the federal resources were shifted there.

Wren saw Rob's crew coming back in from setting a containment fire and went out to meet him. He shook his head, his eyes hollow.

"We fucking need help out there, we can't keep up. It's spreading too fast." His voice was hard and angry at the edges. "Are you about to head out there?"

• • • •

Wren nodded. Her crew was loading up. "Did you hear about the crew south of us? They lost a guy."

"Like he died?"

"Yeah."

"Fuck."

Wren peered at the sky. It was midday but almost as dark as night. A red-orange night. She saw her crew was ready and put her hand on Rob's shoulder, covered by his heavy equipment. He nodded and headed to the tactical tent. She joined her crew and they were shuttled out as close as they could be to the edge of the fire. They proceeded to unload their shovels and other equipment. Wren was relieved to hear a helicopter overhead dropping water. It was a small reprieve and would only help them gain a little ground... if that. It'd take a hundred helicopters to put the fire out.

They joined crews already on the ground and Wren found other crew supervisors for a status update. It wasn't good. They were losing ground by the minute. Towns in the region were being evacuated. Wren thought of Rob and his family, they'd be getting evacuated, too. She was sure he already knew as his family was the most important thing in the world to him. She radioed him anyway and he quickly replied he was on his way to his house. He'd been on a twenty-hour shift, now was having to save his own family. As for his home? It was a crapshoot.

They dug in, working the line of the fire. Hours passed and Wren felt like they'd made no headway. The fires seemed to be bigger each year... faster and stronger. The crews got smaller, which is why the state worked with the prison system to offer the incarcerated *an opportunity*. Some opportunity. Sure, it was a skill and a job, but at what cost? Just a different form of imprisonment. Most of these guys, and the few women, had families. Children

• • • •

they wanted to see grow up. On average, about seventeen wildland firefighters died each year. The number wasn't astronomical, but each of those people died trying to save others. Many of them left behind families, children. The work was hard, it sucked out every ounce of strength and hope to get through each shift.

Wren was relieved she didn't have a family to worry about. She was just starting to rebuild her relationship with her parents. Her little brother, Geoffrey, had moved out east to pursue music. He'd been the smart one. Not intelligence-wise only, but more so because he focused on his dreams and followed them. He didn't let anyone influence how he defined himself. They'd been close but lost connection when she went to prison. He'd tried to write to her then, but she was ashamed and she didn't write back. Between fighting addiction and grief, she didn't feel like she had anything to offer. Eventually, he stopped writing.

"Gretchen? Gretchen Meyer?" A voice yelled out to her.

Wren turned to face a young man holding a clipboard, squinting at her. She nodded and stepped towards him. "Yeah? That's me."

"Hey, I'm the supervisor for the crew out of Phoenix. I was told to reach out to you and see where you want my guys?"

"Oh, right! If you want to go down the line to the west, we're spread pretty thin down there. Check for spot fires and start cutting down trees. Thank you!"

"Sure thing. I'm Dylan, I have twelve in my crew."

"Nice to meet you, Dylan. I actually go by Wren. We're glad to see you out here. We're swamped."

"Wren. Got it. Don't see too many women out here."

"More than you'd think. Hard to tell with our equipment on," Wren explained.

• • • •

Dylan nodded and grinned. He appeared to be in his mid-twenties with short brown hair and hazel eyes. He looked like he should be working at a coffee shop, not leading a crew into hell. Turnover was a bitch. The pay wasn't great and the risk was high. Most wildland firefighters moved on to other jobs within a few years. Wren figured she'd be at it forever. Dylan waved to his crew and they disappeared down the line. Wren slid her goggles back over her eyes and used her chainsaw to cut down trees.

The crew took turns breaking for water and a fast bite. This went on for hours throughout the day and night. Wren let her men take shifts to grab a nap, knowing exhaustion made for mistakes. She didn't want to lose anyone, they were the only family she had at this point. Around midnight, the supervisors met up and shared updates. They had the fire line held in their area but weren't making progress pushing it back. The teams were beat and they were running out of backup. They'd just have to keep cutting and shoveling.

By the time her twenty-four-hour shift was over, Wren was shaking from exhaustion. A new crew had come on to relieve them. The men practically dragged their equipment to the trucks and climbed in. It was war. No one was joking or talking, like on the way in. They sat in silence, most with their heads down. Some leaned back with their eyes closed, attempting to shut out the imagery.

Wren didn't even both to shower when she got in. She shed her gear and crawled into her bunk. She guzzled some water and closed her eyes. She didn't know how they did it. The ones that had families. She had nothing left to give. She'd likely sleep most of the time until her next shift. Shower, eat something. Then it was back out again. It's how she wanted it. It helped her not feel anything. Like heroin. It was a weird kind of high and in some ways, she traded one addiction for another.

Rob woke her up about ten hours later, sitting on her bunk. She sat up and stared at him, her eyes glazed. "Everything okay?"

"Yeah, I got my family to my in-laws in New Mexico. I think we may lose our house. I don't know."

"Damn, Rob. I'm sorry. Any updates?"

"Not really. About the same. The state sent in another helicopter on the north end. That should help. We're getting a crew from the Navajo Nation, as well."

"Really? I didn't know they had their own crew."

"Yeah, about ten men and women."

"Women? Nice." Wren swung her feet off the bed. "When are they coming?"

"I think tonight. Wait, it is tonight. Tomorrow morning?"

It was easy to lose track of time. The sky was never blue with the fire raging. Wren could smell food cooking and realized she hadn't eaten since a granola bar the day before.

"I'm famished."

"There are burgers and hotdogs out there. Some group came out to cook for us. There's cake," Rob replied.

"Cake? I'm in." Wren slipped on her shoes and realized she was still filthy. "Ugh, I suppose I should shower first."

"Nah, come have cake. No one cares what we look like."

They headed to long tables stretched out with food. Wren filled her plate and ate more than she should. She sat with Rob and a couple of members of her team. Everyone was in better spirits after sleep and food. Tomorrow they'd have more help with the volunteers from the reservation and a group from the prison.

Maybe tomorrow they could make some real headway. She checked the forecast, but it didn't look like rain was due any time soon.

After eating, Wren showered and cleaned her equipment. She was looking forward to having some other women around for a while. She'd spent six and half years with only women, and the last close to a year and a half with almost only men. Women firefighters were a unique breed. They were powerful and secure in themselves. After all, they put their lives on the line in an almost completely male-dominated field. They were the only women Wren ever felt like she connected to.

The next morning, Rob headed out with his crew and the team from the prison. Dylan came in with his team, tired and defeated. It was a vicious cycle. Dylan almost passed right by Wren, not recognizing her until she called out to him. He stared at her and his eyes got wide.

"Wren?"

"One and the same." Wren laughed.

"I'd never have known! You clean up nice," Dylan said almost bashfully.

Wren shook her head, hoping it didn't go any further. "Thanks. There's food in that tent and showers over there."

"Great! I don't know what I need first. Shower, food, sleep? Too bad I can't do them all at once," Dylan joked.

"I hear you. I usually crash out first."

"Tempting, but I can't think of the last time I ate."

"There's plenty in there. Nice seeing you again, Dylan."

Dylan nodded and made a straight line for the food tent. Wren's next shift wasn't until the evening, so she grabbed a book and sat on a table at the edge of the camp near the road. About an hour later, a bus came rumbling down the road and pulled in. One

• • • •

by one, the riders unloaded and collected their gear into a pile. Wren watched quietly as they sorted their things, peering around. They were the group from the Navajo Nation. There were seven men and three women. Two of the men had short hair, five had long hair. The women all had long hair. The thing which struck Wren was that many of them were at least in their thirties, a few even older. They talked amongst themselves and Wren realized they probably didn't have a point of contact. She climbed off the table and walked over to them. She headed for the oldest man, sticking her hand out.

"Hi, I'm Wren. I'm a crew supervisor here. Are you from the Navajo reservation?"

The man took her hand and smiled. "We are. I'm Joe. Where do you want us?"

"Okay, well, I have the only women's tent. There are six bunks, so plenty of room. Over on that side are the men's tents. We're pretty full, so you may have to split up into different tents. That there is the tactical tent, as we call it. It's where we meet and get status updates. Food is there. The latrines over there. I can show the women to our tent and once we all get situated, I can show the crew supervisor the tactical tent and where we are with everything. Are you the crew supervisor?" Wren asked Joe.

Joe laughed and tipped his head back. "No. Not at all. You'll want to speak to Elijah."

"Which one is Elijah?"

"Elijah, come over here and meet Wren. She is one of the other crew leaders here," Joe called back to the group.

A young man in his late twenties stood up from checking the equipment and moved towards them. His long, black hair was loose and he frowned as he drew close. He eyed Wren and stuck his

24

hand out to her. She was taken aback by his deep brown, almost black, eyes which sat under a black, straight set of brows. He seemed angry. Wren took his hand and shook it. He glanced around the camp, nodding.

"I'm Elijah. I see you've met Joe. We're ready to jump in wherever and whenever needed."

"Nice to meet you, Elijah. Wren. Let's get you settled, then I can show you where the fire line is and let you know the schedule. I believe you are going out with my crew tonight."

"Good." It was all he said and turned to grab their equipment.

Wren motioned to the women to come with her, so they gathered their things and followed her to their tent. A woman about her age joined alongside her, laughing.

"Hey, I'm Echo. Don't mind Elijah. He's a grump. Too serious all of the time."

Wren glanced over at Elijah, who was carrying his gear to a tent, then nodded to Echo. Elijah made her feel self-conscious and she hoped he wouldn't be hard to work with. He glanced over to see her watching. He grimaced, then disappeared into a tent. There were women on his team, so it wasn't that. Maybe it was just who he was like Echo said.

Regardless, for the first time since she'd left home, he made her feel small.

• • • •

Chapter Three

T he two teams headed out that evening and were dismayed
to see the fire pushed further in. Even though there were
nine crews, totalling over a hundred firefighters fighting the
blaze, they lost any ground as soon as they moved to another area.
Across the southwest and west, fires were burning everywhere and
resources were limited. It'd been one of the hottest and driest
summers on record; many places were in a drought. The winds
were also high, spreading embers into new areas and catching them
ablaze. It seemed hopeless. Wren saw Rob when she climbed off the
truck and he shook his head at her. They needed the big guns...
planes with retardent and ten times the amount of firefighters than
they had. Wren grabbed her chainsaw and went to work.

While she was cutting, she thought about her conversation
with Elijah earlier that day. It was short. Just going over the maps
and resources. He was quiet and didn't say much, but listened

intently. Echo had elaborated in the tent about him. He had an eight-year-old son he raised alone. The mother signed over parental rights shortly after the birth. Elijah was twenty-eight and other than his son, the only thing he was interested in was firefighting. Echo joked he'd been emotionally burned, so he fought fire with fire. Wren asked where his son was when Elijah was out firefighting. Echo shrugged and said mostly Elijah's grandmother.

Wren liked Echo. She laughed easily and didn't take herself too seriously. Her brother was also on the crew. From what Wren gathered, a few of the crew members were related and dedicated to wildland firefighting. They'd grown up on the reservation, which had its own thriving fire department. The ones that came to help were only a portion, some stayed back to make sure the reservation was safe, as well. Joe was Wren's favorite, though, because he treated everyone like family. He was like an older Uncle.

Elijah was tough. They needed to depend on each other out there, but he was basically unreachable. He'd talk strategy and implementation, however, that was all. Wren recognized it had less to do with her than himself, but it was still frustrating. He gave one-word answers to everything she asked and didn't reciprocate. While they were leaning over the map prior to their shift, she'd noticed he'd braided his hair behind him much like she did and watched his face. He was staring down at the map and sighed.

"How many firefighters are here?"

"I think a total of eighty-four," Wren replied.

"Anything else?"

"Just the two helicopters. Mostly they're keeping our ways in and out clear. They aren't making much of a dent."

"Any planes?"

"None."

Elijah nodded, leaning against a stool. "I don't see a way without rain to get ahead of this."

Wren thought about her rain dance joke earlier with Rob and blushed. It *was* offensive. She shook her head. "No, at this point, we're just trying to hold out to keep it from progressing until either more help or rain arrives."

Elijah met her eyes and for a second she saw a crack. This was their common ground. He chewed his lip and stood up. "What time are we heading out?"

"In about two hours. The trucks will bring a crew in and take us out."

"Alright, well, see you then." Elijah walked to the tent opening and paused. "Wren? Is that your birth name?"

"No. My birth name is Gretchen. My little brother couldn't say Gretchen, so he called me Gren, which turned into Wren, and caught on with the rest of the family. It's all I've ever known, honestly."

Elijah turned his head, surprising Wren with a brief smile. "Nice. See you in a couple of hours, Wren."

It was progress. They didn't have to be best friends, but they needed to have enough of a bond to be willing to save each other. Allowing each other in, made them more invested in the fight.

Wren set down her chainsaw and wiped the sweat out of her eyes. They all knew they were barely holding on, but calls for help were going unheeded. They had about what they were going to have. Wren went to the water station and drank as much as she could. It was never enough. Rob's crew had wrapped up and left. The winds were picking up. Wren watched the movement and her stomach sank. The winds were blowing in the direction of the

• • • •

camp. If they got much stronger, they were at risk of the fire jumping and tearing through the forest toward it. She radioed Rob and went over her observation. He checked the weather, the winds were supposed to pick up even more. He told her to stand by as he started making some calls. If the fire breached the line, they'd need to move the camp. They tried to stay close so they could get crews in and out quickly, but it was a risk.

Fifteen minutes later, Rob radioed to get everyone back to camp. They needed to reassess the situation. Trucks were on their way to pick everyone up. It would take two trips. Firefighters don't want to leave the front lines but understood the problem was greater than them at this point. The trucks came and pulled two crews, leaving Wren and Elijah's for the next trip. They kept working until they heard the rumble of the trucks. The crews gathered their equipment and loaded it onto the trucks. As they were driving out, a gust of wind picked up, sending embers flying through the air. As the embers landed, they created spot fires and Wren caught her breath. At this rate, they were barely going to outrun the fire.

On the way back, they could see the fire spreading. Even though they were staying ahead of it, it would catch them not long after they hit camp. Wren radioed Rob with an update. They were already breaking down the tents and moving them out. By the time they hit camp, it was just equipment ready to go. The fire was off in the distance, but from the look on Rob's face, Wren knew it had picked up speed. The camp supplies were taken out on the trucks they'd come in on. Rob ran up to them.

"Fuck, we need to get back in there but it's becoming increasingly dangerous. I think I got them to understand and they're sending in planes with retardants. Let's hope it's not too

• • • •

late. I'm having my crew set up a new camp and the rest of us here are going to loop around to try and set up a barrier. You game?"

Wren and Elijah both nodded. The fire was coming over the hill towards where the camp was. They could try to head it off from there. They grabbed their equipment and cut through the still-living trees to the line. They put out spot fires as they moved and began digging trenches. Rob and Wren used chainsaws to cut down a line of trees between them and the encroaching fire. Elijah and his team started clearing brush. It was exhausting, however, the fire showed no signs of slowing down. As it approached, they paused to see if it would slow but the wind kicked up and blew embers all around them. The fire ate the vegetation in front of them and screamed toward the sky. It jumped the line, immediately surrounding them in flames.

"Run!" Rob yelled and the team ran back towards the camp. They were outnumbered by nature.

They moved as fast as they could, weighed down by their equipment. When they hit the clearing where the camp had been, they paused to catch their breath. The camp area had been reduced to dirt from all the foot traffic, but the fire spread in the vegetation surrounding it. They headed down the road in, as fire breached it and burned on both sides. They made it down when one of the trucks came rumbling over the hill. They ran towards it, scrambling in, as the driver backed down enough to turn around. They were crammed in tight, wide-eyed as the fire engulfed the area they'd just been in. The truck took them to the new campsite as they saw the planes with retardant fly overhead. At least someone had finally listened.

Once at the new campsite, everyone was called in to be briefed. The fire had spread miles in just over an hour. The winds

· · · ·

had picked up, but the planes were still going in to make drops. A call for more crews had been put out, however, since a lot of states were dealing with fires, it wasn't likely much help was coming. Each crew was given a shift schedule and the supervisors were asked to stay back. It wasn't good. They were looking at implementing forty-eight-hour shifts for more overlap.

Longer shifts meant more exhaustion and thus more injuries. It also meant risking losing the volunteer firefighters, who weren't used to such unforgiving hours. Rob met Wren's eyes, shaking his head. She smiled wryly back. Somewhere people were sitting around a dinner table talking about their days, school, their jobs, and had no clue the world was burning.

The bright spot was the planes were still flying even with the wind. Elijah's and Wren's crews were the first to go back out since they'd been pulled in. No one was in high spirits, which wasn't a good way to start a shift. The ride was somber and while they rapidly got to work, an air of dejection was around them. They worked through to morning when Rob's crew joined them. There would be more people on-site at times with the two days on, one day off cycle, but everyone would be more worn out.

This cycle went on for over a week. They were making headway, but Wren didn't know if she was coming or going. When she was at camp, she was sleeping or eating. Even showers had become a luxury because most times she was too tired to do anything. On one of the days in, she went to grab food to take back to her camp when she saw Elijah off to the side on the phone. His face was different, softer. He actually smiled and hung up the phone. He caught her eye and nodded, the smile still touching the corners of his mouth. She held up her food and he jogged over to her.

31

• • • •

"Hey, if you can wait a minute, I'll grab something to eat and we can sit together," he said hastily.

Wren stood, making sure her mouth had not dropped open. She bobbed her head and went to a folding table. Elijah came out and sat down. Wren didn't know what to say and didn't want to talk about the fire. She picked at a corner of her sandwich, watching him. "Echo tells me you have a son?"

Elijah met her eyes and she saw something flash behind his eyes. "I do. Tse. He's eight."

Tse? He said it like *say* with a 't' in front of it. Wren didn't want to be nosy and nodded. Elijah took a bite of his food and stared off. Now, it was awkward. Wren wished she'd gone to her tent. Elijah cleared his throat.

"I was just talking to him. He's with my grandmother, right now. She's getting old but keeps him in line. What about you, any family?"

Wren considered the question and shook her head. "Not really. I have a mother, father, and brother, but I did something which drove them away."

"Like?"

"Like got addicted to heroin and didn't care about anything else for years."

Elijah nodded and raised an eyebrow. "Heroin? That's some pretty heavy stuff."

"It was and got me locked up. It's how I ended up here. There was a program inside prison that allowed me to learn how to be a wildland firefighter. When I got out, they offered me a job."

"It was good for them, anyway. You know what you're doing," Elijah replied honestly but without emotion.

• • • •

"Thanks? I guess it was good for me, too. Otherwise, I would've gone back to heroin," Wren stated flatly.

This time both of Elijah's eyebrows went up and he put his sandwich down. "Seriously?"

Wren nodded. She wasn't interested in sugar-coating her addiction or lying about how she'd turned her life around. She was still an addict. Just an addict without a fix. She met Elijah's eyes hard, waiting on his response.

He watched her, then sighed. "I guess we all have our demons."

That wasn't the reaction she expected. A bit after they ate, Elijah pulled a small pouch out of his bag and opened it. He pricked his finger with a lancet and dripped blood into a small device. Numbers appeared and he shook his head. He drew out a syringe, thumping it with his finger before sticking it in his arm. Wren was speechless and stared at him.

Elijah caught her eye and smiled. "Insulin. I'm diabetic."

Wren blushed. Or course, her mind had gone elsewhere, but plenty of people carried syringes around for diabetes. Her twisted mind immediately went to drugs. She watched as he cleaned everything and put it neatly away.

"Have you always been diabetic?"

Elijah nodded. "Type one for as long as I can remember. My mother was, too, and it killed her. She didn't take care of it, though."

"Is it genetic?"

"Somewhat. Type one is and type two isn't, necessarily. Thankfully, my son doesn't have it."

Wren listened, then stared at the needle on the table and pushed down the urge to stick it in her arm.

••••

Chapter Four

Wren smelled it before she heard it. She sat up in bed and a flutter went through her chest. She took a deep breath, listening. It was there. She shook Echo awake. Echo opened her eyes and instantly registered what was happening. Her face broke out in a huge grin as she sat up.

"Rain!"

They woke up the other women and went outside in their pajamas. It was raining. Steady but gentle. Wren turned her face up to the sky and let the rain fall on her face. She wasn't sure it was going to be enough, but it was something. Echo started dancing with Marie, one of the other women, and Wren glanced over to the men's tents. One by one, the men started to emerge, whooping and hollering. Regardless, any rain would let them make headway. Wren walked over to Rob, ignoring she was barefoot in a t-shirt and sleep shorts.

He was checking the weather on his phone and smiled as she approached. "There's water falling from the sky," he said, holding his hand up to catch it.

"Best thing I've seen in a long time," Wren agreed.

"From the looks of it, we have some decent days of rain coming. We can go out and work the soil to uncover and saturate any coals underneath. We may just get ahead of this."

"Who's out now?"

"Dylan's crew and another from New Mexico."

"We're scheduled out in the morning. I want to stay out and play in the rain, but I suppose we better get rested up," Wren replied and pouted. She wanted to let the rain wash over her.

"Have a beer with me and we can head back to bed after," Rob bargained.

"Okay, but just one."

Rob ducked into his tent and brought out a couple of beers. They stood in the rain sipping their beers, hoping it wouldn't stop. Wren noticed Elijah talking with his team and wondered if this meant they'd be leaving. She hoped not, she liked Echo and they still needed their help to turn the dirt. Plus, she had a feeling she needed to get to know Elijah better. Rob finished his beer and stepped away to call his wife. Wren made her way back to her tent, making sure not to interrupt Elijah's meeting. She stopped at the tent opening and drained the last of her beer. It would make her sleepy, which was good. The meeting broke up and Echo came over, ducking into the tent. She glanced at Wren.

"You coming?"

"In a minute. I don't want to let this go quite yet."

Echo nodded and slipped in, followed by the other women. Unintentionally, this left Elijah and Wren standing outside

••••

her tent by themselves. Elijah was shirtless, revealing his dark golden skin and hard-working physique. He was wearing only pajama bottoms and his long black hair was soaked, sticking to his back. Wren glanced at him and cleared her throat.

"This is great. Should really help. Do you think you'll be leaving soon?"

Elijah's eyes flashed and he stared at her. "Trying to get rid of us?"

Wren blushed, she hadn't meant it that way. "No. Of course not. We can use all the help we can get. I guess I was asking because I know you all have a life to get back to."

Elijah considered this and nodded. "Yeah. We do. After this shift, I'm going to head home to see my son. I'll be back by the next shift, but I need to be there for him."

"I understand. That must be hard leaving him. You know, you may be able to bring him here for a visit."

Elijah shook his head. "I wouldn't have anyone to watch him when we were on shift. This isn't the most kid-friendly place."

Wren pictured the inside of the men's tents with the naked lady pictures and foul mouths, chuckling. "I guess not."

They stood in silence and Wren began to feel self-conscious about standing outside practically in her underwear. She was also particularly struck by Elijah's high cheekbones and strong jawline. Before she made it too obvious, she turned away. She rubbed her arms and smiled. "Morning will be here soon. I'm going back to bed. Night, Elijah."

"Night, Wren," Elijah replied and watched her disappear into the tent. He paused, running his hand over his face, then shook his head before heading back to his own.

• • • •

The next morning, the rain had paused as they loaded up but the sky was still overcast. Everyone was hoping for more rain because only the top layer had been soaked and the coals would run much deeper. Word came down they could move back to twenty-four-hour shifts in the meantime, bringing a collective sigh of relief. They worked on rotating the soil, getting coals exposed without reigniting fires. It was intense, hot work but when it started to rain again they knew it was necessary. As the rain hit the exposed coals, steam rose into the air and they could see the progress they were making. It would still take days with rain and working the land to put it out, but seeing the fires go out as the coals turn black kept spirits up and muscles working.

By the end of the shift, Wren was excited to be able to see fire-free soil, knowing a hot shower and rest were going to come easier. When she was a girl, she thought she'd grow up to be a teacher or veterinarian, but she never imagined she'd be a firefighter. Now, she couldn't imagine being anything else. She leaned back and closed her eyes as the truck rumbled towards camp. As they unloaded, she caught sight of Dylan and he was waving at her. She waved back and he motioned to come over. She headed in his direction, raising her brows.

"Hey, Dylan, what's up?"

"Hey, Wren, how's it looking out there?"

"Not too bad. We made some good headway and if it keeps raining, I think we can move more into recovery."

"Nice. I was hoping to hear that."

Wren watched him, sensing there was more, and waited. Dylan stared at his feet, then peered up at her with his amber eyes. He cleared his throat and glanced away, swallowing hard. Wren hoped he wasn't about to make a pass at her. Not that he wasn't attractive, but she wasn't going down that road.

"I was wondering if you all needed any more people on your team? My team is going back in a couple of days and I'd like to stay out here. I, uh. Damnit, I'm willing to stay on as just a crew member and not a supervisor."

Wren knew they always needed help and couldn't see it being an issue. She shrugged. "I'm sure we do. I can give you the name of our hiring manager."

"Thanks, Wren! I promise if I can, stay I'll be an asset. I don't have much to go home for, you know?"

She didn't, but it was none of her business. Maybe he broke up with his girlfriend or wife. It was his matter and she didn't need her nose in it. "I mean we have space in tents, however, some of the members live in the closest town. The camp breaks down after fire season, though, so you'd need housing then."

Dylan grinned. "I think I can manage that."

"Okay, well let me go get that info for you. I'd love to have you as part of the team. You're hardworking and don't complain. Hold on."

She ducked into the tent and pulled out her binder. She scribbled down some contacts for Dylan, wondering what happened. No. It was none of her business. They could use all the firefighters they could get. When she came out, Dylan was staring at his phone with a distraught look on his face and tried to shake it off when she walked up. His face was pale, his eyes wet and large. Wren handed him the paper and sighed.

"Everything, alright?"

Dylan shook his head, rubbing his nose. "Naw. My boyfriend of five years waited until I came here and ended it. Said he couldn't sit around waiting for me."

"Oh," Wren replied. "I'm sorry."

Dylan nodded and bit his lip. "Me too. Anyway, thanks for this Wren. I hope it works out."

Wren placed her hand on his shoulder. "Me too, Dylan. We'd be lucky to have you stay on."

Dylan smiled wobbly and walked away. Wren watched him go, realizing they didn't know each other all that well. None of them did, really. During their time at the camp, they had one life but everyone had another life back at home. Except for Wren. Well, and now Dylan. She saw him stop and stare at the paper while he dialed his phone. She silently hoped he'd get the job. It would be one more semi-permanent addition to her world. He wandered off, talking on the phone and Wren headed for her tent. Now that there were more women than just her, they had more leeway to the showers. She quickly grabbed a change of clothes and a towel before she missed the window.

After her shower, she grabbed a book and granola, then walked away from camp. She found a clearing in the woods, sat down, munching on dry granola, and opened her book. One thing prison taught her was to appreciate time alone and reading. She turned to her saved page, letting the words take her away. She almost didn't hear the footsteps behind her until they were right upon her. She peered up, blocking the sun with her hand, and squinted. Elijah sat down next to her.

"I didn't want to bother you, but I'm about to head out. I'm taking the bus since that's how we came in," Elijah explained.

● ● ● ●

"Oh, okay. You're welcome to take my car if you want. It's a piece of shit, but it runs and is good on gas mileage," Wren offered.

Elijah eyed her and cocked his head. "That's very generous for someone you hardly know."

"Trust me, if you stole that car, the joke would be on you. Two of the windows don't roll down, the AC hardly works, and the radio doesn't play at all. It's the red Subaru hatchback down by the highway. Keys are in my tent in the box under my bed."

"Can I ask you something?" Elijah asked softly.

Wren nodded and pushed down the anxiety creeping up in her.

"What brought you here?"

"You mean other than the heroin?" Wren asked wryly.

Elijah shrugged. "That is a response to trauma, not a cause. What brought you to heroin?"

Wren fought back tears which invariably forced their way up every time she thought about it. She shook her head. "Long story or short story?"

"How about short and maybe one day you can tell me the long?"

"Short it is. I was a chubby, ugly child and was bullied throughout school. I hated myself, pretty much wished I was never born. By the time I left school, I was broken and miserable, then met a group of people that accepted me for who I was. They liked to get fucked up, so I started getting fucked up, too. Mostly lighter stuff. Then this guy came along and I fell in love. He did heroin, so I did heroin. It killed him but unfortunately left me alive. I tried to die but wasn't any good at it. Police raided the house I was in and I was arrested. The courts sentenced me, which forced me into detox and eventually here."

"The guy, he was special to you?" Elijah asked more as a statement.

"He was. He is."

"You've been alone since?"

"Since and before. It's my destiny, I suppose."

Elijah sighed and stood up. "I don't know you, Wren, but I doubt that's true. We go through fires, but like the forest, eventually they go out and new growth springs up. I also doubt you were an ugly child. You can't let others define you. You may have been different, but you weren't ugly."

"You didn't know me then."

"I didn't have to. You're what's inside, not what's outside. From what I can see, both are beautiful and kind."

Wren was taken aback by this statement. Elijah had been friendly but not overly, almost seeming bothered by her at times. She frowned and stared at him.

"Can I ask you a question then?"

Elijah nodded.

"When we first met, you acted like you were angry at me... like I bothered you? Why?"

Elijah stared off and set his mouth. "It wasn't that."

"Then what was it?"

"Wren, sorry, I need to go. Thank you for letting me use your car and I'll be back in a day. We can talk more when I get back. It's more than can be covered here." He stood up and stared down at her for a moment, his dark eyes unreadable, before turning and heading back towards camp.

• • • •

Wren watched him leave and sighed in frustration. She was more confused than she'd been to begin with. As he disappeared from view, she turned her attention back to her book but couldn't focus. She slammed the book closed and gritted her teeth.

Not since losing the man she loved, had she felt so confused by another human being.

· · · ·

Chapter Five

T he rains brought the fire under control but didn't totally eliminate it. There was still work to be done. The volunteer crews started to phase out and move to other fires, leaving the hired crews behind. Dylan's crew went back to Phoenix and he stayed behind. He had an interview lined up and figured he'd volunteer until he heard back. Rob got his family back to his still-standing home and spent a few days with them before returning to camp. Elijah's crew was the last volunteer group to leave. On their last day, Rob went into town and bought food to have a cookout. Elijah and Wren had continued to be friendly, however, avoided any conversation outside of that. Wren couldn't deny she felt drawn to Elijah on some level, but even she wasn't sure what it was.

Another regional crew kept an eye on things, so the teams could come together for the cookout for a few hours. The hired

• • • •

crews wanted to show their appreciation to the volunteers before they all went their separate ways. One last time at camp as a group. It was always sad when the volunteers left, but this time was exceptionally hard because the fires had been.

Wren brushed her hair out and let it down. She ran water through her hair with her hands to control the frizz. She glanced in the mirror and saw her own pale green eyes staring back at her. They weren't bright, sparkling green like in the books she read; they were dull and pale, almost whitish-green. Freckles dotted her face everywhere, and she couldn't help but see the fair, chubby child of her past, even though her face was leaner. She thought of him, her love who'd died, and sighed. He'd always told her she was pretty but she didn't believe him. He would kiss her freckles and stare into her eyes with such adoration, it almost hurt. She never understood it but was glad he found something in her she never could. When they made love, he held her tightly and repeated over and over how he'd waited his whole life for her. Then why did he leave? Why was she not enough?

Wren shook the thought away. There was no point thinking back. He was gone, dust by now. The hands that held her gently and the mouth that kissed her fiercely were gone forever. She forced the tears back and cleared her throat. It would never not hurt. He was the love of her life, now she was destined to walk the earth alone. She pinched herself on the arm hard to redirect the pain. She focused on the burning on her arm and took a deep breath. Once the pain subsided, she pulled it together and headed out to the cookout. Food was spread out on tables and Rob was handling the grill. She brought him a beer.

"Wren! Nice of you to join us!" he said too loudly, obviously a few beers in. "Did you hear my news?"

• • • •

Wren shook her head and peered around. Elijah was talking with Dylan, and Echo was flirting with a firefighter on the other side of the tables. Joe was sitting, playing the guitar with a couple of guys. She'd miss the Navajo crew. She faced Rob who was trying to flip a burger as it stuck to the grill.

"What news?"

"The misses and I are expecting a baby," Rob beamed.

"Oh! Congratulations. This makes three?"

"Yep! Third and final. Getting snipped after this."

"Ouch."

"Indeed." Rob laughed as he took a sip of beer. "But I can't keep that train running. Kids are expensive."

"I imagine."

"You ever think about family, Wren?" Rob asked seriously.

"No. Absolutely not. Definitely not kids, I'm not the motherly type. I see kids and run the other direction."

Rob snickered and turned back to the grill. "Fair enough. You're a hell of a firefighter and it's hard to be out here with a family."

"I don't know how you do it, Rob."

"Honestly, me either. If it wasn't for Lindsay, I couldn't do it. She's a rock. Keeps everything back home running."

"You're lucky to have her," Wren replied.

"Don't I know it? She's everything to me."

Wren felt a familiar pang and pushed it away. "Alright, going to make the rounds."

She wandered around, talking to different groups, and finally settled with a plate of food by the group playing music. After she ate, she sat back and listened to the songs. When a familiar one was played, she sang along. Joe's eyes opened wide and

45

he smiled at her in awe. In school, Wren was in chorus and had been asked to perform solos, which she always refused. The idea of standing up alone, in front of a school of kids who made her life hell, was more than she could handle. Joe asked if she knew Amazing Grace. She told him she did. He started to play and other musicians joined in.

Wren closed her eyes and let her voice join the music, feeling a part of herself she'd buried rise up. When she stopped at the end of the song and opened her eyes, she was shocked to see all eyes were on her and a few mouths were hanging open. She blushed and glanced at the ground. People started to clap and she peered up, embarrassed. Elijah met her eyes, nodding in appreciation. Wren jerked her eyes away and went back to Rob, who felt like a safety net. He shook his head when she walked up.

"Damn, Wren. I didn't know you could sing like that. Why are you out here in the ashes with a voice like that? You could have a singing career."

"I like it out here in the ash. Besides, that would require me standing in front of people being judged, and I don't have the look."

Rob cocked his head in confusion. "The look? You're stunning with that red hair and pale eyes. Okay, maybe not when you're filthy and covered in soot, but they would clean you up real nice."

"Oh, stop, Rob. This is my home out here, and where I belong."

"I think you sell yourself short. I mean, I know we all have our histories and demons, Wren, but at some point, you need to be willing to put that behind you. I needed to, otherwise, Lindsay wouldn't have had me."

Rob knew her history and she knew his. He'd committed to moving forward, she had not. Just getting through each day was enough. She met his eyes and smiled.

"Thanks, Rob. Maybe one day. Are you hoping for a girl?" Wren asked, attempting to change the subject.

"Whichever. My boys are my life, so either way, this child will be my life, too. I like the idea of another boy, as well. Girls are scary," Rob replied, laughing.

"I think any girl of yours would be wild."

Rob nodded and took a sip of his beer. "Yeah, that's even scarier."

They chatted for a bit, but Wren was beginning to get tired. A few people were dancing to the music and Wren went to sit at a table to watch. Elijah came over to sit next to her. She glanced at him, then back at the dancers. He sat silently and turned to her.

"I wanted to thank you all for being so welcoming and treating us as part of the team."

"Of course. You came and helped when we most needed it. It's us who should be thanking you. This is never easy and we're always short-staffed," Wren said.

"For us it's different. This is our land. The land of our ancestors. It's our obligation to protect it, no matter the cost. We've always had fires but they're getting bigger and faster. I want my son to have land and trees to grow up to. The world is changing, we aren't taking care of it. I worry for his future."

Wren listened and considered what he said. For her, this was a job. It mattered, but she hadn't thought about what it was like to watch the land of familial generations being destroyed. Land wasn't a concept she understood. Her family had a house but not land. Nothing to hand down, nothing which was part of their history. Just a house on a plot next to other houses on other plots. Eventually, it would be sold and someone else would inhabit it. And that cycle would happen over and over indefinitely until the house crumbled. She watched Elijah, feeling sad for his connection to the loss of the land.

"I can't understand on that level, but I'm committed to saving the land," she offered.

"Are you, though? Or is this more about running from yourself?" he asked sharply.

That hurt. It wasn't that it wasn't true, but she'd opened up to him and he was being unfair. She stood up, staring down at him.

"Does it matter? I put my life on the line every goddamn time for land which isn't mine. Which I'll never be part of or own. At the end of the day, I have nothing. You at least can say you're fighting for something which matters to you, which is part of you. I'm part of nothing and have nothing. So, before you get high and mighty, maybe you should consider how fucking hard this is on me," Wren spat at him.

Elijah watched her steadily, not breaking eye contact. He nodded. "That's fair and I'm sorry. But I'm also not wrong." He stood up and placed his hand on her shoulder. "I leave in the morning. I'd like to take you on a hike before I go. If you're willing?"

Wren was confused by the conversation. He was so calm and sure of himself. She wanted to yell at him and storm off, but it would seem ridiculous in the face of his serenity. She nodded and sighed. "Fine. What time?"

"I'll come by your tent at six unless that's too early?"

• • • •

Wren shook her head. "Six is fine. You'd better have coffee."

At this, Elijah laughed and his face changed. "I can do that. In the meantime, would you like to dance?"

Wren wanted to say no and disappear to her tent to put her thoughts together, but also didn't want to break contact quite yet. "Sure."

They walked to where others were dancing and Elijah slipped his arm around Wren's waist. She wasn't sure where to put her hands, so she rested them on his shoulders. They swayed to the music as Wren resisted the urge to rest her head against his shoulder. Dancing was one thing, vulnerability another. But she couldn't take her mind off the heat of his arm on her waist. She dropped her arms to his waist, finding herself a little breathless at the feel of his muscles under his shirt. She instinctively met his eyes and could see he was feeling the same. He kept his eyes locked on hers until the song ended and she pulled away. He was leaving the next day, she didn't need to get caught up in anything.

She stepped back and stood uncomfortably. "I suppose it's time for me to head to bed."

"Wren," he started, then stopped. His face shifted back to its stone facade and he nodded. "Good night. I'll see you in the morning."

"Goodnight," Wren replied and practically bolted for her tent.

Once inside, she took a few deep breaths. What was that? Why had she let her guard down? She rested back on her bed, not being able to deny she felt something for Elijah. It was stupid and reckless. She was trying to make sleep come when she heard Echo

• • • •

come up. She was talking to a man outside the tent, giggling, before she came in and threw herself on her bed.

"Too many absolutely beautiful men here," Echo murmured to herself. She flipped over to face Wren. "I saw you dancing with Elijah. I can't believe it."

"What do you mean?" Wren asked.

"Elijah dancing with you. He doesn't connect to anyone, except his son."

"Why?"

Echo shrugged. "His son's mother did a number on him. She was white like you. He met her right out of high school and they were an item for a bit. She was beautiful. Blond, blue-eyed. She was fast, though. Elijah had grown up on the reservation and had only dated Navajo girls. When he met her, he was smitten. She ended up getting pregnant. They talked about getting married, but right after the baby was born she changed her tune, hooked up with another guy, and signed over her parental rights. Elijah has raised Tse alone since he was a newborn, and he pretty much doesn't leave the reservation except to fight fires. It's only him and Tse most of the time. He doesn't date and if he did it certainly wouldn't be another white woman."

"He asked me to dance. I didn't push myself on him," Wren said defensively.

"I know. That's why it's so unbelievable. You somehow cracked Elijah's shell."

• • • •

Chapter Six

Wren was up and waiting outside the tent at six, as to not wake up the other women. Right on time, Elijah showed up with a thermos of coffee and some biscuits he'd snagged from the food table the night before. Wren had on hiking boots, shorts, a tank, and a pullover hoodie, knowing she'd need to shed the hoodie before long. Elijah was in his usual cargo pants, t-shirt, and sneakers. His hair was loose to the middle of his back. Wren had her hair braided, not wanting to mess with it. They headed out of camp as the sun started its journey into the sky. It was beautiful and neither spoke, appreciating the clear sky and the way the light hit the landscape around them. Elijah led the way, moving up from the camp until they were able to see back down. He brought them out to a jutting rock where they could sit and gaze over the land. They stood for a moment, taking in the majesty of the area. Elijah turned and smiled.

• • • •

"Coffee?"

"That would be great," Wren replied and sat down on the rock.

Elijah sat next to her, pulling out the thermos and biscuits from his pack. He handed her a biscuit and poured them each a cup of coffee. Wren sipped it gratefully and yawned. It was times like these, she didn't feel so out of place in the world. Elijah ate his biscuit and brushed the crumbs off his pants. He watched her for a moment, chewing his lip.

"You asked me before why I seemed angry when I first came?"

Wren nodded and glanced at him. "It's not a big deal. I shouldn't have asked."

"No, you had every right to. I want you to know it's not personal. Or, not in the way you think. I have my own demons, maybe I was jumping to judgment."

"Echo told me about your son and his mother," Wren said, then worried maybe she shouldn't have.

Elijah eyed her, then cocked his head. "She did? I guess that's alright. It's not a secret, honestly. I was young and stupid, got caught up with the wrong person. I loved her but in the end, she wasn't as invested as I was. After Tse was born, she didn't want anything to do with him and since I did, she didn't want anything to do with me. It broke my heart, but Tse is the best thing that has ever happened to me. I chose him and she chose freedom. I was bitter for a long time; I suppose I was projecting it on the wrong people. Because she was white, my anger came out that way when it should've been just because she was selfish. I focused on Tse and nothing else. Except for firefighting. Being around white guy firefighters didn't trigger those feelings, but for some reason when I saw you sitting on the table reading when we pulled up to camp, it brought those feelings of abandonment and resentment up. It wasn't you, it was her, but I still felt it."

Wren listened and understood. She'd immediately put up a wall as soon as a man showed interest in her because she was still dealing, or not dealing, with her own loss. Elijah was angry about what happened to him and Tse, not at her. He had every right to be upset, and maybe getting to know her, would allow him to open his heart a little. She nodded, placing her hand on his arm.

"Thank you for letting me know. I was confused by it but it makes sense now. We create barriers to protect ourselves. Sometimes an unexpected event comes up which challenges that. I have done the same since Gabe died."

She hadn't said his name out loud in years and it tore at her heart. He was just *him* to her, so saying his name ached in a way she couldn't explain. She felt hot tears spring to her eyes as she cleared the tightness in her throat. Elijah met her eyes, taking her hand in his. He could see the pain in her and smiled with compassion.

"I'm sorry, Wren. About Gabe. I can see you loved him. You can talk to me about him if you want."

Wren didn't think she could but was surprised when the words poured out. She told Elijah how growing up she felt hideous and unwanted, how meeting Gabe changed that. How through his eyes, she saw herself differently. How he was gentle and kind. How he laughed easily and had big dreams. How he used heroin to escape from an overwhelming sensitivity, which froze him in place. He wanted to save everyone and everything but in the end, couldn't save himself. She told him how Gabe was the first person in her life who truly knew her, and when he died, part of her died with him. Since then, she was a shell. Just moving through the world until the end. Elijah held her hand and didn't try to interject. When she stopped, he squeezed her hand.

"So, we aren't so different, are we? Maybe that's why I was drawn to you."

He was drawn to her? That was news to Wren. At most, she figured Elijah saw her as necessary company. She peered at him with her brows knitted. He met her eyes and nodded.

"Believe it or not, you're the first person I've opened up to," he explained. "I'd like to continue our friendship, Wren. Even after I leave. Get to know you better."

Wren bobbed her head; she felt the same. "Okay. How far are you from the camp? I'll be there through the fall, then likely get an apartment in town until the season starts again."

"It's about two hours. Maybe we can meet halfway to go hiking, or something, sometimes?"

"Sure. That would be fun. Maybe you can bring Tse."

Elijah eyed her and thought about it. It was obvious he didn't let many people into Tse's life, to protect him. "Maybe. Let's try us first."

"I understand, you need to protect him."

"I do."

They gathered up their things and headed back towards camp, so he could leave with the crew. Wren was sad about them leaving but knew they had their own lives back home. She asked Elijah about his life on the reservation and he proudly talked about his community. They supported each other and worked together to build an inclusive family as a group. They took care of their elders and each other's children. Not to say they didn't have their issues, and Elijah worked to educate the youth on the dangers of addiction and isolation. It made Wren consider she'd never seen him take so much as a sip of beer, though that could have to do with having diabetes, as well. By the time they got to camp, the others had started loading the bus and Elijah went to get his bags.

Wren went up to Echo and hugged her. She'd miss her terribly and hoped they could stay in contact. They exchanged numbers, promising to stay in touch. Elijah loaded his bags, making sure their equipment was secure. Joe hugged Wren and told her she was now family, which made Wren feel her throat get tight. Joe didn't use technology, but gave Wren his address and asked her to write. Rob and Dylan came to say goodbye, and for a moment, Wren wished she could hold the moment with all of them. She imagined it was like leaving summer camp, never knowing if they'd ever see each other again.

By the time Elijah came over, she was on the verge of losing it. Other crews had come and gone, but she'd never felt they were friends. Elijah's crew had become friends, and in some ways, family. He came up to tell her goodbye and she couldn't fight back tears anymore. They rolled down her cheeks as she looked away. He hugged her tightly and whispered in her ear.

"It's okay, Wren. This isn't the end. We've just begun our journey on the same path. I made a friend in you and I don't have many of those. We'll see each other again." His voice was soothing. Wren let her guard down to believe him.

They pulled apart and met eyes. His face was different now. The hardness was gone, his dark brown eyes were open to her. She resisted the urge to touch his face but allowed herself to soak him in. His golden skin, black eyebrows, high cheekbones, and broad smile. She was risking her heart again but she wanted to. To feel something. He placed his fingers on her chin and smiled at her.

• • • •

"Let's exchange numbers. I promise I'll stay in contact," he said.

Wren pulled her phone out and typed his name in. She realized she didn't know his last name and paused.

"Clarke," he answered.

"Clarke? Oh." She'd figured it would be like Little Eagle or something.

Elijah nodded and chuckled, understanding. "Another misconception of Native Americans. A lot of us have names given to us by early whites when they tried to assimilate us. Some changed their names later, but most kept them. Hollywood has done a number on Native American reality. A lot of natives have short hair and are not embedded in our culture or history. I'm trying to give that to Tse, so he is connected to that side of him, but it can take work. I don't want him getting his history from television and movies, which are almost always wrong."

"I'm going to miss you, Elijah," Wren said honestly. She hated that she felt so vulnerable, but she was also relieved she could still feel that way.

"Me too, Wren. Sorry I took so long to get to know you. I promise I'm not such an ass."

Wren laughed at this and Elijah cocked his head. "Don't let anyone ever convince you you aren't the sky," he whispered and turned to go to the bus.

She didn't know what he meant and watched him go. He loaded on the bus, which was being driven by Joe. Rob came over and stood with her as the bus drove away. Dylan headed back to his tent. She saw Elijah raise his hand in a wave and she responded in kind. He met her eyes until they were too far off. Wren sighed, heading to grab breakfast. Rob followed her and touched her arm.

"Hey, Wren. You connected to Elijah, huh?"

Wren blushed. "Just as friends. We found we had some things in common."

Rob squinted his eyes at her. "Okay, then. Breakfast?"

"Definitely!"

They grabbed breakfast and worked out a new schedule with the existing crews. It was her crew, Rob's, and now that Dylan had been hired on, his. They hired him as a crew supervisor and a few new firefighters under him. Plus, the prison crews who rotated out as needed. The camp seemed empty and it gave Wren pangs of sadness when she went back to her tent alone, being the only woman again. She grabbed a nap before her shift that night. When she woke up she checked her phone. No messages, but they should've made it safely back to the reservation.

On her shift, her thoughts turned back to Elijah, how nice her hands felt on her. It was the first time since Gabe died, she'd even thought of another man and guilt rose in her. They were just friends. Two people who'd simply shared their pasts and commiserated over them. She'd love Gabe until she died. Beautiful, blue-eyed Gabe, who'd touched her soul. By the end of the shift, she'd packed away everything inside her neatly into their appropriate boxes and refocused on her duties. She was glad to have a friend in Elijah, but that was all.

When she finally was able to sleep, her mind took her on a turn through her dreams. She was walking through the woods and came to a clearing. She saw Gabe standing on the edge with his back to her. She ran and threw her arms around him, holding him so tightly her arms hurt. He turned and grinned down at her. He kissed her, running his fingers through her hair.

• • • •

"I've missed you, Wren. This beautiful hair and your soft lips."

"Gabe! I've waited so long for you. Please don't leave me again. It's been so hard without you," Wren begged.

"I never really left you. Just my body. I'm so proud of you. For beating that shit and what you've done. I'm sorry I wasn't strong enough to beat it with you. I wasn't fair to you and hurt you deeply. I never wanted to do that to you. You were everything to me, Wren. I thought I'd wake up one day and have the ability to stop. I told myself that every night. Then every morning, it started over. I honestly wanted to run away with you, begin again, have babies. It had me so firmly, I couldn't find a way out. But please know you were my soul. I love you with every ounce of my being. I'll always be part of you."

"Gabe, please don't go. I can't do this without you. I can't do it alone."

"You aren't alone. Let's take a walk. I want to show you something." Gabe took her hand and they wandered through the woods. They came out to an outcrop where Wren could see the whole world before her. Every mountain, every tree, every animal. Gabe smiled at her.

"This is where I am now. I'm part of everything and everyone. It's what I thought heroin could give me, but it couldn't. This is everything. You're here, too. I can be with you whenever I want. Part of you. Your feelings, your skin, your breath. See, Wren, I've never left you. You're not alone."

Gabe drew her in, placing his mouth on hers gently, then went on. "You need to allow yourself to be loved. Heroin was a prison, prison was a prison, now you're imprisoning yourself. I'll always love you. Our love will never die. But you're where you are

• • • •

for some time, and you need to allow others in. To be loved. To not be alone. I need to go now, Wren. Open your eyes and see you deserve more than you're allowing yourself to feel. You have someone out there who'll show you a love like you've never known. Without the prisons. I love you, Wren. Forever."

Wren turned to stop him from leaving but she was alone. She crumbled to the ground in tears, sobbing. Her heart broke into a million pieces. She was alone. She felt a hand on her shoulder and gasped. Gabe had come back. She grabbed the hand and stood up. She turned expecting to see Gabe, but a dark set of eyes met hers, then nodded with a depth of understanding she'd never experienced.

Elijah.

"It's time to go," he whispered in her ear.

Chapter Seven

Wren sat up drenched in sweat and stared around the tent. Her heart ached for Gabe and she sobbed quietly. It wasn't fair. Why would he come to her to leave again? Didn't he know it made her want to end it all? She considered what she had at her disposal to take her life. She just wanted to be with him again. This living life was too hard. This being alone. She picked up her phone to check the time and saw a message flashing. She clicked on it.

"Are you alright? I had a weird feeling," Elijah texted.

"No. Bad dream. Well, good dream but bad waking up."

"Do you want to talk about it?"

"Honestly, Elijah, I'm tired of it all. Gabe was in my dream and waking up is like a knife to the heart."

"I'm sorry. Can I call you?"

"No, don't. I'm not in a good place."

"Wren, that's why I need to call. Please answer."

The phone rang a few seconds later. Wren considered not answering it but didn't want to be rude. "Hello."

"Hey, Wren. Thank you for answering. Let's talk, okay?" Elijah's voice was soft and gentle. "Tell me about the dream."

Wren walked him through it and started crying again when she got to the part where Gabe left her. Elijah waited while she worked through it, his voice was just above a whisper when he spoke again.

"What do you think it meant?"

"That I'm always fucking alone."

"I know it feels that way but you aren't. You have people who care very much about you. Rob, Dylan, Echo. Me."

"Not the same," Wren replied bitterly.

"No, it's not. I know. But we all want you around, do you understand? You're part of our lives and you would be very missed," Elijah said, understanding where her head was at. "Can I see you? Can we meet to go hiking?"

Wren just wanted to bury herself and not think. She was off the schedule that day and nothing was stopping her from meeting with Elijah, except her brain. Part of her wanted to see him. Part of her knew it would make her face everything.

"There's one more thing about the dream, Elijah."

"What's that?"

"After Gabe disappeared, I felt a hand on my shoulder and thought he'd come back, but when I looked up it was you."

"Me? Did I say anything?"

"You told me it was time to go."

"And is it?"

"I don't know."

● ● ● ●

"So, can you meet today?" Elijah pressed.

"I guess. I'm off."

"Okay, I'll text you directions where to meet. Please, Wren, meet me there. Get out and get some breakfast. Go be around some people until then."

"I will," Wren promised. The sun was coming up anyway, and she needed to get out of the tent. "Bye, Elijah."

"See you *soon*, Wren."

After they hung up, she dressed and left the tent. The cool air helped her clear her head and she walked to the food tent. Dylan was in there drinking coffee at a table and grinned at her. She grabbed a muffin and coffee, heading over to him.

"Coming or going?" she asked as she sat down.

"Coming. Just got off shift and was too amped to sleep. A small fire caught but we got it out. Mostly mitigation, but I saw a family of deer which was cool," Dylan replied, his eyes twinkling.

"Nice. Yeah, I'm off today, too. Going hiking shortly."

"Yeah? Where at?"

"Not sure, meeting Elijah."

"Elijah? He's a good guy. Tell him I said hello," Dylan said and downed his coffee. "Well, let me try and grab some sleep. Hey, you know, Wren, if you ever want to go hiking or anything here, I'm game."

"Thanks, Dylan, I may take you up on it."

Dylan got up and rinsed his cup. He waved at the tent door and headed out. Wren ate and checked her phone. Elijah had sent the directions. She grabbed her bag and went to her car, not wanting to stick around camp for too long. Her brain was all over the place and she felt like it was visible to everyone. The drive was a

• • • •

good time to regroup. By the time she got to the location, she felt more put together.

When she arrived, no one was there, so she grabbed her thermos of coffee and climbed onto the hood of the car, still hot from the drive. She sat staring out at the mesas. Arizona was so beautiful. Tress and green in some areas and painted desert in others. She hadn't grown up there. Her family was from Texas and she didn't end up in Arizona until she caught a ride with a group of kids, heading to Phoenix for a concert. That's where she met Gabe and never went back to Texas. There was always someplace to crash.

Gabe was from California but didn't talk about his family much. He'd moved out at fifteen to get away from an abusive stepfather. The other kids were half-siblings and much younger than him, so he didn't talk about them, except to say they were treated differently. Better. He'd ended up in Phoenix much the same way. With someone heading there for something or another. It was the same version of the story for the rest of the people they hung out with. What tied them together was the drugs. The escape from a previous life.

A small, white truck came rumbling into the parking area, and Wren cautiously prepared herself in case it wasn't Elijah. Dust kicked up and once it settled, she saw a figure climb out of the truck. Elijah. She waved at him and walked over. He immediately embraced her, his face lined with worry.

"I wasn't sure you would come," he said.

"Of course. I wouldn't leave you hanging."

"I was worried you might not be able to. That you might be incapacitated."

• • • •

Incapacitated? Oh. He knew where her head had been. Wren smiled nervously. "I'm here. Thank you for reaching out. I needed a friend."

"I know. You know you can always call me, day or night. Just so you understand, I've had days like that. If it wasn't for Tse, who knows where I'd be? Or if even would be," Elijah said and met her eyes.

Wren nodded, letting their eyes lock. She had to remember everyone had their burdens and their demons, not only her. Elijah let his hand drift up and placed it delicately on the side of her face.

"Your eyes are like stone. Unreadable," he whispered.

"I was just thinking, I need to remember I'm not the only one who suffers. I know you have been through a lot, too, and are here offering me support."

Elijah nodded, then dropped his hand. "I didn't only mean in that way. Your eyes are the palest green I've ever seen... like there is no end or beginning."

"Oh." Wren blushed. "I always thought of them as plain and lifeless."

Elijah laughed, shaking his head. "You're so strange. No, you hold the cosmos in your eyes. The earth, the sky, the sea. You have to be kinder to yourself, Wren."

Wren wanted to tell him she found his eyes to be a constant draw inwards, like a cave in a storm. Chaos and comfort at the same time. But she didn't want him to think she was coming on to him. Not that she didn't want to wrap her fingers in his hair and kiss his full mouth, but that's not who they were. They were friends, she needed to keep it that way. She lost people who got too close. Keep everyone at arm's length and they stayed around.

• • • •

"Thank you, Elijah. Are you ready to hike?" she asked, diverting his attention.

He took notice of her discomfort and tipped his head. "Let's do it."

They headed up into the rugged terrain, matching each other's strides. While they hiked, Elijah told her the history of the Navajo, how the land was as much part of them as their bodies were. Wren listened intently, not even knowing what her family's history was. Her last name was German and she had Scottish ancestors, she knew that much, but that was about all. Elijah knew everything about the land, his ancestors, and customs. He told her hadn't always felt so connected because as a kid and teen all he could think about was leaving the reservation, being part of the world he saw on television. His mother was diabetic and died young, his father was an alcoholic and was in and out of Elijah's life until he died at sixty from heart failure. Elijah told Wren how he himself was a father by twenty.

Wren talked about her family, how they'd written her off for years. She was thirty years old and was trying to rebuild that relationship with them. At this point, it was just letters and an occasional phone call during the holidays. She expressed how she didn't want children and saw herself being alone for pretty much the rest of her life. Elijah didn't question it and listened, offering support. They made it to the top of the mesa and the view took Wren's breath away. A breeze picked up, blowing sweaty strands of hair off her face and she closed her eyes. If only life could be like this moment.

She opened her eyes and glanced at Elijah. His hair was blowing back and he was staring intently across the land with his hands in his back pockets. She wanted to reach out and touch him

• • • •

but knew boundaries needed to be maintained. Elijah turned and smiled at her; for a moment she was captured by his beauty. His eyes had an almond shape to them and under his black eyebrows, they were striking. She blushed and looked away. He moved towards her and touched her arm.

"You ready?"

Her mind was befuddled as she stared blankly at him. "For what?"

"To go?"

She nodded and met his eyes. "Thanks, Elijah. For being there for me today. You're a good friend."

Elijah brushed a piece of hair out of his face, seeming like he wanted to say something but just watched her. Wren began to feel self-conscious and glanced away. Elijah moved and started back down. Wren observed him go, admiring his muscular back under his t-shirt, and sighed. She needed to not destroy this. When they reached the parking area, Wren wasn't ready to go and thought of a way to stall. Luckily, Elijah was two steps ahead.

"Hey, I packed a cooler of food if you want. We can sit in the back of my truck," he offered.

"Good! I'm hungry for sure. I didn't even think to pack food for the hike."

Elijah took the cooler out of the cab of the truck and climbed into the bed. He pulled out his blood testing kit and pricked his finger, allowing a drop of blood to fall on the testing strip. Satisfied with his results on the meter, he packed it away to lay down a blanket and began taking food out. Wren climbed up into the truck, grateful for his foresight. He'd made sandwiches and had cut fruit and crackers. There was a canteen of water and a couple of cups. Wren ate a sandwich and enjoyed the ease at which they were with each other. She couldn't deny she was attracted to him but neither seemed to make it a deal-breaker. They talked about the fire season and plans for the winter.

Elijah checked the time, then sighed. "I need to head back and pick up Tse. He was spending the day at a friend's. I want to do this again."

"Me too," Wren agreed.

Elijah stared at her, biting his lip. "When? Do you want to make a set day a week, so I can make arrangements for Tse? My grandmother is getting older, so I'm trying to make alternate care for him when I'm gone."

"You can always bring him," Wren offered again, already knowing the answer.

Elijah shook his head. "Not yet. I want time for us to get to know each other better. He'll be back in school soon, anyway, and we can meet then."

Wren understood but also felt slighted he didn't want her to meet his son. She was being silly. He had every right. She also wanted time alone with him. "I usually have Wednesdays off. How about then?"

"That sounds good. We can meet here on Wednesdays at the same time if it works for you."

"Sounds like a plan. I can pack food next time," Wren offered.

"Deal."

They put away the remaining food and climbed out of the truck.

Elijah turned to Wren. "Next week. Call me before then if you need to talk. I mean it."

"I will. Same to you."

• • • •

Wren did something she never did and stepped forward to hug him. He returned the hug, rubbing her back. Wren drew back and glanced at him. He climbed into the cab of his truck and smiled. She smiled back, raising a hand as she stepped away.

Wednesdays. It was something she could hold on to. She turned and walked to her car, pausing to fish out her keys. She dropped them and when she stood back up from retrieving the keys, he was gone.

Chapter Eight

T he rest of the summer was a series of fighting fires, land control, and meeting up for hikes with both Elijah on Wednesdays and Dylan when they could at the camp. Dylan was open and funny, allowing Wren to feel like the big sister she'd robbed herself of being because of heroin. He was twenty-four and regaled her with tales of his adventures. His adventures were mainly finding ways to get into trouble and unintentionally hurt himself. He'd met his ex-boyfriend his first year of college and they rapidly blew off school to find different ways to get into shit. They'd gone to Vegas and convinced guests they were staff to save them trips getting change and buying game chips. Guests would give them money to do this instead, and Dylan and his boyfriend, Grayson, racked up over a thousand dollars before their jig was figured out. In running from casino security, Dylan tripped over a curb and broke his arm.

• • • •

Then there was the time they got cornered by a bear while camping and threw beer cans at it until it got frustrated and left. The time their car broke down in the desert, and they were picked up by a guy they were sure was covered in blood. The stories went on and on. The one thing Wren could see was that Dylan was still madly in love with Grayson and grieving for their life together. Every time he said Grayson's name, his voice changed a little. Wren knew the feeling.

"Have you talked to Grayson since you broke up?" Wren asked.

Dylan sighed, shaking his head. "No. I mean, what's the point? He ended it and me calling him would seem desperate and needy."

"That's fair. What about writing to him? Telling him how you feel?"

"This isn't the eighteen hundreds, Wren. Nobody writes anymore," Dylan teased.

"Dylan! Yes, they do. I still love getting letters."

"Yeah, but what are you, like, ninety?"

Wren's mouth dropped open and she laughed. "You'd better watch it, mister, before I pull out my ruler and smack you on the knuckles with it."

"I don't even know what that means. Is that some kind of kinky sex thing, you perv?"

Wren laughed so hard, tears streamed down her face. Rob came in and stared at the two of them falling off their chairs, clutching their sides, and shook his head.

"What did I miss?" he asked as he sat down with them.

Wren was laughing too hard to answer and pointed toward Dylan.

• • • •

"Wren is coming on to me, promising to spank me or something," Dylan replied, which only made Wren laugh even harder.

Rob glanced between them. "You're so fucking weird."

Wren finally composed herself and wiped the tears away from her eyes. "Seriously, though, Dylan has some stories to tell. Surprised he never got locked up."

"Nope, free and clear," Dylan replied, holding his hands up. "Not that I didn't deserve to be."

Rob and Wren glanced at each other and smiled. They'd done their time, neither intended to ever go back. He nudged her foot under the table. They'd all been young once and made stupid decisions. Wren met his eyes, nodding. They never took freedom for granted. Dylan was lucky he wasn't caught and sent to prison, but none of them really should've been. They were still just kids; guidance would've gone a lot further. Wren was an addict and Rob was trying to survive in a system of poverty.

"Shit, I need to get ready for my shift. Thanks for the hike and the talk, Wren," Dylan said as he stood up.

"Think about what I said about writing a letter. I think I have some ink and a feather in my tent you can use. Maybe some parchment," Wren replied.

Dylan busted out laughing and leaned down to kiss her cheek. "Thanks, Wren. I shall write it by candlelight for effect."

Rob frowned, staring at the two of them. "I don't even want to know."

Dylan left and Rob turned to Wren. "He's a good kid. Hell of a firefighter, too."

"I'm glad he joined us. Brings a little lightness to us old folk."

"Ha, speak for yourself, lady," Rob replied.

"You are older than me by a few years, old man."

"True, true. Not ready for a cane yet, though. Besides, with the baby on the way, I have to stay spry. She's going to put me through the wringer."

"She? You found out the gender?"

"We did. Lindsay is beside herself, buying every girl thing she can find. I have to admit, it's a little intimidating."

"Aw, you'll do fine. When is she due?"

"February."

"Good timing, before the season starts," Wren replied.

"You'd think we'd planned it, right?" Rob joked.

Wren needed to think more about the end of the current season. Last year she'd rented an apartment in the nearby town, but she didn't like her neighbors. Most firefighters had a home to go to. She'd chosen to just stay at the camp previously, but now wanted a place she could call her own. She'd saved money staying at the camp and considered purchasing a small house.

"So, Rob, I was thinking. I have money saved and was wondering, how hard is it to buy a house?"

Rob raised his eyebrows. "Thinking of buying? We bought ours, but honestly, with my history, I don't know if we could have without Lindsay's parents helping us out. I had no credit and coming out of prison didn't have much of a work history."

"Oh," Wren felt deflated. She wanted to put that part of her life behind her.

"I mean, maybe there are programs or something. You work hard, now. Look into it. Sorry, didn't mean to make you feel bad."

"No, it's reality, I guess. I have less than two years of work history and a prison record. Not sure anyone will take a chance on me."

"Sorry, Wren. I know it sucks. I'll ask around and see what's out there."

"Thanks, Rob. I hate that decisions I made in my late teens and early twenties are going to haunt me forever."

"Don't I know it? If it wasn't for Lindsay, I think I would've gone back to that life. I don't know what I'd do without her."

"Give yourself some credit. You're a devoted father and husband; you work your ass off. The system sets people up to fail," Wren reasoned.

"You're right. I'd do anything for my family. I was lucky to have a lifeline out," Rob said softly. "Your time is coming."

"Let's hope so. Alright, I need to shower and get some rest. Thanks, Rob. It's nice having someone around who understands."

"Anytime, Wren."

Wren showered and climbed into bed. She laid on her back and stared up at the top of the tent. If she could go back, would she change things? The truth was through her bad choices she'd also met Gabe, which was the best part of her life. She wouldn't give that up. He'd forever be part of her and she'd serve a million sentences for the time she had with him. In a way, she now was. His death was her sentence. She closed her eyes and pictured his face. The way he always cocked his head slightly when he was laughing. She imagined his arms around her and ached to feel him close. The way he'd rub the back of her neck when she rested her head on his chest. She sighed and wiped away the tears. Missing him was her penance.

• • • •

The next morning she lay in bed, trying to figure out what to do after the season. She could rent a house but didn't like having a landlord. Frustrated, she sat up and got ready for her shift. Something would come to her. There was no point dwelling on it. She shoved on her boots and met her team for their shift. At least that was something she could count on.

A few Wednesdays later, she met Elijah for a hike but it started to rain when she got there. He drove in and waved her over. She ran to his truck and climbed in.

"I guess we should've checked the weather," she said and laughed, pushing wet hair out of her face.

"You want to take a drive? There's a halfway decent diner in town and we can grab a bite to eat," Elijah replied.

"Sure. Beats steaming up your truck."

They drove for a bit and pulled into a small diner with a sign flashing the word "coffee" over and over. Coffee actually sounded good. They ran through the rain and grabbed a booth near the windows. Wren twisted her hair, feeling water drip out, and looked at Elijah. He was striking with his wet hair pushed off his face to his back. He met her eyes and smiled.

"Still good to see you," he said.

Wren grinned and touched his hand. "Breakfast will be nice. I wanted to talk to you, anyway. Trying to figure out what I'm going to do after the season."

"What are you thinking?"

"Well, I was wanting to buy a small house but hitting some dead ends with that. With my history no one may want to take a chance on me, you know?"

Elijah nodded. "Yeah, I've heard that in the past."

• • • •

"I really don't know. I don't want to rent again, I feel like it's time to settle down. Have something of my own. I'm still looking into some types of loans for people in my situation, so hopefully, something pans out."

Elijah didn't reply but peered out the window in thought. The waitress came up and took their order. She brought coffee back while their food was being made. Elijah sipped his coffee, then glanced at Wren.

"I'm trying to think about what I'm going to do long-term myself."

"Really? Like what?"

"I think it's time to leave the reservation."

"Oh! Why? It's your home."

"It is. But I want Tse to see the world, too. The reservation will always be my home and I can go back. But I've isolated myself there for eight years. I want him to understand the big picture. To be able to make choices. My grandmother is getting too old to live alone and her house is too small for Tse and me to live with her much longer. Not to mention it's falling apart. I could invest all of my money in fixing it up, but then I'd have no money for Tse and me. Or, I could buy a house and move her in with us."

"Elijah, you have such a big heart."

"It's the way it should be. She took care of me after my mother died and has helped with Tse. It's my turn to take care of her."

"Where? I mean, where would you buy a house?"

"That's the thing I need to think about. What my future holds."

Wren nodded. Buying a house was a commitment. He'd want a place Tse could grow up. She hoped it wouldn't be far away

75

but didn't want to say anything since it was a hard enough decision. Their food came and they ate as they conversed about the world. Elijah was very committed to preserving the land and while Wren hadn't thought about it to the level he had, she understood. The land was what gave her back her life.

As they wrapped up breakfast, the rain showed no sign of letting up, so they headed back to the parking area where Wren's car was. Even though they didn't get to hike, Wren always enjoyed Elijah's company and his ability to be a sounding board. They sat in his truck as the rain beat down and talked so much, the windows steamed up. Wren laughed.

"Someone's going to think we're making out in here," she joked.

"Maybe we should prove them right," Elijah teased.

"Better watch yourself. You might get us in trouble," Wren replied, laughing.

Elijah reached out and touched her face, rubbing his thumb across her cheek. Wren paused and watched him. Heat filled the small cab as Wren held her breath. When he leaned in and kissed her lightly on the lips, she didn't stop him. He sat back and sighed.

"I like you, Wren. You've been the best friend I've had in a long time. I don't want to mess that up. I'm attracted to you, but your friendship means the world to me."

Wren nodded, she knew what he meant. "I feel the same. On both fronts. We've both had our hearts broken in the past and our friendship is everything to me. I don't want anything to ruin that."

Elijah watched her and she reached out, running her fingers across his lips. He grinned, taking her hand. The heat of the

• • • •

moment caught them both off guard. They knew they couldn't risk it. They'd newly found each other as friends, so jumping into anything else was detrimental to the tender connection they'd made.

Elijah cleared his throat, meeting her eyes. "I want you to meet Tse."

Chapter Nine

Elijah brought Tse along on the next hiking trip. If Wren had expected a shy, timid child, she was greatly mistaken. When she pulled into the parking area, Elijah and Tse were already there. Tse was standing in the back of the truck while Elijah tested his blood sugar. Wren parked and walked over to them, hearing Tse chatter away. Elijah frowned looking at his blood meter but smiled when she came up.

"Wren! Hey. Tse, this is my friend Wren," Elijah said, attempting to get Tse's attention.

Tse glanced at Wren and smiled with his adult front teeth just starting to grow in. He was a striking child with long brown hair and eyes that could only be described as bronze. He had light freckles across his nose, his skin a light caramel.

"Hi, Wren."

"Hi, Tse."

• • • •

He went back to telling his father something about the clouds and Wren glanced at Elijah, who was focused elsewhere. He gave himself a shot of insulin, then packed his supplies away.

"Everything okay?" Wren asked quietly so as to not let Tse know.

Elijah shook his head. "It will be. I'm having a hard time keeping my blood sugar in range."

"Do you know why?"

"Not really. I just need to keep an eye on it. Nothing to worry about," Elijah said and met her eyes. "It's good to see you."

Wren blushed. "Good to see you, too."

Elijah hugged her and she breathed him in. Regardless of their friendship, the feelings were still there.

"Daddy, can we go?" Tse asked impatiently.

"Yes, come on, let me get you down." Elijah helped Tse down from the truck and the three of them started walking.

At no point did Tse stop talking. Wren didn't mind because she was afraid she'd have to try and make conversation with a child who didn't know her. He pointed out everything and spouted off facts about whatever they saw, plus some. He was a bright child, very outgoing. They stopped for lunch and Wren noticed Elijah checking his blood sugar again. Her stomach knotted until he seemed relieved by the results. They ate and she noticed he'd altered his diet. He packed sandwiches for her and Tse but was eating a salad with nuts. She didn't know much about diabetes, however, wanted to make sure she was being supportive.

"Hey, when I bring food next time, what should I pack for you?"

Elijah looked uncomfortable. "I think, for now, I'd better pack my own food. No offense."

• • • •

"I'm not offended. Worried, but not offended."

"Don't worry, Wren. I need to be more careful. Watch my supplies better."

"Insulin?"

"Yeah. I need to stay on top of checking my blood sugar and not space my insulin so much."

Wren chewed her lip, nodding. Tse started talking about birds, then paused to stare at her. "Wren? Like the bird?"

"Yep, like the bird," she replied. "My name is actually Gretchen but I've been called Wren most of my life."

He turned his head, considering, and went off on a tangent about different birds. Elijah laughed and shrugged. He was used to it. He laid on his side, bracing himself on his elbow, and listened to Tse. Wren sat cross-legged, enjoying watching them interact. She pictured Elijah at twenty with a newborn baby and now with his very active son. He was a good father; it was hard to believe this was the same man she'd met months before, who seemed angry and distant. He glanced over at her and their eyes met. Heat flushed through her as she cast her eyes away.

Tse started to get bored, so they collected their blanket and packs to head back down to the parking area. Tse climbed in the truck and rested his head against the seat. They'd managed to wear him out. Wren stood with Elijah on his side of the truck. He was leaning with his back against the door and reached out, taking her fingers in his own. He met her eyes and ran his thumb across her fingers.

"Wren, this isn't going away."

"What?"

"This feeling. I think about you a lot."

• • • •

Wren bobbed her head. "Me too. But I can't lose you. I've been down this road... it ends badly."

"No, Wren. That road ended badly. We have no idea where this journey will take us. I think we need to talk more about this."

Wren reached up and touched Elijah's cheek. This time she leaned in to kiss him. They let their mouths linger and she drew away breathless. She hadn't felt this way since Gabe. Gabe. Guilt washed over her and she stepped back. Elijah pulled her back.

"This doesn't change anything about Gabe. You love him. He was part of your life and is part of you now. I'm not trying to replace him. You can hold both of us in your heart," he said gently.

Wren peered at him. He was so different from Gabe. Gabe was funny and energetic. Elijah was steady and calm. Wren felt her head spinning into chaos and winced.

"Elijah I..."

He stood up and hugged her tightly. "We don't have to figure this out today. Or tomorrow. We have time. I love you, Wren. As a friend, as a person; I want you in my life. This is hard for me, too. To trust anyone. Let's take it slow and see what happens. No matter what friends first, okay?"

"Okay. I love you, too, Elijah. I just don't want us to do anything which forces us away from each other."

"I know... me either. I'll come alone next time and we can talk. Maybe kiss a little," he joked tenderly.

Wren laughed. "I'd like that."

Elijah turned and opened the door. "Hey, Tse, Wren is going home, okay?"

"Bye, Wren. Bird Lady," Tse said, his voice small and tired.

"Bye, Tse. It was nice meeting you."

• • • •

Elijah climbed in, touching her hand one last time before shutting the door. Wren went to her car and climbed in. She thought about Gabe and let her heart hurt for a bit. She knew Elijah was right in that she didn't have to give up Gabe for him, but it still ached. It was recognizing Gabe was truly gone and she'd never get to hold him again. She allowed herself to cry on the drive home. She'd always love Gabe. It was like he took a trip far away, where she couldn't go but he was still there, part of her. In her mind, she kissed him and wrapped her arms around him. She could feel his breath on her neck, his lips kissing her forehead.

She was afraid to go too far with Elijah. To let him in and be vulnerable, but this all seemed to have a mind of its own. They'd talk and figure things out. As he said, there was no rush. They were both bruised and battered. It would take time. For now, she'd stay focused on work and meet him to hike. Everything else would find its way.

When the phone rang in the middle of the night, she almost didn't answer it until she saw it was her brother. He never called, so it had to be serious. She picked up the phone and answered, "Hello?"

"Wren, it's Geoff. You need to come home. Dad's in the hospital. He had a heart attack."

Wren held her breath for a moment. "Alright. Let me pack and I'll leave as soon as I can. How's Mom?"

"Numb." Geoff gave her the hospital information and they hung up. Wren went to Rob's tent and woke him up.

"I have to go, my father is in the hospital," Wren whispered.

Rob sat up, rubbing his face. "Damn. I'm sorry, Wren. Do you need anything?"

"No, I need to leave. Can you get my shifts covered?"

"Sure. Be safe and let me know when you get there, okay?"

"Thanks, Rob," Wren replied and hugged him.

She loaded up the car and drove out of camp in the dark. It was hours away and she hadn't been back since she'd hitched a ride to Phoenix ten years earlier. She still wasn't ready to go back. She texted Elijah to let him know she wasn't sure how long she'd be gone. He texted back he loved her and he wasn't going anywhere.

By the time she got to the hospital, she was road weary and emotionally drained. Her father was in ICU and the prognosis wasn't good. Her mother was by his bedside. Wren paused at the door watching them. They looked so much older and frail. Geoff came up from behind her and handed her coffee.

"You look terrible," he said quietly.

"Thanks, Geoff. How did you get here so fast?"

"I flew. It's not good, Wren. He had a massive heart attack and he is in and out of it. If he doesn't pull through, I'm going to ask Mom to move back east with me."

Wren peered at Geoff. He was younger but was always the one who handled things. He had to when she was fucked up, then in prison. "I'm sorry, Geoff. For being such a shit sister. You deserved better."

Geoff nodded and shrugged. "It's okay, Wren. We all have our struggles. I never blamed you. You should never have been locked up. You needed help, not punishment, you know?"

Wren smiled wryly. She knew. It destroyed eight years of her life, probably more. "Thanks, Geoff."

"I'm proud of you, Wren. For beating heroin and turning your life around."

She didn't want to correct him. To tell him she didn't beat addiction, only had been removed from it long enough to be forced down a different path. She never would've done it on her own. If someone sat in front of her right now with heroin, she figured it was a fifty-fifty chance she'd go back to it. Maybe more so. Everything had been out of her control. Which had been good. Her control was *no* control. But she appreciated his faith in her, it made her feel not so alone.

Her mother looked over at her and her eyes got wide. "Gretchen."

That one word made tears fall down Wren's cheeks and she went to embrace her mother. Her mother's red hair had faded to mostly golden-gray and lines surrounded her eyes. Wren hadn't seen her family in a decade. Her mother touched her face and smiled.

"I've missed you."

"I missed you, too, Mom."

They went to her father's side. He was pale, his face showed no signs of life. The machines he was hooked up to beeped and blinked, showing he was still alive. Wren reached out and squeezed her father's hand. For a second his eyes fluttered open and he stared right at her. His mouth moved but nothing came out. Wren made out the word "Gretchen" and burst into tears. She'd allowed her shame and fear to keep her from her family. There was no going back. She'd wasted those years.

In the early morning hours, her father let go and passed away. She was sleeping on a chair in the room when she heard the nurses come in. She sat up and they were consoling her visibly distraught mother. Geoff was on the other side of the bed with his head down. Wren got up and went to him, putting her arm over his shoulder. He turned and hugged her, crying.

For the first time since he was a small child, she was able to be the one to offer him comfort. She stared at her father's lifeless body and swore she wouldn't waste any more time. Now, Gabe and her father were on the other side.

But she was on this side and needed to wake the fuck up.

Chapter Ten

Wren's mother agreed to sell the house and move back east with Geoff. It took a couple of months to get everything situated. Wren stayed to help since she felt she had nothing else to offer. She missed her crew, Dylan, Rob, and Elijah, but she felt she owed this to her family for all she'd put them through. Geoff already had a fully furnished house, so they sold off almost everything which wasn't sentimental and packed up the rest. Geoff rented a truck and they loaded it to the brim. On the morning he and her mother were driving the truck back east, they sat eating breakfast sandwiches in the empty kitchen and reminisced. Wren thought she'd be sad about the house being sold, but it had been gone long before to her.

They locked up the house and left the keys in the box for the real estate agent. Wren hugged her mother and Geoff, promising to come to visit. She didn't know if it was true, but she hoped it was. They drove off, waving at her one last time. Once the truck was out of sight, she glanced back at the house, up to what used to be her bedroom window. She'd shed so many tears in there, just wishing to be accepted. To be loved. Now she was. She texted Rob she'd be heading back to the area, knowing the season was already over. They shifted to daily work but with no camp, so she needed to figure that out, too. He mentioned Dylan might be looking for a roommate. She texted Dylan after and he asked her to please come stay with him.

Lastly, she texted Elijah. They'd been in contact while she was gone, however, she sensed a distance may have grown between them. She asked if they could resume their Wednesday hikes and it took him a while to respond. It was only one line when he did.

"Let's talk when you get back."

The drive back to Arizona was long, but Wren wanted to push it in one day. Dylan sent her his address, so she headed straight there. By the time she arrived, it was late evening and she was afraid he might not be awake. She knocked on the door and waited. He flung the door open and gave her a huge hug.

"Man, have I missed you!" he exclaimed, grinning.

"Dylan! You're a sight for sore eyes. Thank you for letting me stay."

"Are you kidding? I've been lonely since camp broke down. I have an extra room and an air mattress if that works."

"Anything works. I'm beat but if you aren't tired, I'd love to stay up and talk."

"For sure. Are you hungry? I made spaghetti earlier, there's some left over."

"Yes! I haven't eaten since early this morning."

• • • •

Dylan showed her the kitchen and where everything was. He heated the food and they brought plates to the living room. Wren told him about her trip; how she was glad to be back where she belonged. His eyes lit up.

"I forgot to tell you! Grayson and I are talking again. Only as friends, but he opened up to me about how lonely he was every time I left. How he felt like I wasn't thinking about his feelings. Which was probably true. I did take him for granted, always on the adrenaline chase."

"Do you think you'll get back together?"

"I don't know. I have some growing up to do, but I love him and am glad he is at least open to talking."

"I'm happy to hear it. Relationships are hard and for some reason, as humans, we insist on making it harder."

"What about you? Were you and Elijah ever officially an item?"

"Not officially. Just really good friends. I also had some growing up to do. I may have blown any chance by being gone for so long. As long as we remain friends, I guess it's good," Wren said truthfully.

"You know, Wren, it's okay to fight for something you want."

"I don't know how to do that. I've always been a runner... if something good came my way, it was by sheer luck."

Dylan nodded and grinned. "I get that. But you'll know when the time comes."

They stayed up into the early morning hours until Wren couldn't keep her eyes open. Dylan showed her the extra room and she crashed on the air mattress fully clothed. By the time she woke up, he'd headed out to work. He left her a note, letting her know when he'd be home. She called work to see when she could return and they agreed to the following week. It was already mid-November and she was starting to burn through some of the money she'd saved to buy a house. Not that it seemed likely anymore. She texted Elijah to let him know she was back in Arizona and staying with Dylan. He didn't reply. After a few hours, she decided to go for a walk and see what was in the area. There was a grocery store within walking distance and a small park. She watched the mothers with their children at the playground, feeling no sense of motherhood.

By the time she got home, she had a message from Dylan, saying he'd pick up pizza on the way home. Rob said he'd swing by to see her, too. Still nothing from Elijah. He'd been supportive while she was in Texas dealing with her father's death, but maybe he'd decided to move on. She tried to not read too much into it. The next day was Wednesday, the day they normally hiked and his lack of response let her know they wouldn't be meeting.

Dylan came in with pizza and drinks, followed shortly by Rob, who gave Wren a bear hug. She was so relieved to be back around her family. They dug into pizza and Rob filled her in on the happenings for the team. The rains had been a welcome relief and they'd gotten the fires out. They were working on clearing the forest floor now. Wren couldn't wait to get back to work. Rob headed out to his family and Wren and Dylan stayed up to watch a movie. He cracked jokes, pointing out every way they failed in making the movie. Wren glanced at him, grinning.

"I missed you, Dylan."

"I missed you, too, Wren. You're like the big sister I never had. Well, I have two sisters, but they're bitches," he joked.

Wren laughed, shaking her head. "You're so weird. Alright, I'm heading to bed. I'm still travel tired."

"Sounds good. I have an early morning, too. Can't wait until you're back out with us. Not the same without you," Dylan replied.

"Trust me, I need to find my feet again."

Wren headed to the room and flopped down on the mattress. She was about to doze off when her phone lit up with an incoming message. She clicked on it.

"Hike tomorrow?" Elijah asked.

Wren wanted to not respond or to say no, out of spite for him not responding sooner. But ultimately she wanted to see him. To figure out what was going on. She typed one word, "Sure."

The next morning she got up with Dylan as he got ready for work. Seeing him in his jeans and boots made her long for getting back out to the land. She let him know she was going hiking with Elijah and he raised his eyebrows. She shook her head, shrugging.

"I don't know. He's being odd. I guess I'll know more after today."

Dylan bobbed his head. "People act strange when they're protecting themselves. You know that."

"I do. Anyway, we shall see."

"We shall," Dylan replied and winked.

He headed out for work and she left right after to drive to the meetup spot. It was cold, so she slipped on a coat over her t-shirt and pants. When she pulled into the parking area, she saw Elijah was already there. Her heart started to beat fast and her hands were sweaty. She'd missed him but now didn't know what she was walking into. He was standing outside of his truck, his hands in his jacket pockets, watching as she got out. He walked towards her as she made her way to him. They paused a few feet away from each other. It was awkward, making Wren wonder if she should've come. Elijah gave her a quick hug, their eyes meeting for a second.

"You want to hike? We can talk on the way," he asked.

Wren nodded, then followed him up the trail. They didn't speak for some time and Wren didn't know how to break the ice. Finally, she took a deep breath. "How's Tse?"

"Good, he's back in school now, which makes things easier. For work and things."

"That's good. He's so bright."

Elijah didn't reply, so Wren dropped it. When they got to the top of the hill, they stopped to watch the sun make its way into the sky. Elijah turned to her, silently observing. Wren didn't know if he was going to say something and furrowed her brow. Why were things so hard? She'd only been gone a few months. Finally, he spoke.

"I missed you, Wren. I wasn't sure if you were coming back."

"Oh. This is my home now, my job is here. I love my family, but I felt nothing there. There's nothing left."

"So, is that why you came back? Because there is nothing there? For work?"

Wren didn't know what he was getting at and cocked her head. "I guess so. I mean, this is all I know anymore."

Elijah nodded. He didn't say anything else and Wren felt something hanging between them. She was confused and stared at him. Dylan's words echoed in her mind. Sometimes you have to fight for things. She didn't know how to do that. Elijah sighed and checked the time.

"It's time to go," he said, turning to go back down the hill.

Suddenly, everything that had ever happened in Wren's life came together. The love of her parents, the bullying in school, her brother thinking she hung the moon and stars, the drugs, loving and losing Gabe, prison, firefighting, meeting Elijah, her father's death. It all came to a point, an arrow showing her the direction she needed to go. She stopped in her tracks and watched Elijah moving down the hill away from her.

"Elijah!"

He turned, confused, and stared at her, his eyes shadowed. "Wren?"

She ran to him and wrapped her arms around him. She hugged him tightly, feeling his arms slide around her waist. She looked up at him and kissed him deeply, relieved when he responded.

"I came back for you. For you and Tse. Not because this is what I have known or for work. I came back for us."

Elijah's face relaxed, his eyes staring into hers. He leaned down and kissed her, letting his mouth cover hers and stay there. Wren felt her knees waver and pulled away for a breath. Elijah wound his fingers in her hair and drew her in against him. He kissed her again, then rested his cheek against her hair.

"I thought you were gone. I couldn't go through that again, Wren. When you left, I realized how much I loved you. Then when you didn't come back for months, I prepared myself for losing you. That you might never come back."

Wren rested her head against his shoulder. "I'm sorry. I had to wrap those things up. But I missed you every day and wanted to talk to you all the time. Elijah, I love you. I want to be with you."

Elijah pulled back and met her eyes to make her understand. "I can't go through another heartbreak, Wren."

"Me either, Elijah. I guess we need to learn to trust each other. That's the first step."

Chapter Eleven

T he thing about wildland firefighting is the danger exists year-round. Heavy equipment, unstable ground, and unpredictable weather can turn a regular day into a fight for life. By the time the holidays rolled around, Wren was back at it full-force and glad to be with her crew. Rob was relieved to have her back as he'd covered for her while she was out, working long days and not seeing his family. Over the holidays, she and Dylan agreed to cover the shifts, so those with families could spend time with their loved ones. Wren had no plans to see her family and Dylan admitted since coming out as gay, his family had been a little uncomfortable. He'd been spending previous holidays with Grayson, but they'd agreed to take a break this year.

It was a skeleton crew and the focus was on clearing brush, pulling vines and dead wood away from trees. They headed up into the hills and Dylan and Wren took turns using the chainsaw to clear deadfall, while the others used shovels and hoes to clear the ground. It was a quiet day and they were coming to the end of their shift when it happened.

Dylan was clearing deadfall with the chainsaw near the edge when the ground he was standing on gave way. He reached out to grab ahold of a branch, but it broke off in his hands and he fell with the chainsaw down the cliffside. Wren saw him reach out, his eyes meeting hers in panic, and ran to him but he was gone by the time she got there. She grasped onto a tree trunk and peered over the edge. His body was down below, his right leg twisted behind him, blood gushing from a wound on his stomach.

"Dylan!" she screamed but he didn't respond. She grabbed her radio and called for help. She glanced around for a way down to him, realizing she'd have to go back down and around. She notified the other guys and began the trek down. It was arduous and seemed to take forever. By the time she got to him, she could hear a helicopter off in the distance. She ran to his side and touched his face. He was lifeless but if she leaned close, she swore she could feel breath on her cheek. His leg was broken and mangled. There was a large gash on his stomach, caused by the chainsaw when he fell with it in front of him.

She stood up, waving frantically at the copter as it got close. They lowered a gurney with a paramedic on it. His face looked grim when he saw Dylan, and Wren helped him move Dylan's body to the gurney. The paramedic quickly strapped Dylan in and straddled the gurney, motioning for it to be raised. Wren ran back up the hill to her guys and grabbed her things. They'd all ridden out together, so they loaded up and headed back to the meet site. From there, Wren got on the radio and found out where they were taking Dylan. She texted Elijah and Rob to tell

• • • •

them what happened as she drove to the hospital. She kept picturing the fear on Dylan's face as he tried to grab on to keep from falling.

Rob met her at the hospital and they ran inside. Recognizing Wren's uniform, the nurses escorted them back through Emergency to a waiting room. A nurse gathered as much information as he could and asked about next of kin. Rob took over and made some calls to try and find out how to reach Dylan's family. They were informed he was in surgery but that he'd lost a lot of blood. Wren was in too much shock to cry and sat staring at the floor. She should've grabbed him or told him to not stand so close to the edge. But he couldn't have known, and she was too far away. The ground had been stable. Or so they'd thought.

Hours passed with no word. Rob was able to get ahold of Dylan's parents and they were on their way. Finally, a doctor came in and asked for Dylan's family but they hadn't arrived yet. Wren stood up and walked to the doctor.

"I'm his roommate and we work together. We were on site when this happened. Is he okay?"

The doctor shifted uncomfortably, knowing he needed to speak to the family first, but could see the desperation in Wren's eyes. He met her eyes and shook his head slightly.

"I'm sorry. He lost too much blood and the wound in his stomach had perforated the intestinal wall. He didn't pull through."

Wren stood frozen, attempting to understand the words the doctor had said. She shook her head and whispered, "No!"

The doctor reached out to her and she jerked away. He was wrong. She stepped back into Rob, who'd heard. She turned and saw tears streaming down his face. It was true. Dylan was gone. She started to sob and pushed her way out of the waiting room. She ran down hallways, not knowing where she was going, and got lost. She crumpled to the ground and sobbed into her knees. They'd just been talking about what to do for dinner. Trying to convince each other it was the other person's turn to cook. It was his, but she'd played along. She cried until her eyes and nose were raw and peered around. As she looked up, she saw Elijah coming down the hallway, his face twisted in concern. He came and sat down in front of her, gathering her in his arms.

"Wren, I'm so sorry about Dylan. I know you were close. I remember working with him this summer, how he was always laughing and cutting up. Rob is with his family. They're being told now."

Wren felt a fresh wave of tears coming and leaned against Elijah's shoulder. First Gabe, now Dylan. She was cursed. Anyone she got close to. Rob was different because he had his own family, but Gabe and Dylan had become hers. Elijah. What would happen if he got too close? She sat back and met his eyes.

"I'm a jinx. Anyone who lets me in will suffer."

Elijah pushed wet, teary hair from her eyes and shook his head. "There's no such thing. You simply love with all of your heart. You work a dangerous job. You know the risks, so did Dylan. He didn't deserve this, but you had nothing to do with it."

"If he'd gone back to Phoenix and never worked for us, he'd still be alive," Wren replied.

"You don't know that. Something may have happened in Phoenix. Wren, this sucks and it's going to hurt, but you can't blame yourself."

Wren rubbed her nose, feeling dizzy. She tried to stand up but lost her balance. Elijah put his arm around her and helped her

• • • •

get her balance. She was mentally exhausted and didn't want to have to face Dylan's parents. She searched around for an exit. Elijah, sensing what she needed, guided her through the halls and out a side exit. The sun and fresh air hit her face and she leaned into the bushes, vomiting.

"I can't go home. Can you let Rob know to tell Dylan's parents there is a key under the mat? They can go in and get anything they want. I can't go back there. Not right now."

Elijah settled her on a bench and called Rob. Rob would take care of everything. Elijah came and sat down. "I called Tse's friend's mom and asked if he could stay the night, considering. They said it was fine. We can get a hotel room if you want. Or a cabin. I know of some not far from here."

"A cabin. I can't face people, right now. Are you sure? Tse will be alright?"

"He'll be delighted to have a sleepover. We can take my truck. Do you need anything from your car?"

Wren thought about it. She did have a change of clothes she kept in case she needed them while working. She nodded and they headed for her car. She grabbed the clothes, realizing Dylan had left his phone in her car when they rode out together that morning. She slipped his phone into her bag and locked the car. Elijah led her to his truck and they climbed in. She stared at the hospital, knowing the body of one of her closest friends was inside and she began to cry again.

Elijah started up the truck, placing his hand on her leg as they drove out of the parking lot. He wound through the town and headed out. They drove for about an hour when he pulled into a state park and went into the office. He came out with keys and they took a winding road up into the trees. They ended up in front of a one-room cabin with a screened-in porch and got out. Elijah had brought a bag with him, maybe aware he'd need to stay with her.

The cabin was small but clean, and Wren immediately went to lie in the bed. She took off everything except her tank top underneath her uniform and her pants. She lay on the bed and stared at the wall. Elijah told her he was going to leave for some food but that he'd be right back. She heard the truck fire up and drive away. The silence was deafening. She kept picturing Dylan lying at the bottom with his leg twisted and blood pouring from his stomach. His eyes open, staring off at nothing. She sat up in bed and peered around the cabin. She couldn't hide forever, but for now, she couldn't go back to their apartment.

She remembered the day she found Gabe like that. Staring empty. She'd called his name and shook him, but he wouldn't wake up. She'd called 911 and screamed into the phone. When the paramedics came, they knew and looked at her with disregard. They took his body away and since she was only his girlfriend and a "junkie", she'd had no rights. She never saw him again and wasn't told about a funeral or anything. He'd been her everything and just like that became nothing. She pulled Dylan's phone out of her bag and turned it on. There was a message from her to pick up bread. There was an unread message from Grayson, saying he hoped Dylan had a nice holiday. She didn't want Grayson to feel like she did after Gabe died. Like he didn't matter.

She dialed the number and held her breath. A young, male voice answered. "Hello? Dylan?"

"Is this Grayson?"

"Uh, yeah," he replied, thrown off by a female voice coming from Dylan's number.

• • • •

"This is Wren, Dylan's roommate. I needed to call to let you know..." Wren couldn't get the words out as tears bubbled up. She cleared her throat. "Grayson, there was an accident. Dylan fell and was killed."

The line went dead. Wren looked to make sure she was still connected and she was. "Grayson?"

She heard heart-wrenching sobs coming from the other end and she held the phone to her ear, not knowing what to say or do. She cried with him and wished she could be there to ease his pain. She remembered crying for Gabe all alone in the apartment, then using heroin to try and mask her pain.

"Grayson, I want you to know how much Dylan loved you. He talked about you all the time and was happy you reconnected."

Grayson mumbled something unintelligible and Wren paused to listen. He was still crying and all she could make out was how he'd made a mistake, how Dylan was the love of his life. Wren understood, wishing she could let him know that. But his grief was too raw and she needed to just be present. She let him cry and speak. Finally, he let out a heavy breath and said he needed to go be alone. Wren let him know she'd send him any information she got, and if he needed to talk she was there.

Elijah came back with groceries and eyed her sitting on the bed. He came over to sit next to her. "Hey. I'm here for you."

She took his hand and squeezed it. "I know you are. I called Grayson, Dylan's ex-boyfriend. They were trying to work things out. He's pretty devastated."

"I'm sure he is. It *is* devastating. There are no words to make it better."

• • • •

"No, there aren't. Dylan was a kid with his whole life in front of him. This stupid fucking job took it all away. I hate this job. I hate that we're always short-staffed and overworked! I hate that he believed he was doing something and now his parents have to bury him. I hate all of this. I hate fucking breathing!" Wren yelled and covered her face with her hands.

She threw herself back on the bed and tried to hold her breath as long as she could. Body won over mind and she gasped. Elijah lay down next to her, sliding his arm around her. She didn't open her eyes or move. After a bit, he got up and went to the kitchen. He began making food and she opened her eyes, watching him. He went to his bag, pulled out his blood testing meter, and pricked his finger. She watched as he dripped blood into it and frowned at the results. He took out a syringe and gave himself a shot of insulin. Worry lined his face and he didn't know she had her eyes on him. He ran his hands through his hair and sighed. She knew this meant his sugar was too high. He didn't want to let her know and cause concern.

She felt that familiar feeling creep up in her. The feeling that anyone who got close to her would die. She rolled over on the bed and bit her lip until she tasted blood. If Elijah was to survive, he'd need to get as far away from her as possible.

Chapter Twelve

Most firefighters are aware of the risk and are clear with their wishes in the event of death. Dylan was no different. He'd expressed he wanted to be cremated and his ashes scattered in the trees. His family obliged and held a service there, so the other firefighters could attend. Wren sent the information to Grayson in case he wanted to come. On the day of the ceremony, Wren woke up in their apartment and sat on the edge of the air mattress. She wasn't ready to face the reality, however, she needed to for Dylan. She and Elijah had spent the first night in the cabin, but she knew she couldn't run from the pain forever. The next day, she had him take her to her car at the hospital and let him know she needed to do it alone. Elijah headed home to pick up Tse, and Wren came back to the apartment. It didn't look like anyone had been there, the items they had left scattered in their rush to get to work on time were left undisturbed.

● ● ● ●

She'd bawled when she poured out Dylan's half-drunk cup of coffee and punched the mirror in the bathroom when she saw he'd left the cap off the toothpaste. Things she'd teased him about and now would fix for the last time. Part of her wanted to leave everything as it was, but there was no point. Dylan was dead. Twenty-four years old and gone. She lay in his bed, wanting to smell him, but she couldn't draw him up. She was tired of crying and tired of hurting. When her father died, she was sad but part of her had always prepared for that. Losing Gabe and now Dylan so young, there was no way to prepare for it.

She dressed for the ceremony, knowing all the firefighters would wear their uniforms to honor Dylan. To honor a kid who had just started living life and chose a profession with no regard for him as a person. She asked Rob to pick her up, so she wouldn't have to drive. She made her uniform look sharp and went to Dylan's room. How would she get through this? She wiped tears away and sat on his bed.

"Dylan, I'm sorry."

It was all she could get out. There were so many words in her, but they knotted together in a lump she couldn't untie. She opened the bedside table and drew out a necklace with a Saint Florian medal, the patron saint of firefighters. She slipped it into her pocket and closed her eyes. There was no way out of this but to go through it. She'd been through it before and would need to force her way forward. She heard a soft knock at the door and went to answer it. Rob was standing there in his uniform; she could tell he'd been crying. She stepped forward into his arms and they held onto each other, not wanting time to move.

The ride to the funeral ceremony was quiet. Lindsay held Rob's hand, her stomach huge. Wren stared out the window and tried to figure out a way to hide in herself. What she would do for heroin, right now, she thought. Part of her knew if she tried hard enough, she could get some and obliterate any feelings in her. Part of her knew she needed to suffer to make sure she never let anyone get close again. Both thoughts were wrong, she knew that, but it was the only way she could get through the day. Besides, did it matter? If she did heroin? Who was she really hurting? She tried to shake the thought, but it stayed in a corner of her brain as an option.

The ceremony was up a hill under the trees, looking out over the land. Similar to where he died. Wren swallowed the bile pushing its way up her throat. She was truly afraid she'd start screaming. A podium had been brought up and placed at the front near the edge. A picture of Dylan in his uniform had been blown up and was placed near the podium. Even in that serious photo, Wren could see he was trying to not crack up. It reminded her of the nights they sat up talking and laughing so hard her sides hurt. Dylan was the funniest person she'd ever met. His parents and sisters stood near the photos, their faces blank and in shock. Dylan had said how they loved him, however, his being gay made it hard to connect.

She joined the firefighters on the other side of the family as Rob held her hand. This was their family. She felt more firefighters standing behind her and turned to see Joe, Echo, Elijah, and the rest of the Navajo Nation firefighting crew in their uniforms. She hugged Echo tightly, not being able to hold back her tears. Joe placed his hand on her shoulder and she met Elijah's eyes. They were dark and unreadable. He gave her the pained smile one only sees at funerals. Before she turned back, she saw a slender, young man standing at the back in a navy blue suit. He had shaggy, blond

• • • •

hair and gray eyes. She didn't recognize him, then remembered a picture from Dylan's bedside table. Grayson. She met his eyes and nodded. He nodded back and wiped tears off his face. God, they were just kids. Then again, she was in prison by that age.

Members of the Forestry Service spoke, along with a firefighter chaplain. Then members of the family. Wren couldn't relate to a lot of what they said because it wasn't the Dylan she knew. Rob went up to speak; Wren knew it was going to be tough to hear. He cleared his throat, stared out at the crowd, and met her eyes.

"When I was asked to give a eulogy, at first I didn't think I could do Dylan justice. It's hard to wrap up someone's soul in a few words. But I will try. Dylan came to us during one of the worst wildfires I've seen... the area has seen. He came with another crew, and afterward, he asked to stay on with us. We were grateful for his help but more so were grateful for *who* he was. Being a firefighter can turn the brightest heart dark, but not for Dylan. No matter day or night, he was cracking a smile, telling a joke, or simply there for others. He had the biggest heart and for one so young, his soul was eons old. It takes a special person to be willing to walk into the gates of hell and come out victorious. That was Dylan. There was no fire too big, no task too hard, he wouldn't face. Outside of the job he was goofy and mischievous, but once in uniform, his dedication was like none I've ever seen. He cared. He laid his heart on the line to protect. And while his heart has stopped beating on this side, it continues to beat in all of us. His soul can not be extinguished. He was my friend, my little brother, a warrior, and a force to be reckoned with." Rob's voice cracked and he stared down at his notes as tears spilled out. "He will be missed forever."

• • • •

He stepped away from the podium, off to the side to compose himself. Wren stopped even trying to wipe the tears off her cheeks. She moved to the podium and gazed at the crowd.

"Thank you, Rob... that was beautiful. I was asked if I wanted to give a reading as Dylan's friend, sister firefighter, and roommate. I'm not one for speeches, but I found this poem by Rumi and it says it all better than I could:

> *Your body is away from me*
> *But there is a window open*
> *from my heart to yours.*
> *From this window, like the moon,*
> *I keep sending news secretly."*

Wren wiped her face and went to stand by Rob. He grasped her hand and squeezed it. She saw Grayson with his head hanging low. When he looked up, his eyes were red-rimmed and he nodded at her. He reminded her of herself after Gabe died. Now, the pain was his burden to bear. She met his eyes and tried to smile but her mouth just twitched.

Dylan's father spread the ashes over the edge into the trees and Wren's heart ached for Grayson, who knew Dylan best. He wasn't acknowledged, even though he'd spent almost five years with Dylan. The ceremony was over and Dylan was put to rest. But she knew better. Those close to him would be haunted forever. The family lined up for condolences and Wren went to find Grayson. She didn't want him to go away feeling isolated. He was walking down the hill when she caught up to him.

"Grayson, wait."

• • • •

He turned and faced her, his eyes tired and defeated. "Wren, right?"

She bobbed her head and put her arms around him. "I'm sorry, Grayson. Dylan loved you so much. He always hoped he'd grow up enough to be worthy of you."

"Worthy of me? He was everything to me. It was just hard being the one home alone week after week. I should've been patient. Stayed by him. Then he wouldn't have stayed here and he'd still be alive. If I hadn't been such a selfish dick, he'd still be here."

Wren knew the mind trick. She'd been there. It's easier to blame yourself than to believe sometimes life has other plans. "I know it hurts, Grayson, but it isn't true. We can't see the future and have no idea how things will play out. You loved Dylan and he loved you. It was okay to ask for boundaries. He understood that. He was a firefighter and put his life on the line every day, no matter where he was."

Grayson eyed her. "Do you understand what it's like to lose someone because they can't give up something?"

Wren nodded. "The love of my life was addicted to heroin. Even though he always thought it was something he could give up, he never did, and it killed him. I guess we all have our addictions. At least Dylan's was to help others and not himself."

"Either way, he's still dead."

Wren understood. She'd traded heroin for the adrenaline of firefighting. She wasn't sure she could survive without either and knew both were a dance with death. She pulled out the Saint Florian necklace and handed it to Grayson.

"This was Dylan's. I wanted you to have something today. I can't say anything to make this better. I know that. Grayson, he loved you."

• • • •

"Then why was I not enough?" Grayson replied bitterly and stared at the medal.

That's a question Wren knew only took one down a maze of confusion and despair. She'd struggled over that question for years. There was only one thing she ever came to. "It's not that you weren't enough, it's that they were fighting inside themselves to figure out if they were enough. To find their worth."

By they, she meant Dylan and Gabe, who weren't so different. Funny, sensitive... and lost. Grayson nodded and met her eyes. He slipped the necklace over his head and leaned forward to kiss her on the cheek.

"You were the only one who included me, or even really knew I existed. Thank you for that. Now, I walk alone."

He turned and moved down the trail. She wanted to call after him. To say not to give up, but she knew it would fall on deaf ears. He was right, he was alone. He'd be alone in a sea of people. At least for a while. Hopefully, one day he'd find love again. But there was no way to it but through it. She couldn't face going back up and found a rock to sit on to be alone in her thoughts. As the family and friends made their way down, she slipped out of view, not wanting to have to make pleasantries. They were heading to a location to meet and commiserate, the firefighters were heading to another. It was two separate worlds. Once the family passed and she knew it was only firefighters left, she headed back up. She found Rob and hugged him. She glanced around, seeing Elijah and his crew standing near the edge. It appeared they were saying a prayer of sorts and she waited until they were done. Elijah turned and came to her, wrapping her tightly in his arms.

"Wren," he whispered in her hair. "I'm so very sorry. I'm here if you need me."

She nodded, letting her head rest against his chest. Now, she was just tired. The group made their way to the old campsite, following one another. Tables were set up as a fire was started. Joe pulled out his guitar and began playing. Food was set on the tables and everyone shared their Dylan stories. Tears and laughter were shared around and Wren finally felt like they were truly honoring Dylan. She asked Joe if he could play a specific song, to which he nodded. He started to play as she joined in, singing *Wherever You Will Go* by The Calling.

Her voice stopped everything, its higher lilting timber and acoustic guitar accompaniment giving a haunting difference from the original rock song. She closed her eyes and pictured Dylan in her mind, allowing the words to pour out of her. When she finished and opened her eyes, there wasn't a dry eye. For the first time that day, she felt like Dylan was near. She took a deep breath and wiped the tears off her cheeks. That song had meant something to her when Gabe died, now it was a connection to Dylan.

She saw Elijah watching her and a pang hit her heart. She couldn't lose him, either. It would kill her. She thought of Grayson and a darkness fell on her heart. If she allowed anyone in, she'd end up alone. Not just alone. But walking through the world unseen with a broken heart. She couldn't go through that again. What was it Grayson said before he left?

"Now, I walk alone."

•   •   •   •

Chapter Thirteen

T he thing about grief is everyone experiences it differently. There is no defined path, and what works for one may not work for another. The phases don't have set timelines and are not at a forward-moving pace. Grief spirals, it circles, it jumps back and forth. Wren tried throwing herself into work. But she kept seeing Dylan reach out time and again, his eyes panicked as the branch crumbled beneath his fingers.

She couldn't focus and started to make stupid mistakes. Realizing she was putting herself and her crew in danger, she put in her notice. They told her they understood and she was welcome back any time. She packed up her and Dylan's things, letting the landlord know she'd be moving out at the end of the month. She had no idea where she would go and didn't care. Everything from Dylan's funeral forward was a blur, and the new season was quickly approaching.

••••

Elijah reached out repeatedly, but she always made excuses as to why she couldn't meet, though she suspected he knew. She was deeply in love with him but was afraid her presence would somehow lead to his demise. She had enough money to start over somewhere or get totally fucked up on heroin and forget the last few years. She hadn't made the call yet. Rob contacted her when he heard she'd put in her notice, however, with the birth of his daughter looming, his mind and time were elsewhere. Everyone had their own lives and Wren was a side thought. Or at least, that's how she felt. She spoke to Geoff one night and he told her she should move out east to be close to him and their mother. She said she'd think about it.

A week before the lease was up, she heard a knock at the door and groaned. The landlord had been showing the place but he usually called first. She opened the door, hoping to shoo him away, and came face to face with Elijah. God, he was beautiful. Part of her was glad he came, part of her knew there was no way to make excuses in person. He stared at her and asked if he could come in. She opened the door, knowing he'd immediately see the place was packed and empty. He stepped inside and spun to face her.

"Wren? What's going on?"

She shrugged not knowing what to say.

"Are you leaving?" he asked, confused and hurt.

"I don't know. I don't know what I'm doing."

"Rob called me, he said you quit?"

Wren nodded. She didn't want to hurt Elijah, but in her messed-up head, she thought she was saving him. "I just can't do it anymore. I hurt people around me. If I'd stayed, someone else would've died. I'm cursed and if people are too close to me, something happens to them."

• • • •

"Like me?"

Wren met his eyes, he knew what she was getting at. "Elijah, I know you think I'm wrong, but I've only ever lived with two people except for my parents, and they're both dead. One was the love of my life, the other one of my best friends. Since you're both to me, I have no doubt I'd lose you."

"Have you ever considered both of those people made choices in their lives which put their lives in danger? Gabe was a heroin addict and Dylan a firefighter. Maybe it has less to do with you, and more to do with the types of people you love," Elijah reasoned.

"You mean like being diabetic and a firefighter?" Wren replied, pointedly.

Elijah winced at this. "Fair enough, but I can quit being a firefighter and am doing everything in my power to take care of my health. Is it worth leaving me and breaking both of our hearts to fend off some imaginary curse?"

"Tse needs you more than I do."

"Yes, he does, but if I'm going to die, it is going to happen with or without you. Maybe he needs you, too. Like I do."

"Elijah, I'm not as strong as you. When Gabe died, I did everything in my power to kill myself, short of blowing my brains out or jumping off a bridge. Losing Dylan not only hurts because I love Dylan, but because it brought up everything I went through with Gabe. If you died, I'd blame myself and find a way to end it. I feel that way now, knowing I'll never see Dylan again, and am pushing the one person who can help me away."

Elijah stood stone-still and looked at her. "Just so you know, I'd follow you to the ends of the earth. You can't push me away. Would you be willing to take a trip with me, so I can show you something?"

Wren considered it, figuring it was the least she could do for him. She nodded and he told her to pack a bag. They'd be gone for a few days. Wren threw clothes and necessities in a bag and glanced around the empty apartment. She'd offered Dylan's things to Grayson since his parents didn't seem interested. He was to meet her a few days later to go through them. She locked the door and followed Elijah to his truck. She climbed in, waiting while he put her bag in the back. He slid in next to her, his eyes focused on her face.

"Wren, I'm not telling you to not hurt or question things. I know you need to work through this in your own time and way. What I'm asking is, please don't shut me out. Even as a friend. We've come a long way together, I'm not turning my back on you now."

Wren met his eyes and nodded slightly. She didn't deserve him but needed someone to lean on. He put his hand out and she took it. They drove for a couple of hours when they crossed into the edge of the Navajo reservation on the Arizona side. It crossed over multiple states, but Elijah had grown up in the Arizona part. He explained how his people had come to the land and made it their own. It was striking and massive, but Wren was overcome by the level of poverty she saw. Elijah drove for a while on the reservation until he pulled up in front of a falling-down shack.

"This was the home I grew up in," he explained.

Home? It was more like a shed and looked like it had been piece-mealed together. Wren frowned and stared at him. "I don't understand. You lived there?"

• • • •

"We did. Mostly my mother and me. As I said, my father wasn't around much and wasn't too good to my mother. She worked hard and eventually diabetes took her life. After that, I moved in with my grandmother. I'll take you to meet her."

"Elijah, if diabetes took your mother's life, why are you so sure it won't take yours?"

"I'm not, but I have the education to try and stave it off. My mother grew up poor and she didn't know how to take care of it. She often didn't take insulin when she needed to because it was hard to get without a car. She also didn't trust the doctors and sometimes wouldn't take it, believing it was hurting rather than helping her. That took its toll and damaged her body. She lost her foot by the time she was thirty. She died shortly after."

"Do you ever have to do that? Not take it when you need it?"

"I have. Being remote, if I run out or something happens, I've missed doses. But having Tse makes me take it seriously. I can't risk slipping into a diabetic coma being alone with him."

"Why has it been worse lately?"

"Honestly, I think with the stress of the job, maybe not eating as healthy as I should, might be the cause. I've been trying to keep up with my grandma's house, take care of Tse, firefighting, and a lot of traveling. I think it's time to buy some land and a house, move my grandma out with me."

"Traveling? Because of me?"

Elijah met her eyes and thought about how to answer. "Wren, you are the one thing, next to Tse, which reduces my stress. I want to be closer to you. I don't want you to leave. I brought you here because I want you to understand I've never had it easy. I grew up poor and have had diabetes pretty much my whole life. I'm ready to find a way to preserve the land without always putting my life on the line. I love the reservation, but I want something I can leave to Tse. When I was a kid, I wanted to grow things. I loved the trees and plants, so being a firefighter seemed natural to protect that, but it's gotten bigger than all of us. We can't just put the fires out, we need to fix the earth to stop them. Plant the right things, the right way. Rejuvenate the soil. We're so busy trying to mitigate the injury, however, we aren't healing the land."

"So, you want to be a farmer?"

"Of sorts. Maybe an agriculture warrior," Elijah replied and winked, making Wren smile. "I've applied for a land grant to start. I've been taking classes on regenerative agriculture and think I can make this work. I want you to join me."

"On the farm? As an employee?" Wren asked, confused.

"An employee, a friend, maybe more."

Wren considered this and was intrigued. She liked the hard work of preserving the land, so the idea of running a farm piqued her interest. She shrugged. "I need to be out of my place in a week. I don't know where I'm going after that. How long until you think you'll start the farm?"

"I already made an offer on land and put down a down payment. Hopefully, the land grant will come through soon. Either way, I've been saving for years to get to this point. I can take you out to the land tomorrow if you want. My grandma is making dinner and would love to meet you tonight."

"She knows about me?"

"Of course, Wren. I love you. I want you in my life."

Wren blushed and stared out the window. Even with her pulling away, he'd not doubted his love for her. She slid over next to him and kissed him on the cheek. "Thank you, Elijah. I know I haven't been fair. I do love you and want you in my life. I just don't want to be the reason something happens to you."

"Wren, the world is bigger than you. I know you're hurting, but if you put your ego aside, you'll see you're on your own path and I'm on mine. If our paths join, they come together as one but don't necessarily influence the other. We're companions on a journey, you can't change my journey from how it's been decided. You can hurt me but if you love me, nothing you do will change my path."

Wren leaned against his shoulder and sighed. He was right, she was giving herself too much credit. She'd fight for him, to keep him safe and healthy. He kissed her forehead and fired up the truck. They drove to his grandmother's house, which wasn't much bigger than the shack they'd left. Tse was playing in the front yard and waved ecstatically at Wren. She smiled and waved back. As soon as they were out of the truck, Tse was talking a million miles a minute, running between them. Elijah hugged him and took Wren's hand.

"Let's go introduce you to the other woman in my life," he joked.

They went inside and a small, black-haired woman was standing over a stove, cooking. She was in a long, black skirt and a purple blouse, squinting in the pot she was stirring. She smiled as they walked in, her wrinkled face beaming at Wren. She set her spoon down and came over, extending her hand.

"Hello, I'm Anna."

"I'm Wren, it's nice to meet you."

"Sit, sit."

Wren sat in the chair she was pointing at. Elijah smiled at her and kissed his grandmother on the cheek. He set to chopping vegetables and she slapped his hand, telling him he was doing it wrong. He switched to the way she was showing him, then laughed.

"Grandma, it's fine. They will taste the same."

She peered at him and scolded, "They won't *cook* the same."

He shrugged and cut them the way she wanted, giving Wren an exasperated look. Once dinner was ready, they called Tse in to wash up and join them. The four of them barely fit around the small table and Elijah's knee was pressed against Wren's. Elijah talked about the land and said there was an old farmhouse still on it. It was on thirty-seven acres and had been a single-crop farm previously, which depleted the soil. His goal was to bring in goats, chickens, and multiple species of plants to rejuvenate the land. They could sell eggs, goat's milk, and cheese, allowing the animals to wander the land free range. Their hooves and manure would add carbon to the soil and help the plants grow.

When bedtime came, Wren realized there were only two bedrooms, one for Anna, one Tse and Elijah shared. The living room was a tiny couch and chairs. She had no idea where she'd sleep.

Elijah took her hand and led her to the bedroom. "Tse is going to camp out with Grandma tonight, you can sleep in the room with me if you're comfortable with that."

"Next to you?" Wren asked, flustered.

"Clothes on. Over the covers, if you want," Elijah offered.

It was chilly and she didn't want him sleeping without blankets. She eyed him, cocking her head. "Clothes on, under the blankets is fine."

• • • •

Elijah grinned. They went to the room and each shed only enough clothes to leave them completely covered. They slid under the blanket and Wren rested on her back tensely. Elijah made no move to touch her. She relaxed and rolled over, sliding her arm around his waist as she yawned.

"Thanks," she whispered.

"For what?"

"For not giving up. For coming for me."

• • • •

Chapter Fourteen

E lijah showed Wren the land on a map. It was a large piece of land with a creek running through it. It had a mixture of plowed fields, brush, trees, and desert. His goal was to bring in native vegetation, including edible plants, keeping the soil covered year-round to prevent erosion. Farm animals would roam the land freely to feed the soil with their droppings. It would support itself with the sale of plants, vegetables, and products made without harming the animals. Elijah let Wren know he'd stopped eating meat to help with his diabetes and was moving to a sustainable way of life. He wanted to be able to live and work solely off the land. She peered at the map but it was hard to picture. He tapped his finger on the paper and gazed at her.

"Do you want to go out there? I have a tent, we could camp and hike the property," he asked.

"We can do that?"

• • • •

"They accepted my offer and I put a payment down, so I can't see why not. No one lives there anymore, I can see if we can get the key to the house to look inside."

"Okay, yeah, I'd like to see it."

"Tse is going to stay with a friend tonight. He may not be up for all the hiking."

Wren considered that and knew it was good to be alone with Elijah. They needed to talk to see what the future held for both of them. Elijah packed the truck with a tent, sleeping bags, a stove, cooler, table, and chairs. Wren wondered if she'd packed well for camping, but Elijah assured her he had extra sweatshirts and longjohns if needed. By the time the truck was packed, Tse's friend's mother came to pick him up. Anna sent them with leftovers and Elijah had bags of food ready to go. The drive to the land took over an hour, with the landscape constantly changing.

"What kind of crop did they grow on the land before?" Wren asked, knowing rainfall was unpredictable.

"I believe it was alfalfa."

"What are you going to plant?"

"Everything that'll grow. The more plants the better. My goal is to keep it planted and nourish the topsoil. No tilling, which causes erosion and turns soil into dirt. Plants keep the soil covered to prevent loss of topsoil."

"You have thought a lot about this," Wren replied.

"I have. Fighting fires is one thing, trying to nourish the earth to reduce fires is another."

Wren nodded and fell silent. Purpose. She thought firefighting was her purpose and maybe it still was, but watching Dylan die took the power out of it. What else could he have accomplished with his life? And ultimately, except to those who loved him, he was merely a statistic. An annual number of deaths, justified in the name of fighting fires. On average, seventeen a year. Seventeen Dylans, Robs, Wrens, Elijahs, Echoes, Joes. People who just wanted to be able to go home at the end of their shift. Hug their kids, fall in love, chase their dreams. Elijah was right, it was getting worse. The land could only take so much abuse and it had hit its max.

They pulled down a long drive to an old farmhouse. It had seen better days, but it was still standing. The realtor had given Elijah the code to the key box and he retrieved the key, opening the door. The house was empty, had been for a long time. A thick layer of dust was on the floor and the house was devoid of any human smells. There were a few broken windows and missing boards on the outside, but the floors and walls were stable. There were three bedrooms and one bathroom. No appliances. The water came from a well and Elijah flipped on the faucet which sputtered brown sediment and water. It became lighter the longer it ran, so the well was still good. A bedroom was on one side of the house, the other two on the other side, along with the only bathroom. There was also a small study off of the isolated bedroom. Wren could picture Elijah turning it into an office to run the farm and smiled. This would be his room and office. The other two rooms were down the hall off of the living room and faced each other, the bathroom at the end. One for his grandmother, one for Tse. The kitchen was eat-in style and there was a basement with a root cellar. It wasn't big, but it was perfect for what he needed.

The house wasn't officially Elijah's, so they locked it up and drove out to the land to set up a camp. They got the tent staked into the ground and set up the table and chairs. They decided to hike first to check out the creek and fields. As they

• • • •

walked, Elijah explained the process behind regenerative agriculture, which seemed to make the most logical sense.

"So, why do farmers typically grow only one crop?" Wren asked, confused.

"Subsidies, mostly. They're paid to grow corn, soybeans, wheat, etc. Just by growing one of those, they're given money, then money for the harvest. What they don't realize is they're still making nothing per acre. Regenerative agriculture doesn't have subsidies, but the payout is higher. Working with the land this way is good for both the farmer and the land. It's hard to teach an old dog new tricks, you know?" Elijah replied.

"But you applied for a grant, right?"

"I did. There are those seeing the benefits and trying to get farmers to switch over."

"It's impressive."

They made it to the creek and Elijah squatted down to scoop some water in his hands. He took a sip, then nodded. "It's clean. That's the other thing. Regenerative agriculture doesn't cause runoff into the waterways. It naturally filters rainfall through the soil to clean it."

Wren caught water in her hands and drank. It tasted cleaner than what came out of the tap. "How long did this all sit empty?"

"From what it sounds like, the parents got too old to farm. The father passed away and the mother lived her years out here but not farming. The kids weren't interested in farming, so it's been for a couple of decades at least. The soil should be in good shape and we'll only make it better."

We. He obviously meant him and Tse. Wren appreciated his vision and smiled at him.

• • • •

"You're incredible, Elijah."

He blushed and stared at the water. "I want you here, Wren. I know you're ready to leave and we're still new, but I think you could help me bring this to fruition."

Wren stared hard at him. She didn't know what he was saying. Like work for him? Or something else? It was too much to sort out. "Hey, I'm getting hungry, do you want to head back?"

Elijah stood up and watched her. "Sure. Think about what I said. I think your destiny is healing the land."

She shrugged and followed him away from the creek. The land was stunning, stretched out untouched for miles. She'd want nothing more than to be a part of it, but she didn't even know where she and Elijah stood. They'd held each other and kissed. He stood by her and didn't let her fall away. Ultimately, what did it all mean? She observed him walking ahead of her and paused at the ease with which he moved through the land. Like he was sprung from it. She stopped with admiration, sliding out her phone to take a picture of him. She snapped a couple before he turned to check on her as she kept taking pictures. He was majestic, timeless. He grinned and shook his head.

"Put your phone away and come take my hand. I want to walk with you through this land," he said, reaching his hand out to her.

She took a couple more pictures and slipped her phone into her pocket. She caught up, placing her hand in his. He pointed out different plants as they wandered and identified them. A snake crossed their path, disappearing into the brush. Some type of bird flew overhead, calling out as it cast a shadow across the desert floor. Even though Wren spent a lot of time in nature, something about this walk was magical.

• • • •

They made it back to camp ravenous and immediately began preparing food. Wren took notice of how Elijah cooked and the ingredients he used, so she would know how he needed to eat. He checked his blood sugar but didn't give himself insulin, which she took as a good sign. They sat and ate plates of steaming vegetables with beans and salsa. Elijah sprinkled pine nuts on top which gave the meal a nice crunch.

When they were done they rinsed their dishes, packing everything away to not attract any wild animals, then built a fire. Wren let Elijah talk about his plans for the land and could picture everything in her mind. Her excitement bubbled up but she didn't want to convince herself of something which might not come for her. Instead, she pictured Tse growing up on the land, becoming part of something great. By nightfall, they were both tired and climbed into the tent. They each had a sleeping bag and faced each other. Elijah reached out, touching Wren's face.

"I've never seen anyone who looks like you. It's like you were dropped off here from another planet," he said and ran a strand of her hair through his fingers.

"Nope, plain old Texas. Born and raised."

Elijah laughed. "Even so, you have the most beautiful hair and eyes. Like fire and jade."

Wren blushed. The things she felt made her ugly, he found beautiful. Like Gabe had. She met his eyes and she saw a sincerity in the deep brown depths. She twisted her fingers in his hair.

"We're opposites. You with your black hair, golden skin, and dark eyes. Me with my freckles, pale eyes, and curly orange hair," she murmured.

He pulled her close and pressed his mouth against hers, then whispered. "Our souls are the same."

• • • •

That much was true. If there were two halves to a whole, it would be Elijah and her. She wrapped her arms around him and moved in close, only the sleeping bags separating them. They kissed and let their hands wander but stayed in their own spaces. Wren was breathless and stared at Elijah.

"What did you think when you first saw me?"

"On the table, reading? You appeared like a goddess. Your hair was flowing around you and you were sitting cross-legged, intent on your book. When you looked up at the bus, I was stunned. You seemed like you were carved out of marble."

"Oh. When I first saw you, I was intimidated. You were so sure of yourself and powerful. You had the most intense eyes and moved with such force. I'd never have guessed you have such a sensitive heart."

Elijah laughed and for a moment he seemed like an innocent child. Wren found this endearing and wanted nothing more than to protect him.

He rested his forehead against hers and sighed. "Don't leave, Wren. Please. I want you here. I want to hold you and know you're part of my life."

"What does that mean, Elijah?"

"I don't know exactly, but I do know I don't want to live without you. That much is clear."

"I don't want to live without you, either. You're my best friend and outside of that, I like you as a person. I like your mind and your soul. I love your passion and how committed you are to things you care about. I don't know what I believe in, but I know I love you," Wren replied.

● ● ● ●

"I love you, too. I believe in us if that matters. I think together we could truly make a difference. I just have to know you won't get spooked and run away."

"Like a horse?" Wren teased.

"Yes, like a horse," Elijah replied.

"I'm not a runner when I have a reason to stay. I have my issues and am scared to let people in, but you are in, Elijah."

He reached out, placing his hand on her chest. She placed her hand over his. It was too late to jump ship. She'd suffer all the same. He took her hand and placed it on his chest.

"This is yours. My heart. I trust you with it and am asking for you to please stay."

"I'll stay," Wren replied softly. "But I need a place to live."

"You are here."

• • • •

Chapter Fifteen

F urther exploration the next day uncovered an old barn and long chicken house. Neither were in great shape but would work initially for bringing animals to the farm. The goats could use the barn and the chickens the long house. Once, when Wren was little, she'd visited a chicken farm on a school trip and was horrified at how many chickens were crammed into the houses, barely able to move, with their beaks cut off. She was grateful they could change the story for the chickens they'd bring to the farm. The goal was to free-range all of the animals, so they could cover the area. Wren suggested burros, too, mostly because she liked them. Elijah laughed at her reasoning but agreed they'd make sense. She pointed out she had money in savings and wanted to invest if she was going to stay on the land. Elijah made a call to the realtor to see if renting the farmhouse was an option until they closed. About an hour later, it was approved.

• • • •

They didn't see the storm clouds rushing towards them in time and got stranded in the tent. Unfortunately, water seeped in and they realized they wouldn't be able to stay the night in the tent, quickly packing up camp. It was late and neither relished the drive back to his grandmother's tiny house, so they made haste to the farmhouse to get out of the weather. Everything was soaked and they had no dry bedding. Elijah had covered the wood at the campsite and brought it into the house. He ran out to the truck and grabbed an atlas he'd shoved under the seat and a hatchet he carried in his toolbox. The living room had an old fireplace and he opened the flue, burning pages from the atlas to make sure the chimney was clear. When the smoke rose, he built a fire to dry their things. They spread the sleeping bags and clothing out in front of the fireplace, using the camp stove to cook dinner.

Despite the circumstances, the fire warmed the little house and they felt safe from the storm raging outside. Elijah called his grandmother to check on her and called Tse's friend's house to make sure he wasn't wearing them out. Wren found an old broom tucked in a pantry in the kitchen and started sweeping the dust out the door. She watched Elijah check his blood sugar and held her breath. He packed up the supplies, catching her eye.

"It's fine. I need to check regularly, but I've been less stressed and taking care of myself," he assured her.

She nodded and sat down on the sleeping bag by the fire. It was dry but her clothes were still wet. She checked through her bag and found a tank top and knit skirt which had managed to remain mostly dry and decided to change into them. There was no electricity, so she found a corner of the room where she could still see but also not change out in the open. She slipped off her wet clothes, put on the tank and knit skirt, then came back to the fire.

• • • •

Elijah handed her a cup of coffee which she gratefully drank. He was still wet and she could see he was considering what to do about it. He only had sleep shorts which were dry. He changed into those and pulled his hair over one shoulder to dry by the fire.

Wren tried not to stare, but in only his shorts he was stunning to look at. His broad shoulders and slim waist glowed in the firelight. She wanted to reach out and touch him. She clasped her fingers around the coffee cup, watching the fire. When she glanced back, he was observing her with the same intensity she'd felt just moments earlier. She met his eyes, thinking he'd look away but he didn't. She couldn't break the gaze and sat her coffee cup down. She reached out, drifting her fingers down his arm. He grabbed them, holding them tight.

"Wren..."

She leaned forward and kissed him, not wanting to stop. He followed her lead and wrapped his arms around her, drawing her closer. The speed at which they dropped their inhibitions was breakneck, and they didn't stop except for air. Wren pulled off her tank and they kneeled to explore each other. Elijah cupped her breasts and kissed her neck. Wren ran her hands over his smooth chest, entwining her fingers in his hair. They pressed against each other, letting their skin touch and their mouths consume each other. Wren slid off her skirt and gasped when Elijah placed his hands on her buttocks, pulling her to him. She slid off his shorts and sat back to admire what she had yet to see. He blushed as she stared and she ran her hands over him, drawing him to her. It had been years since she'd been touched by a man, and this man was bringing her desire to new levels.

She leaned back and urged him forward with her hands, letting her legs part. He kissed her hard as she let him in. Wren was shocked by how her body responded. She matched his movements, wanting to feel him more, and used her hand on his buttocks to drive him deeper. She didn't want it to end and couldn't get enough. She twisted her fingers in his hair as she felt waves rush over her and her face flush. Elijah placed his hand behind her neck and kissed her throat as he released, his back dripping with sweat. He rested his face on her cheek and sighed.

"Damn," was all he said.

Wren laughed and kissed his face, tasting salt. She ran her fingers down his back and didn't want him to move. When he rolled over next to her, she wondered how long she'd have to wait until they could do it again. He rested his hand on her side and watched her. She turned to face him, grinning.

"You better keep your energy up. I'm going to want to do that a lot," she teased.

Elijah ran his fingers through her hair and smiled. "Me too."

Wren slid her leg over Elijah, pressing herself against him. Being sober and making love was a feeling she'd never experienced. All of the sensations, the feel of his skin as she lightly traced his muscles, those were things she'd never felt. She and Gabe had made love but what she remembered was still fuzzy. They were always fucked up.

Elijah closed his eyes and dozed off, so Wren took that time to appreciate him in his full form. He had an athletic body, but one that comes from hard work and not hours at the gym. In looking at his body, she developed a new appreciation for hers. She was fit but also had the soft curves that came from being a woman. Her hips were rounded and her bottom was full, even though she could carry as much as a man and kept the pace of the male firefighters around her. She realized what she'd thought was chubby as a kid, was her becoming a woman with the curves and softness that came with it. She hadn't been a thin child, but the baggy clothes she wore were hiding a natural progression from childhood to womanhood.

Gabe had seen it and appreciated her body. She never gave him credit for that. She'd always assumed he was settling because they got along so well. He told her time and again how beautiful she was and she'd brush him off, never really understanding how such a handsome boy could find her pretty. Now, she could see. She'd been different but in a way to be celebrated. She was unique. She thought of Gabe and smiled. Her first love. The first boy to open her heart. She gazed at Elijah and felt the same love. In a way, Gabe led her to Elijah.

Elijah stirred and rolled over. She pulled the sleeping bag over them and rested her head against his back. It dawned on her they were in *their* home. Where they'd bring Anna and Tse to start a farm. Wren had never really believed in marriage and was pretty sure she didn't want children of her own, but she liked the idea that she and Elijah could build something together. She could help raise Tse. Fear suddenly gripped her and she pulled away. It was that fear, the one that told her things wouldn't work out. That she was setting herself up for a fall. She could only depend on herself. She tried to push it away but it gnawed at her.

Elijah sensed her shift and turned over. "You okay?"

Wren nodded, then shook her head. "Just anxiety."

"You want to talk about it?"

"It's the same old shit. Don't get your hopes up, don't make plans. Things fall apart, have an exit strategy."

•   •   •   •

Elijah watched her, his eyes unreadable. He sat up and ran his hands through his hair. "I get that, too, you know."

"You do?"

"Absolutely. Every time you didn't respond or pushed me away, I started planning how to forget you. Focus on the farm, raise Tse, move on. I guess it's our way of protecting ourselves from being hurt."

Wren listened, then sighed. "So, how do we know when to stop looking for the lifeboats?"

Elijah laughed. "I don't know. Maybe never. Maybe it stretches out over time. I do know, I wouldn't do what we just did with someone unless I thought it was forever."

"Wait, so how many people have you been with?" Wren asked.

"You and Tse's birth mother."

"That's all?"

"Wren, I only want to share that with someone I love, someone I trust. How about you?"

Wren wrinkled her nose and almost laughed. "You and Gabe."

"See? So, why would it be different for me?"

"Because you look like you. I'm sure plenty of women had eyes for you," Wren replied.

Elijah nodded. "Probably, but believe it or not, I'm shy. After being burned by Tse's birth mother, I wanted no part of dating and hooking up."

"What was her name?"

"Tse's mother? Mandy."

Wren tried to picture what a Mandy would look like with the little bit of information Echo had given her. It made her chest feel tight and she pushed it away. She pictured a blond movie star with a wicked smile and long, golden legs. It wasn't helping.

"Wren, don't go there. It's like when I think about Gabe. We'll always make them out to be something they weren't. They were part of our past and each of them gave us something we moved forward with. We can leave it there. You're the only woman I think about, want to touch, need to share my life with."

Wren smiled and stroked his cheek. "I loved Gabe as a girl, but I love you as a woman. You've brought me to places, body and mind, I've never gone to. You're the only man I want to do things to me."

Elijah laughed but saw she was serious when she slid her hand down, insisting he rise to the occasion. He responded rapidly and they buried under the covers for another round. The fire was blazing and they were now too hot and stripped off the sleeping bag as they took each other to new limits. They lay naked in front of the fire spent and famished. Elijah slipped on his shorts and opened the door to let in fresh air, which smelled like rain, to cool them. They sat up talking and cooking until the sun was climbing in the sky. After finding reasons to make love, they finally fell asleep in each other's arms as the day began.

When they woke it was afternoon. They gathered their things to head back to the reservation. Wren wanted to ask Elijah how to explain it to Tse and their friends moving forward but felt uncomfortable with the conversation. She peered out the window trying to broach it.

"Elijah?"

"Yeah?"

"What are we? I mean, to each other. Like, how do I answer the question if Tse or Anna asks?"

• • • •

"You're planning to move to the farm with me, right? To share a bedroom?"

Wren nodded. That much was clear. "Of course, but I think girlfriend sounds too high school and we aren't married. So what are we?"

Elijah considered and shrugged. "Wren, I don't want to be with anyone else in this lifetime or the next. You're the woman I love. I know your feelings on marriage, but it's just a thing, you know? A piece of paper. We can or we don't have to. It doesn't change how I feel for you. You can be my partner or you can be my wife. Either way, it's the same. I'll love you until I die."

"Don't say die. You can simply love me forever."

"Fair enough, I love you forever. So, which will it be, partner or wife and husband? It's our journey, we decide."

Wren sighed. Her fears about marriage were the same as her fears about letting anyone close. In her world it meant loss. Or at least it used to. Legally, marriage made sense because it gave them more rights in the eyes of the law. It would protect one another in the event of something happening. Maybe that's where the fear came from, admitting something could happen. She watched Elijah and realized paper or not, something could happen. Or they could grow old together. She took his hand and squeezed it.

"I say it can be both."

Chapter Sixteen

E lijah added Wren to the offer on the land and house, closing on the deal a month later at a lawyer's office in Phoenix. The next day, they popped into the courthouse to get married. They didn't tell anyone and in lieu of rings, had four dots tattooed on their ring fingers. It was legal but didn't change how they planned to move forward. Wren chose to keep her last name and take Elijah's, making her Gretchen Meyer-Clarke. She felt it sounded like the name of a pharmaceutical company and couldn't stop giggling in the officiant's office. There were a lot of Rs and Es. Even though they married for legal reasons, Wren couldn't deny the romance of the moment she swore her life to Elijah's and his to her. They kissed, and as they walked out of the courthouse the weight of what they did made her feel a little dizzy.

The night in the farmhouse, she'd expressed her desire to not birth children of her own. Elijah shrugged and told her it was

• • • •

her body and he didn't feel any pressing need to have another child. He loved Tse, that was enough. Wren said she wasn't opposed to fostering older children or adopting eventually, but she hadn't felt the drive to have a baby or be pregnant. She'd had an IUD placed when she was with Gabe and never had it removed. Elijah held her and reiterated he supported whatever choices she made with her body. He had a complete family and didn't believe genetics made a child more theirs. If they wanted to foster or adopt, he was open to it.

Elijah asked if she would consider adopting Tse in the long run and Wren agreed. She'd never been one drawn to children but Tse was different. He made it easy. He was smart and energetic, he carried the room when he was in it. The drawback was, it would bring Tse's birth mother back into their life, as the court would notify her of the pending adoption even though she'd signed over her parental rights. Elijah had been happy to let sleeping dogs lie and was afraid hearing he was happy might make her want to cause issues. At first, after she'd left, he'd tried to send her pictures and notes about Tse. In time, those came back unopened. Time had passed and she might feel differently, now.

After the ceremony, they drove out to the land to celebrate privately, towing a trailer of furniture they bought at a thrift store. Anna had some furniture in her house but it wasn't enough to fill the house and was on its last legs. They bought a large wooden table and chairs, bed frame, mattress, and couch. The only thing they bought new was the mattress out of a sense of sanitation. They also got Tse a headboard and matching dresser to surprise him. He'd been sleeping in either Elijah's bed or Anna's and didn't have a bed of his own. Elijah's old full bed would become Tse's since Elijah and Wren now had a queen. They spent the evening

• • • •

hauling furniture in and cleaning it. By the time they were done, their arms were exhausted and the idea of cooking was something neither wanted to do. They were remote, so ordering food was out of the question. Even though they'd been sleeping on Wren's air mattress there, they'd bought appliances as soon as they'd signed the lease.

Wren checked the freezer and grabbed a casserole she'd made a week before to throw it in the oven. They were committed to not eating or buying processed foods, taking a day a week to prep foods to freeze. There was no trash pick-up this far out, so they considered everything they bought to make sure it was necessary and came in the least form of packaging. Eventually, they hoped to grow most of their own food and compost the scraps. Now that the land was theirs, they could start planting. It was early March and Elijah had seedlings growing everywhere in the house, ready to go in the ground after the risk of frost had passed.

The table could seat six and with the added leaf, eight. They kept the leaf out and sat to eat the heated casserole by candlelight. It would have been romantic, but they were too worn out to care. They ate, climbed into their new bed, and cuddled up, falling asleep within minutes. The next morning they made love with the rising sun and dressed their sore bodies for the next round of moving. Even though they'd rented the farmhouse for the previous month, Elijah thought it best to not bring Anna and Tse out until the deal was finalized in case it fell through. Some nights they were there camping in the home and others at Anna's.

A few days after they'd stayed the first night in the farmhouse, Wren met with Grayson at her and Dylan's apartment to go through Dylan's things. She insisted Grayson take the first pick of Dylan's belongings. Then she grabbed a few items she wanted to keep, including a picture Rob had taken of the two of them standing on a ridge in full gear with chainsaws. It was her favorite picture. She and Grayson shared tears and laughter, and by the end of the day had a budding friendship. She told him she wanted him to come to the farm once it was up and running. He loaded his car and turned to her.

"Wren, thank you."

"For what?"

"For reaching out to me. No one else would have. Dylan's family knew about me, but wouldn't have considered my feelings in all of this."

"You loved Dylan and he loved you. This would've been what he wanted. He talked about you all of the time, I think he would've been devastated had you been shut out."

Grayson nodded and hugged her. "Please stay in touch. You're the only person who connects to Dylan. Besides, I like you. You're easy to be around."

Wren laughed, shaking her head. "Not always. But I do have my moments."

Grayson headed out and as he drove away, Wren felt like if she turned Dylan would be standing there, watching his taillights disappear with her. To hold onto the feeling, she put her head down and pretended he followed her into the apartment. She spent the evening cleaning and loading the rest of their belongings. She took a bag to the thrift store and dropped the keys at the apartment office. That chapter closed and her heart ached over it.

Rob's wife had the baby a couple of weeks later, and as the fire season ramped up many of the firefighters from the year before didn't return. Rob talked about switching to a local fire department to be more involved with his children. With him,

Dylan, and Wren gone, a new batch of wildland firefighters rose in the ranks and took their places. The Phoenix paper did a big spread on the prison-to-firefighter program. They called Wren to see if she wanted to be interviewed. She didn't. She was ready to put it behind her.

Elijah and Wren drove back to the reservation with the trailer, ready to load Anna's household items and move them to the farm. Tse was bouncing off the walls, asking about the farm and where he'd go to school. The farmhouse was so remote there were no nearby schools. Elijah and Wren had agreed to homeschool him at least the rest of the school year, then figure out over the summer what to do for the next. Anna was sad about leaving her home but recognized she could no longer live on her own. With Elijah moving, it was best to go with him.

Once her house was packed and loaded it looked bigger, but also appeared that the furniture and belongings were almost holding it together. The living room floor sagged and the kitchen was at a slant. It wouldn't have lasted much longer, either way. Elijah had patched and repaired it as he could over the years, but it simply was falling apart. No one on the reservation owned their land, so once this house fell it would likely be cleared and a trailer would take its place. Elijah wanted his family to have more. A legacy to leave behind.

Wren drove Anna in her car and Elijah took Tse in his truck, pulling the trailer. Anna reached out and touched the four dots on Wren's finger, having noticed the same on Elijah's. Wren met her eyes, as Anna smiled brightly.

"You make him very happy."

"He makes me very happy," Wren replied.

"After Tse's mother, I told him he needed to stay away from bilagáana women. I'm glad he didn't listen."

Wren knew the word. It basically meant a white person in Navajo. She understood Anna's reasoning but was glad he didn't listen, as well. She watched the trailer in front of her with the man she loved driving it and let out the breath she'd been holding. They were on to their new life. A life neither of them foresaw the summer before when his bus pulled into camp. It was slow going but as they pulled in the drive to the farmhouse and Wren saw Anna's eyes light up, she knew they'd made the right choice. This was the family farm. A place Tse could grow up and know was his. She hated that he wouldn't be able to go to school and as an only child would be alone. She thought to bring up the option of being foster parents with Elijah again.

Once everything was inside and in its place, it officially felt like home. Tse was over the moon about having his own room and in awe of his furniture. Elijah had scored an old toy box and repainted it, adding Tse's name. Tse sat on his bed, and for the first time since Wren had met him, he was awake and silent. Wren sat down next to him.

"Are you okay?"

Tse nodded and stared at her. "Wren, are you staying with us, now? Like forever?"

"I am. I love your daddy. And you."

"Are you going to be my mom, now?"

Wren watched him, not sure how to answer. She didn't want to lie but also felt like it wasn't her call to make. "What do you think about that?"

Tse grinned. "Yeah."

• • • •

"Okay. You know I love you, Tse. You're very special to me."

Tse put his small hand in hers and leaned against her. "Other kids, they have moms. I have a grandma, but not a mom. Sometimes they teased me about it. Told me I was weird."

"Tse, a lot of children don't have moms or dads. Families come in all different forms. Did all of those kids have moms and dads?"

"Most had moms. Some had dads, too."

"You know, sometimes kids are just mean. It's not about you. They look for things about you to pick on, so they feel better about themselves. That's about them not liking themselves inside and has nothing to do with you. Do you like yourself inside?"

Tse's eyes lit up. "Yes! I'm smart and can run faster than all of them."

Wren hugged him and for the first time had motherly feelings. "That's all that matters. You may have other kids pick on you, but you need to remember you're special and loved. They're doing that because they feel empty and sad. I know it doesn't seem that way because it hurts when they're mean to you, but I promise their words don't matter. You do."

Saying those words to Tse, put Wren back to when she was young and bullied in school. She was saying those words as much to herself as she was to him. It had never been about her. It had always been about their insecurities. Had she known that then, it would've saved her years of suffering. But then she wouldn't have met Gabe, gone to prison, become a firefighter, and met Elijah. It was a double-edged sword. Now, she was sitting in her home with her husband and son; she wouldn't trade that for the world.

She glanced up to see Elijah standing at the door. He put his hand out to her and she stood up, taking it. He watched Tse.

"Hey, little man, why don't you unpack your toys into your box, we'll be eating soon, okay?"

"Okay, Daddy!"

Wren and Elijah left him to unpack and went out to the small front porch. It had a swing on one end and a couple of rocking chairs. They sat in the chairs, looking out over the land. Elijah turned to Wren.

"I heard you talking with Tse. That was nice, Wren. He'll benefit from you being in his life."

"He asked me to be his mom."

"I heard. I like that you let him make the decision. I know I'm overprotective of Tse, but it's time for me to let someone else into his life."

"I was thinking. I don't see school being an option out here with him having to be shuttled back and forth for so long. His days would be excruciatingly long. I think we should school him out here."

Elijah thought about it, then nodded. "I think you're right. But he'd be the only kid out here."

"So, there's more. I think we should foster and maybe adopt. I know there is a need for homes for children over three years old."

"I'm not opposed but a lot of those kids have been through stuff, Wren. Abuse, neglect. They'll have special needs."

"I know. But that means they need us more. It may take adjustments, but I think we could offer children a safe, loving home and teach them to be a part of making their world better."

"What about your prison time?"

"I looked into it. Being convicted of drug charges can stop me, but I can petition for a "good cause" exception. I want to try, Elijah. I want Tse to have siblings." Wren could feel shame rising in her and fought back tears. If she could go back and change things, she would.

Elijah stood up and kneeled in front of her, placing his hands on her legs. "We will, Wren. There are scores of people who'll stand up and say what an amazing person you are. I'll be the first in line. We all make bad choices when we're young. That was nine years ago. You're a different person now."

Wren met his eyes and wiped a tear away from her eye. She hoped he was right. She'd done her time and didn't want to keep serving that sentence the rest of her life. The system sometimes meant never having freedom.

• • • •

Chapter Seventeen

Wren knew nothing about farming and watched in awe as
Elijah gently communicated with the plants and land. He
didn't till the soil, but rather made shallow dents where to
plant, which were filled back in once the seedling was in the
ground. He researched the soil and planted the right things in the
right places. It was slow going, not like the massive machines which
could till and planet in swaths. He used organic compost and
manure when they had it, truly working with the land. He taught
Wren, Tse, and even Anna how to plant and tend. Wren would
sometimes look up and see them all working together and it made
her smile. Anna was surprisingly agile for her age and never
complained. Wren could see the pride in Anna's eyes when she
watched Elijah. Tse found it to be the most exhilarating task. When
the rest of them were standing up to stretch their backs, he was
running them in circles, begging to do more.

• • • •

Wren saw the tenderness with which Elijah handled the plants and spoke about the land. "You really have found your home, haven't you?"

He grinned and nodded. "I have. I think this was all I ever wanted, outside of someone to love. Don't get me wrong, fighting fires was a passion, too, but you can only see so much destruction without it wearing on you."

"I understand. There is something healing about putting a plant in the soil."

"Exactly. We aren't so different, you know?"

"How do you mean?"

"Well, like take you, for instance. You beat heroin but that's like putting out the fire. It doesn't bring you back to life. You have to work at that also. Nurture yourself, be loved, find joy, purpose. Put those plants in the soil, so to say. The land is like that. We can stop doing things to it, but until we make an effort to heal the damage, we're not making it any better. Does that make sense?"

More than he knew. Or maybe he did. Wren wrapped her arms around Elijah and rested her head against his shoulder. "We can't expect things to grow if we don't tend to them. It lies fallow until it is given what it needs to regenerate."

Elijah chuckled, kissing the top of her head. "See? You and I are the same."

As summer rolled in, many of the previously empty dirt fields were growing things and they started to reap the rewards of their hard work. They brought in burros and goats, using their manure for the plants, but keeping the notorious eaters away from the fields. Chickens roamed freely, their droppings enriching the soil. By the time they could start harvesting and selling their first vegetables, they invited all their family and friends out to have a

145

••••

farm day. It wasn't a large crew but Wren was happy when Rob, Grayson, Joe, and Echo all confirmed they could come. They invited anyone who wanted to bring tents and stay overnight.

The morning of the farm day, Tse was up running through the halls, ecstatic to see other children. Rob was bringing his whole family, and Echo was bringing along her nieces and nephew. Some of the firefighters who could come were also bringing their families. For the first time in a while, Wren had a pang for firefighting. It was another bad year and every time she heard about what was happening, part of her wanted to be back on the front lines facing it. The other part of her was glad she was back in her own bed each night.

Long tables were set up and Anna made too much food. No doubt it wouldn't go to waste, but she cooked like she was feeding a hundred. As guests arrived, they also brought food and drinks. It was too hot for a fire, but that didn't stop Joe from making a circle of chairs and logs to sit at, so they could play their instruments. Rob's boys seemed to be out of the car before it rolled to a stop, having never been to a farm before. Tse showed them the goats and burros; they screamed and giggled with excitement. Rob reminded them the goats had horns and liked to headbutt people. Soon the farm was filled with children, music, and laughter. An empty field was designated for camping and multicolor nylon domes began to appear.

Grayson came and stood off to the side until Wren introduced him around, getting the conversation going. Echo brought a couple of nieces and a nephew, as well as her boyfriend and his two small children. Wren recognized him as one of the firefighters from New Mexico, who'd volunteered the summer before. Before long, the conversation turned to firefighting, so

• • • •

Elijah and Grayson wandered off to talk about the fields. Grayson was fascinated by the type of agriculture and wanted to learn more. Elijah was happy to oblige.

Rob came up, placing a baby in Wren's arms. "Here you go. This is my daughter Hayden. You can hold her, my arms are tired, and I need a beer."

Wren laughed and bounced the baby, noticing Lindsay was taking the chance to eat a plate of food in peace. Lindsay grinned at her and waved. Wren waved back and entertained the baby. By entertained it was mostly walking, bouncing, shifting, holding, other arm, knee, other knee, and repeat. Finally, Rob relieved her and took the baby naturally as he sipped his beer.

"We've missed you out there, Wren. I didn't think I'd go back, but honestly, I was bored with regular firefighting."

"I have missed you all, too. Sort of. I like farm life, to be honest."

"Who wouldn't? This is the life. Hard work though?"

Wren rubbed the callouses on her hand and nodded. "God, yes."

Rob laughed. "You're the right person for it."

He wasn't wrong. She loved working hard and aching by the end of the day. She figured that was her purpose. Proved she was doing something. She watched Elijah and Grayson traverse the fields, deep in discussion, and smiled. She didn't know much about Grayson, but from their conversations, she could tell he was struggling with what to do with his life. He was bright and could do just about anything he put his mind to, however, he lacked passion for one particular path. He seemed to find it talking to Elijah. Elijah caught her eye and waved her out to join them. She headed out towards them. Grayson was asking a million questions, taking mental notes. Wren went up and touched his arm.

"You know, you're welcome out here any time. We can always use the help," she offered.

Elijah nodded. "I was just telling Grayson that. We need another farm hand and if he is good with room, board, and a little extra, we could put him up."

Wren thought about it. Where would he sleep? She eyed Elijah and cocked her head. He laughed.

"We were trying to figure that out. The house is full, however, we might be able to get a small structure up pretty fast. It would be rudimentary at first, but by winter we could have it snug."

"Grayson, are you even considering it?" Wren asked, confused. "I mean, I'd love to have the help, but is this something you're interested in?"

Grayson stared at his feet, chewing his lip, then met her eyes. "I love this idea. Healing the land, working with the animals and plants like it should be. I went to school for a year, focusing on horticulture but this is the next step. I'd like to get the experience and maybe take it further."

Wren glanced between the two of them and shrugged. "I'm on board, but I want you to know what you're getting yourself into. It's hard work and low pay. But I have no doubt Elijah could get you set up quickly. He is tenacious when he puts his mind to it."

"Thanks, Wren," Grayson said softly.

He was a mystery, but Wren could see he was determined. She glanced back at the crowd and took her leave as they continued discussing topsoil, crops, and manure. She wandered over to Joe and listened to him play, remembering the last time she sang was after Dylan's service. She didn't feel like singing today and just listened. Today was about healing, regrowth. Tse and a group of children were playing tag and she sat down, watching them. Tse was comfortable anywhere but around other children, he was in his element.

She'd spoken to a lawyer and they'd filed a letter to petition her to be able to foster and adopt. It'd be months and she might have to go in front of a judge, but everyone who knew her was quick to write a character reference for her, so the lawyer felt her chances were good. Now, it was a waiting game. She still had no desire to have a birth child and wanted to give a home to an older child. Someone closer in age to Tse, who was now nine. Kids like the ones he was playing with.

The evening ramped up and while parents put their children to sleep in tents, the group around the circle grew and more joined in with instruments and singing. Elijah came and put his arms around Wren, resting his chin on her shoulder. At this moment it seemed perfect, a protected bubble in the world. Wren let her guard down and enjoyed being with their family and friends. Anna took Tse in for bed and for the first time, he didn't fight or bargain to stay awake. He was beat. It was after midnight and most of the adults showed no sign of going to bed. Wren stared at the stars, holding her breath. Let it be like this. A community coming together for the right reasons, for happy reasons. Children playing without a care in the world. People considering each other, trying to make things better. Wren knew it was mostly a fantasy, however, at this exact moment, it seemed possible.

By two in the morning, she was exhausted and snuck away to sleep. Elijah followed shortly after; they cuddled in bed and

• • • •

listened to the chatter around the circle. Wren buried her face in Elijah's hair and fell asleep. Despite the lack of sleep, she was up with the sun and put coffee on. She made her way to the porch and gazed out over the fields, at the now quiet tents. Knowing so many people she cared about were sleeping on their land made her feel whole. She poured the first pot of coffee into a thermos and put another on. She had a feeling at least a few were going to need some this morning. When she came back out with coffee, Grayson was walking towards the house fresh from sleep.

"Hey, Wren. Coffee?"

She handed him a cup and the thermos. "Grayson I want to make sure you didn't feel pressured into coming out here to work. Elijah can be very persuasive."

Grayson chuckled, shaking his head. "He can be, but no. I actually mentioned it. I've been lost since Dylan died. Nothing seemed to hold any purpose for me, but coming out here I just feel connected. Like it matters."

Wren nodded. "I know what you mean. You don't know a lot about me, but before I was a firefighter..."

"You were in prison," Grayson finished. "Dylan told me. About that and the heroin."

"Oh." Wren felt a fresh wave of shame come over her.

"Wren, don't feel like that. He told me because he was in awe of your strength. How you could overcome addiction to become such a leader and friend. He talked about you all of the time. You mattered to him."

Wren shook her head, trying not to let the stinging in her nose turn into full-fledged tears. "He mattered to me. He was my little brother."

"He told me. He said one of the reasons he wanted to stay on with that crew was because of you. Because he admired you and wanted to learn from you."

This was all news to Wren. She and Dylan were friends, they joked around and gave each other shit, but she never knew he looked up to her. Her heart squeezed and she sighed.

"Thanks for telling me that, Grayson. I didn't know."

"You don't give yourself enough credit, Wren. Maybe the reason you went through the hell you did was because you care so much. It's not a bad thing."

She met Grayson's eyes and nodded. He was the same way. So was Elijah. And Dylan. And Rob. They had certain exteriors but the same compassionate drive. It's why they were drawn to each other. To find others who understood and could help them heal.

The tents started to open up; little by little the inhabitants came out in search of food and coffee. Anna brought out fruit and coffee cake while Wren kept the coffee flowing. Noticing Elijah hadn't emerged, Wren slipped back to their room where he was fast asleep. She climbed under the covers and wound her arms around him. He kissed her and smiled. She brushed the hair off his cheek, admiring the angles of his face. He yawned, closing his eyes as he held her tight against him. Wren ran her fingers delicately along his spine.

"Hey, you better get up. Everyone is eating and getting amped up on coffee. You promised tours of the farm. Of your great handiwork."

"Our handiwork."

"Mmm, I just dig the holes. You create life."

• • • •

Elijah laughed, cupping her buttocks. "Hardly. Simply a humble servant to Mother Earth. I couldn't do this without you, Wren. Let me hold you a while longer."

Wren didn't mind. At this moment, it felt like anything was possible. Like nothing could touch them.

· · · ·

Chapter Eighteen

T he battle between human desire and the fragility of the
earth is not won overnight. People don't want to have to
give up their conveniences, and companies are more than
happy to oblige. After all, the almighty dollar is the ultimate
religion. The more humans deny their impact on the earth, the
more it shows its suffering. Year after year, the climate shifts,
increasing natural disasters. This was felt by the firefighters in
Arizona and around the country, as fewer people returned to the
job, but the need became greater. The wildfires grew in intensity,
challenging existing alert systems and staff. Wren always felt a desire
to help but couldn't risk her growing family. Rob ended up going
back to the wildland crew, not only for the action but lured by the
sign-on bonuses they were offering, as he tried to make ends meet.

Grayson moved out to the farm and within a week he and
Elijah built a small cabin-like structure. An electrician came out to

run wiring from the house to the cabin, allowing it to have lights, AC, and small appliances. The goal was to move it, and the farmhouse, over to at least partial solar, but in the meantime, they didn't want to cook Grayson in the small space. They installed a window AC unit, adding a dormitory-sized fridge and hot plate. Grayson was invited to all meals, however, they knew sometimes he'd need his own space. The cabin fit a full bed, a small table with a chair, and a wood stove. Plus the corner with the fridge and small counter over it. It was tight, but Grayson insisted it was all he needed and planned to be in the fields as much as possible. True to his word, he spent very little time there, except sleeping and reading on rainy days.

The night all hell broke loose, they were fast asleep and not expecting to face losing everything. Wren awoke to banging on the door and crept out of bed to see what was going on. She answered the door and Grayson was in a panic, pointing to the hills which were on fire. There had been a fire burning but it was miles away; they hadn't been alerted it was heading in their direction. She ran to the room to wake Elijah up.

"We need to get everyone up! The fire has breached the ridge."

Elijah jumped out of bed, throwing on pants and a shirt, then ran outside. The winds were picking up, moving the fire at a fast pace in their direction. Elijah rushed inside and woke up Anna and Tse, telling Anna to get Tse to the reservation. Anna resisted, but as soon as she saw the fire she bundled Tse up and loaded him in the car. They needed to move, now! She packed bags for them and let Elijah know she was about to leave. He hugged Tse tightly, fear crossing his face. He kissed Anna and told her to keep by the phone. She drove off with Tse peering out the back window, sleepy and confused.

Grayson, Elijah, and Wren made a plan of action. They knew it was safer to leave, but if the fire made it to the farm it would destroy everything. Wren grabbed whatever fire gear they had and doled it out. She gave Grayson Dylan's hat, boots, and jacket, which she'd kept to remember him by. Grayson noticed but didn't say anything as he put them on. Elijah had full gear, as did Wren, and they grabbed shovels and chainsaws. They took a Mule vehicle out to the fireline and assessed the situation. They immediately began putting out spot fires, as Wren called on the radio to see if any crews were in the area. There were a few, but they were hunkered down fighting the fire in different areas; no one was directly near them.

Grayson wasn't trained, so they gave him a shovel and had him go closer to the farm where he could use irrigation hoses to put out the spot fires as they appeared from flying embers. Wren and Elijah moved nearer the fire, taking down trees with the chainsaws and digging trenches along the farm line. The issue was the wind was carrying embers overhead, they could only hope Grayson was able to get the ones out that didn't extinguish on their own. They kept the line and encroaching fire back, hoping it was enough. After a couple of hours, they could hear a crew moving in towards them and Wren ran to meet them. She filled them, informing them she and Elijah needed to get back to the farm to check on things.

They took the Mule back to where they left Grayson and could see he was quickly becoming engulfed on all sides by landing embers, causing spot fires. They jumped out and started helping put out the fires, taking down any vegetation which could spread the fire quicker on the ground. They worked tirelessly for hours

• • • •

and heard the planes coming in to make drops. The winds shifted, redirecting the fire away from them, but there were still spot fires burning everywhere. It was daylight before they were able to see how much had burned, devastated by what they'd found. The buildings were still standing, but at least half of the planted fields were burnt.

They spent the next couple of days checking for spot fires, turning the soil to make sure fresh moist soil was on top. It was too late in the season to replant the summer harvest, and they'd lost much of the winter plants. If they wanted a winter harvest, they'd have to get plants in the ground within days. The money they'd made from previous sales had been rolled back into the farm, it was going to be tight. Grayson offered to work for free as long as they could feed him, and they were too short to turn him down. Wren told Elijah she thought she should go back to firefighting. He stared at her and shook his head.

"It's too dangerous. I need you here."

"Elijah, just for the season. They're so short-staffed, they're offering sign-on bonuses. That would cover the plants to get back in the ground. We can't risk losing the farm and you know way more than I do about farming. I need to do this. For our family."

"Wren, I'm scared to let you go. I can't lose you."

"You won't. But we *will* lose everything if I don't. Just one season. Okay?"

He knew it was the truth and couldn't fight her on it. "Would you go back to your old crew?"

"I would prefer to. I know them and how they work. It would mean I'd be at camp, except on my days off. It's too far of a drive to come back more than that."

• • • •

Elijah did something Wren thought she'd never see and began to cry. Wren was shocked and watched him, frozen. Finally, she came next to him and put her arms around his waist. He buried his face in her hair, clinging onto her.

"Wren, I don't know what to do. I put us in this situation, now you're having to put your life on the line to fix it."

"No, we chose this life together. I'm choosing to make sure we don't lose it. I love you, Elijah. I love our life here; for the first time, I have something to fight for. Please understand and let me go."

Elijah met her eyes and she could see the pain in them. If she didn't come back, he'd never forgive himself. She wiped the tears off his cheeks and looked to him for approval. She was her own person, but she knew she was putting her family through fear by making this choice. Elijah sighed, then bobbed his head.

"I don't have much choice do I?" he asked, his voice raspy.

"We. We don't have much choice because this is everything we have. This is for our family. For Tse."

Elijah held her to his chest and kissed her cheek. "Don't be a hero. Just do what you have to and come home to me."

"I will," she promised, hoping it was the truth.

When she called Rob to see if he could get her back on the team, he sounded haggard and discouraged.

"I can. But Wren it's bad. Worse than last season. We lost about a quarter of our guys since last year and are relying heavily on the prison crews. How soon can you get here?"

"Day after tomorrow. I need to help out with some things on the farm first."

"Alright, plan to be here. I know there is no doubt they'll be ecstatic to have you back."

157

"Thanks, Rob. Make sure they have a tent for me."

"Oh, we have a couple of crews from the women's prison, too. You have a place ready and waiting."

Wren hung up and sighed. She didn't want to go, but they needed the money. She went to find Elijah and held him as tight as she could. They had the rest of the day and the next before she had to go. Anna and Tse came back once they knew it was safe and dinner that night was somber. Tse asked her when she'd be back.

"I'll be back a couple of days a week, okay, Tse?"

He nodded and pushed a pea around his plate. "Will you miss me?"

"Of course, I will. I'll think of you every day and I'll call before you go to bed."

Tse watched her, his little face too serious. "Will the fire hurt you?"

Wren didn't know how to answer and stared at Elijah helplessly. He put his hand on Tse's back, clearing his throat.

"Tse, it is dangerous, but Wren has done this for years. She knows how to fight the fire. She doesn't want you to worry. Maybe you can write to her every day and give her the letters when she comes home?"

"I like pictures, too," Wren added.

Tse smiled but his eyes were still concerned. "Okay."

Wren was mentally worn out by the time they went to bed and lay on her back staring at the ceiling. Elijah came in and climbed next to her, placing his arm around her waist. She turned and curled into him, needing to feel protected. He rubbed her back rhythmically. She met his eyes and kissed him gently. She'd been alone for so long, yet couldn't imagine not lying next to him at night. He brushed the hair off her face and watched her.

• • • •

"It will be okay, Wren," he said, though she thought he was trying to convince himself more than her.

"Elijah, I'm going to miss you so much. Your arms, your eyes, your hair, your lips."

Elijah leaned in and kissed her deeply. This ignited a need in her to feel him as part of her. She entwined her fingers in his hair, pushing herself to him. His body responded and they touched each other everywhere they could. Wren felt like she was vibrating and moaned. Elijah slipped his fingers between her legs and she arched to meet him.

"I need you, Elijah. Take me... remind me what I'm going to miss."

He met her eyes and guided her legs open. He slid inside her and grasped her as he thrust roughly. She felt her cheeks get hot and clung onto his back as he moved them both with such force, she felt like she might break. Wren cried out with pleasure. She felt he might truly become part of her as he took her with such ferocity, she didn't know where she ended and he began. Waves of heat surged through her and she wept. Elijah shuddered and met her mouth as his body let go inside of hers. Wren was sore but didn't want it to end. She wrapped her legs around his buttocks, holding him there as she trailed her hands up and down his back. He rested on her and met her eyes.

"Come home to me."

Wren could see the world in his eyes and nodded. "You are mine, Elijah. There is no place without you in it. You opened something in me I didn't know was there, now you hold the key."

She loosened her grip on him and he rolled down next to her. She had a feeling walking the next day was going to be a little rough. She felt raw from where he was inside of her and looking at

159

• • • •

him, she saw he bore the tenderness, as well. She slipped her arm around him and buried her face in his hair. It was damp but smelled like him. She wanted to remember that smell.

"Can I ask you something?" she wondered out loud.

"Of course."

"Is it wrong to have you cut a strand of your hair I can put into something to take with me? To feel close to you?"

She wasn't sure if it was wrong to ask but he knitted his brow and tipped his head.

"Anything for you, Wren. Will you cut a piece of yours for me?"

Wren nodded. Elijah got out of bed and grabbed a pair of scissors and some twine. They sat across from each other crossed-legged. Elijah braided a strand of his hair from underneath and cut it close to his head. He handed Wren the scissors and she did the same. Elijah tied each end of his braid with twine as Wren tied hers. They handed each other their braids at the same time and leaned in, meeting each other's mouths. Wren ran her fingers over Elijah's smooth, black braid and met his eyes.

"You're mine, heart and soul, Elijah. Now, I can carry you with me."

"You always did, Wren."

Chapter Nineteen

T he following months were a blur of home and fire. Wren almost fell asleep at the wheel a couple of times and often would wake up not knowing where she was. She did her best to balance work and family but was beginning to crash mentally. Grayson and Elijah overturned the soil in the burnt fields, replanting about half of what they lost. It would be enough to carry them through the winter.

Wren was grateful for her time back on the farm, however, her mind was always fighting fires. Now that she had something she cared about, it seemed so much harder to keep going. She wondered how Rob did it for so long. When she asked him, he chewed his lip and sighed.

"To be honest, Wren, this will be my last season. I've been taking classes in electrical coding and hope to get my electrician's license soon," he told her. "With my daughter joining us, I decided

• • • •

it was time to watch my kids grow up. Give up firefighting altogether."

"Oh. That's good. I mean, for you and the family, the team is going to miss you."

"They will but at the end of my life, I want my kids to know me, to be alive. How about you? Just this season?"

Wren laughed. "God, yes. Seriously, this is so much harder than I remember. I don't know if I'm coming or going."

Rob chuckled and nodded. "Try having a baby on top of it."

"No thanks," Wren replied and shook her head vehemently. "There is no way a baby is coming out of me."

On the next drive home, Wren considered what Rob had said about being there for his family. She had no desire to keep doing this and was counting the days until the end of the season. They needed the money, but after that, she was ready to be done once and for all. Rob was smart to go to school to be an electrician; she considered if she should seek additional training as a backup. Something which would have her home at night.

By the time she got home, it was late and she slipped in as to not wake Tse or Anna. Elijah was up waiting for her, reading in the living room. He saw her come in and got up to greet her. He wrapped her in his arms, burying his face in her hair.

"You smell like smoke," he murmured.

Wren peered at his face and furrowed her brow. He didn't look well. Dark circles lined his eyes and his skin had a strange pallor. She placed her hand on his cheek and met his eyes. "Are you alright? You look ill."

"Just tired I suppose, we've been working twelve-hour days to get things back. Probably pushing too hard."

• • • •

"Are you eating okay? Keeping an eye on your blood sugar? Taking your insulin?"

Elijah sighed and took her hand. "Enough of the twenty questions, Wren. I'm doing the best I can."

She knew his avoidance meant he hadn't been. "I'm worried about you."

"We're all making sacrifices," he snapped, then turned away. "Just drop it."

"Whoa," Wren replied and put her hand on his chin, turning his face back towards her. "I will not drop it, Elijah. You're my husband and I get to be worried about you. I get to demand you take care of yourself."

Elijah's face softened and he put his arm around her. "You're right. I'm just exhausted and missing you. I know we need to do this, but it's tearing me up every day worrying about you. This wasn't the plan."

"We plan, God laughs," Wren said, quoting a saying she saw on a sign in a gift shop once.

Elijah chuckled, running his fingers through her hair. "I'm glad you're home. How many days this time?"

"Two."

"Never enough. Are you hungry or anything?"

"No, I want to climb in bed with you."

"Come on then," Elijah took her hand and led her to the bedroom.

She stripped off her clothes and considered hopping in the shower but was too tired even for that. She slid under the cool sheets and yawned. There truly was no place like home. Elijah gathered her close, intertwining his legs with hers. She felt a desire stirring, but neither of them had it in them to follow through. She

• • • •

rested her head against his shoulder and closed her eyes. She didn't remember falling asleep but was woken up by a loud crash in the hallway. She sat up, reaching out for Elijah. His side of the bed was empty but still warm. She slipped on a nightgown and clicked on a light.

"Daddy!" She heard Tse scream and she bolted out to where his voice was coming from.

Elijah was sprawled out in the hallway, unconscious. She ran to him and checked his pulse. It was thready and erratic. Fuck. She checked his pupils and ran to get his insulin and blood meter. After a quick check of his blood levels, she was shocked to see his blood sugar was skyrocketing. She asked Tse to go get Grayson and gave Elijah a shot of insulin, doing what she saw him do. Grayson ran in, wearing just his undershorts and she yelled at him to call 911. Anna stumbled out of her room from all the commotion and stared wide-eyed. Wren didn't know enough about diabetes and didn't know when, or if, she could give him more insulin. Grayson was talking with 911 and while they were sending an ambulance, Elijah could be dead by then. She asked him to see if they could guide her on what to do. They asked what she'd done and she explained his blood levels, that she gave him insulin. They told her to wait and check again in fifteen minutes.

Elijah remained unresponsive and Wren started to panic. What if they didn't make it in time? She fought back tears and prayed to a god she didn't even believe in. It seemed like hours when she heard sirens coming down the drive. Anna ran out to wave them in as Wren checked Elijah's pulse and blood levels. His pulse was faint and his blood sugar levels were still too high. The paramedics came in and took over, assessing Elijah's condition and loading him onto a stretcher. One look at their faces and Wren knew Elijah might not make it.

Wren gathered Tse in her arms. His eyes were huge and wet; she knew this would scar him forever. She told the paramedics everything she knew and asked Anna if she would stay with Tse, so Wren could follow the ambulance to the hospital. Anna took Tse's hand and murmured something in Navajo to him, guiding him to the kitchen. Grayson stood helplessly in the hallway.

"Wren, do you want me to go with you or stay on the farm?" he asked, his voice tight with worry.

"Can you stay here and make sure to keep an eye on things?"

"Of course. I'll pick up where Elijah and I left off yesterday. Please let me know what is going on when you get there. Elijah has become like family to me."

"I know, Grayson. I will."

Wren threw on clothes and packed a bag of things for her and Elijah. She didn't know if they'd keep him there. Or if he even would survive. It didn't look good. They said he was in a diabetic coma. That's all they told her before they rushed him out the door. Wren kissed Tse on the head and met Anna's eyes. She knew. She'd seen Elijah's mother die from diabetes, her eyes told the tale.

The drive to the hospital was miserable, the road stretching out for miles. Wren felt tears slip down her cheek and thought back to Gabe. The irony that a prick of a needle killed him and the need for a prick of the needle might kill Elijah, didn't go unnoticed to Wren. She screamed and cursed as she drove, pounding her fists on the wheel. If she'd just stayed on the farm, he wouldn't have become so physically and mentally exhausted and would've taken better care of himself. Checked his blood sugar, took his insulin, rested more. The wildfire may not have burned their home, but it was still taking them down. Defeated, she called out to the only person she could think of.

"Gabe, I need your help. I need you to speak to the powers that be and help Elijah get through this. I lost you, I can't lose him, too. Tse can't lose his father. Please, Gabe, if you can hear me, do something! Pull some strings. Talk to the big guy, or girl. I don't fucking know. Just help me!"

Tears poured down her cheeks and she bargained anything she could think of. She'd be better. She'd try harder. She'd give up anything asked of her. At this point, she was shooting in the dark, hoping something would land. She thought of Dylan, her father, and the grandparents she really didn't remember and asked them to please help. Rage and panic filled her and she screamed at the top of her lungs.

"Can anyone hear me? Is anyone even out there listening? Please!"

Her voice disappeared into the dark and she scrubbed the tears off her face, causing her skin to burn. She couldn't do this again. Bury someone she loved. The night closed in around her and she felt completely alone in the world. No one else was out there. She was driving into the abyss, nothing was on the other end. The road went on for miles, stretching into oblivion. She convinced herself she was heading into the mouth of hell when she saw the lights of the town on the horizon and shook her head. She needed to get it together. She guided the car into the hospital parking lot and ran to the emergency room. It wasn't the same hospital, but it reminded her of the day Dylan died, and she fought back the panic of familiarity.

● ● ● ●

"My husband Elijah Clarke was brought in?" she barked at the guy behind the desk as he tapped away on his keyboard and nodded.

"Please take a seat. They'll come to get you as soon as they can," he replied flatly, used to being berated and abused by people.

Wren found a seat and clutched her bag, jumping every time a doctor or nurse passed through the doors from the exam rooms. She texted Grayson that she was waiting and to let Anna know. She'd send updates as she got them. Too much time passed and Wren impatiently went to the desk.

"My husband Elijah was brought in. Are there any updates? Elijah Clarke."

The guy eyed her and checked the computer again. He shook his head. "No ma'am. Someone will come to find you when they have information."

Wren glared at him and sighed heavily. She paced the waiting room, watching people come and go. Still, no one came. She was just about ready to reach across the desk counter and strangle the guy when a nurse came out and called her name.

"Mrs. Clarke? Mrs. Elijah Clarke?"

Wren bolted towards her and waved her hands. "Me. That's me."

The nurse smiled politely and nodded. "Please follow me. The doctor would like to speak to you."

Wren's heart dropped. She wasn't being taken to Elijah, she was being taken to speak to a doctor. That wasn't good. The doctor would be there to break the news to her. Her palms were sweaty and she took shallow breaths. This couldn't be happening again. She was led to a small office and the nurse motioned for her to sit down.

• • • •

"The doctor will be right in."

Wren wiped her hands on her pants, noticing black streaks as she did so. Ash. She'd never showered and was still covered in a thin layer of grime and soot. A light knock came at the door, a small woman with black hair and caramel skin came in. She met Wren's eyes and nodded.

"I'm Dr. Marri. I have been attending to your husband."

"Is he okay?" Wren asked, knowing the question was stupid.

The doctor peered at the file in front of her and shook her head. "Mr. Clarke suffered a diabetic coma caused by diabetic ketoacidosis. His blood sugar was dangerously high and quite possibly high for some time."

Wren felt her throat tighten and nodded slowly, afraid to ask the only question that mattered.

"Did he die?"

Chapter Twenty

T he doctor frowned at her and shook her head slightly, almost like she didn't comprehend the question. "No. He is currently still in a coma and we're working to get his blood sugar under control. I can't say if he'll pull through, but we're doing everything we can. I must tell you, even if he does come through this, there is a risk of brain and organ damage. Do you know how long his sugar was out of control?"

Wren shook her head. "I just got home tonight. I was gone for a week as a firefighter. He didn't look well when I arrived, and he admitted he'd not been watching it as closely as he should."

"Mrs. Clarke, I need you to be aware of what is going on. With type one diabetes, most patients are at risk of a shortened life span. Organ damage, loss of limbs, blindness, are all risks, as well as heart attacks and bodily failure. Any lapse in insulin, any time blood sugar levels get too high, put the body at risk."

"His mother died young, as well. She had type one," Wren explained.

"I see, do you know at what age?"

"I don't, but Elijah was young. His grandmother pretty much raised him."

The doctor made notes on Elijah's chart. She took her glasses off and rubbed her nose. "I know this is scary and we're doing our best to get him well. If he does pull through, he'll need to rest to let himself heal. Let's try to focus on this incident and move forward from there."

Wren nodded. Incident. Like he wasn't fighting for his life. The doctor stood up and smiled wearily. She slipped her glasses back on and tucked the folder under her arm. She didn't stick her hand out or offer any sort of comfort. Just the facts ma'am.

"I'll have the nurse show you to another more comfortable waiting room. There are vending machines down the hall. If anything changes, I'll let you know. I know it seems hopeless, but he is still breathing. Hold on to that."

"Can I see him?"

"Shortly. We're moving him to the ICU. Once he is there, we will bring you to him."

The doctor left and the nurse showed Wren to the waiting room, passing the vending machines on the way. It was all crap food. Chips, candy, and soda. A hospital should have healthier options, Wren thought bitterly. She was only in the waiting room for about fifteen minutes before she was taken up to the ICU. Each room, or pod, was small with the patient's bed in the center, a couple of chairs on either side, and a sliding glass door leading to the nurses' station. Wren was taken to Elijah's pod and she paused at the door. He didn't look good. Suddenly, all she could see was

Gabe's lifeless eyes staring at her and she fought back a scream. The nurse, used to family reactions, told her to come to the nurses' station if she needed anything and left.

Wren called Grayson and filled him in. Not that there was much to report, but she needed to talk to a familiar voice. Grayson was quiet for a moment and then breathed out heavily.

"Hang in there, Wren. Elijah is a fighter. He has a lot to live for."

"So did Dylan."

Silence grew between them and Wren recognized she was out of line. Dylan was doing his job and it took him. He wasn't given the chance to fight. "I'm sorry, Grayson, that was shitty of me to say. I know Dylan would still be here if had been given even a second to hold on."

"I know you didn't mean anything by it. You loved Dylan, too, and the situations are different. Go be with Elijah, talk to him, hold him. Make him come back."

"Thanks. Can you let Anna know and maybe have Tse help you on the farm to keep his mind off it?"

"Of course, but he's a bright kid. He's asking questions and he knows."

Wren went back into Elijah's room and stood next to him. She ran her fingers through his hair and held on to the ends. *You're a curse,* her mind told her. She shook it off and brushed her lips against his forehead. If she was a curse, she needed to break it.

"Elijah, I'm here. I need you to listen and come to my voice. Tse is home worried about you and he needs his daddy. You know what it is like to grow up without one and lose your mother so young. Anna and Grayson are taking care of him, but he needs you. He needs *us*. If I lose you, I'll be no good for him. It will kill me inside and he needs whole people, not broken people. I'll shatter into a million pieces without you. I'll become dust and blow away. I need you. You're my best friend and the one person who truly understood me. I loved Gabe and he loved me, but we were two wandering souls. You were my other half. You *are* my other half, I mean. With you, I found my path back to myself. But I needed your help. You can't leave me now. I'm not strong enough, I'll slip away." Wren couldn't hold it together and leaned her head on the bed, bawling. She cried so hard she shook the bed, causing the wires and tubes to swing back and forth. "Please, Elijah. Fight to come back to me. I promise I'll stay by your side for the rest of my life. We'll find a way."

The machines continued their steady beeping and Elijah stayed away. Wren gave a shuddering sob and rubbed his fingers. This was real life, her words weren't enough to bring him back to the surface. A nurse came in to check his vitals. She asked if Wren needed anything. Wren shook her head and watched the nurse move around Elijah like he was a car going for an oil change at the mechanic. The nurse wasn't being dispassionate, however, the reality was Elijah was an inert object, right now. Wren waited until she left and moved back to Elijah's side. She wracked her brain, trying to think of a way to get down past the body to the soul. She rubbed her fingers across his lips and let her hand rest on his cheek.

"Elijah, you have to be like the seed in the ground. I know you're down deep in the dark, now it's time to start your journey to the sun. It's time to start growing upward. Push through the darkness, through the cold, towards the top, and the warm sun. You can do this. A seed is the most powerful being. A whole world encased in a tiny grain. You may feel trapped, but you're just getting your strength back to burst out of the ground and bloom. I know it. I feel it. I'm not giving up on you. It's time to heal. It's time to come back."

The doctor standing was at the door and cleared her throat. "Mrs. Clarke. I hope I'm not interrupting."

Wren shook her head and stepped back. The doctor came in and stood next to Elijah. She smiled at Wren but it was the hospital smile... part pity, part lies.

"Good news, we are getting his blood sugar and ketones under control. I'm concerned because even so, he isn't coming out of it which could signal brain damage. If he doesn't start responding in the next hour or so, we'll need to run some tests to see. Are you planning to stay?"

Where the hell would she go? She nodded and bit the inside of her lip. The doctor went out and spoke to the nurses on duty, pointing back at Elijah. The nurses nodded and one met Wren's eyes with a gentle look. Wren glanced away and walked up to Elijah, placing both hands on the sides of his face firmly.

"Fucking wake up, Elijah! Goddamn it, open your eyes!" She knew she was yelling but she didn't care. One of the nurses started for the room but the doctor put her hand out, stopping her.

Wren leaned in close to his face. "If you don't fucking wake up, I'll find you on the other side and drag you back. You belong here. You owe it to Tse, you owe it to me. I swear, Elijah, you'd better get your ass back, right fucking now! You don't want to face my wrath if you don't. I will find you."

Wren grabbed his hand and squeezed it as hard as she could, hoping to make him feel something. She felt a power surge in her she'd never experienced and pinched the side of his leg, hard. She didn't know what the machines were specifically measuring, but she saw one of the lines going across the screen jump slightly.

• • • •

She squeezed his hand again and held it tightly. The activity on the monitors increased and the nurses and doctor watched with bated breath. Wren leaned in and nipped his neck with her teeth and whispered hoarsely in his ear.

"It's time to go."

With that, the monitors started to jump around and the doctor and one of the nurses came in. Wren refused to move or let go of Elijah's hand. They moved to the other side and at the moment the doctor peered into Elijah's eyes, Wren felt him tighten his hand around hers. She made the medical staff work around her as she wasn't letting him go. She raised his hand to her mouth as she bit the tips of his fingers firmly but not enough to draw blood. One way or the other, she was bringing him back.

"Ow," a voice muttered and the doctor stared at Wren then back at Elijah. Wren peered at Elijah and bit his thumb. His eyes fluttered and his mouth moved.

"Wren, okay. I hear you... stop."

Wren wanted to cry but wasn't convinced. She squeezed his hand and he squeezed back. She did it again and this time he gripped her hand firmly and drew her towards him. She put her other arm around him, clutching him tightly. His hand drifted to her hair and he rested it on her head. Wren could hear his heart in his chest; unlike his pulse earlier, it was steady. She pulled her head back and stared at his face. His eyes were barely open but tracked her movements. She kissed his fingertips.

"I'm sorry, I had to. You weren't coming back to me."

He nodded his head slightly and the corners of his lips twitched in an attempted smile. "Hurts."

"I know."

"Love you." His voice was weak.

"I love you."

She met the doctor's eyes in question. The doctor nodded an affirmation that he should be alright. Wren leaned in and kissed his lips.

"I need to call Anna and let her know. I'll be right back."

Elijah didn't let her hand go and Wren laughed. "I promise. Tse needs to know his daddy is okay."

Elijah let go and Wren slipped out the sliding door to call Grayson. When he picked up, she could hear Tse in the background and was relieved she had good news to share.

"Grayson, he's awake."

"He is? Oh, thank goodness, Wren! Do they think he'll be okay long-term?"

"They haven't given me much information but he spoke to me and knew who I was. He squeezed my hand." She left out the part about biting his fingers and yelling at him because it sounded demented.

"Can I tell Tse?" Grayson asked quietly.

"Yes, let him know Elijah is awake, however, the doctors still need to take care of him for a while. He isn't out of the woods but the doctor seemed encouraging. Please let Anna know. I'm going to stay here with him until I can bring him home. Can you manage the farm?"

"Yeah, for sure."

"I don't know what we would've done without you, Grayson."

"We're family. Go be with Elijah, I have this."

Wren hung up and made her way back to the room. Elijah was slightly propped and the doctor was asking him questions. He was answering slowly but correctly. He saw her and watched as she approached. She slid the door open and went to his side. He reached out to her and she took his hand. The doctor kept asking questions, checking his eye movements. She motioned to Wren.

"Do you have a minute?"

"I do. I'll be right back, Elijah."

They walked out of the door and the doctor glanced in at him. "He's doing remarkably well. I don't think there is any brain damage, but we'll need to keep him here to keep an eye on his organs and how he responds to treatment. Maybe a week, less if he seems to be responding well."

"Okay, can I stay with him?"

"Of course. ICU isn't set up for overnight visitors but we do have a lounge with couches you can sleep on. Once we feel he is stable, we will move him to a regular room and those have cots for visitors."

"Do you think he'll be alright?"

"Hard to say, but when I spoke to you earlier, I thought I'd be preparing you for losing him. I shouldn't say that but I'm impressed he pulled through. This is a lifelong condition and he needs to treat it as such. No slip-ups, no missed insulin. Every single action stops a tidal wave."

Wren bobbed her head, glancing at Elijah. The doctor stepped away to talk to the nurses. Wren went back in and climbed into bed with him. She rested her head against his shoulder, trailing her fingers up and down his chest. He placed his hand over hers in mid-stroke, holding it in place.

"I can't do this without you, Wren."

• • • •

Chapter Twenty-One

T here is nothing more touching than seeing a child's eyes when they land on a parent they thought they might never see again. Grayson brought Tse to the hospital after a couple of days, once the doctor felt Elijah was in the clear. Tse immediately clambered up on the bed and wrapped his arms around Elijah's neck. Elijah laughed and held him close, whispering in Tse's ear. Tse nodded, resting against Elijah's chest. He waved at Wren. She came over and gave them each a kiss on the forehead.

Elijah had been moved to a private room and his tests were coming back good, except his kidneys showed some damage from the stress on them. The doctor talked with them about eventual kidney failure as a risk and recommended they get tested for compatibility in the off chance that risk became a reality. Wren had no doubt she would, even though Elijah was concerned about her health. They were not guaranteed to be a match, but she wanted to be tested. Grayson stepped forward and offered to be tested, as well. At that moment, Wren understood how much he cared about their family. He'd grown close to Elijah working the farm, and she wondered about his own family. He hardly spoke about them. His parents were divorced and he had an older sister. That was all she knew. While they walked to the cafeteria as Elijah and Tse watched cartoons, she thought to bring it up.

"We love having you in our family. You've saved us through all of this."

"Thanks, you guys mean a lot to me," Grayson replied, his gray eyes turned down at the corners, making him look perpetually sad.

"What about your family? Don't you think they would want to know if you donated a kidney?"

Grayson shrugged and ran his hands through his almost shoulder-length, bleached-out hair. He swallowed hard and met her eyes. "I suppose. Don't get me wrong, I love my family. We just don't connect. Both of my parents remarried and went on with their lives. They weren't thrilled when I came out as gay, but honestly, I didn't think it mattered all that much because I was an adult and wasn't really on their radar anymore. They were never the invested emotional kind of parents. As long as we did well in school and stayed out of trouble, they were happy to leave well enough alone."

Wren could relate, that's how her parents were, as well. "Did they ever meet Dylan?"

"No. What was the point? I wasn't looking for a Norman Rockwell family gathering. I loved Dylan and that was all that mattered. We lived our own lives away from both of our families. I

• • • •

think of family more as people we connect to and less about blood, you know?"

Wren did. Like him, she loved her family but she didn't miss them. The holiday calls and monthly check-ins were more than enough. She loved her little brother but felt less close to him now than she did Dylan or Grayson. Would Tse feel that way about them when he grew up? The thought made her sad and she shook it off. They had a different relationship. He wasn't just a kid and them the adults. He was part of their inner circle now. His thoughts and feelings mattered and were considered in making decisions. They spoke to him with respect and genuine interest. Still, he might grow up and feel disconnected from them. Ultimately, it was his right as a person. He was on his own journey.

"Why us, Grayson? I mean we all loved Dylan, however, you seemed to just naturally become part of our family."

Grayson blushed, staring at his shoes. "I don't know. When you reached out to me about Dylan, I felt an immediate connection to you. Then when I met Elijah and he taught me about farming, I felt like he was my big brother. He has a way about him which makes me feel like I'm smart and he sees it."

"You *are* smart. You already understand way more about the plants, soil, and land than I do. I love the planting but left to my own devices, we'd have a helter-skelter of randomly placed plants which made no sense. I need a chart to follow to understand."

"You're the business side, is why. Without you, we'd just be planting and harvesting, but not know how to source it out."

That was true. Wren organized all of the orders to restaurants and CSAs. She mapped out their expected product and had it spoken for before it was out of the ground. She knew how

• • • •

many eggs the chickens would lay, and how to rotate the goats so none of them had to produce milk for more than a short time after weaning their babies. The goal was to give the animals a good life while working with them to help run the farm. It was a system of ins and outs, only she seemed to understand. Even when she was fighting fires, she was always getting messages about the how-tos. A bubble of pride filled her chest, knowing she was an integral part of the farm.

"I'm glad we found each other, Grayson, but if I could give you back Dylan and have never met you, in a heartbeat, I would. I lost my first love to heroin, not a day goes by I don't miss him. But then I met Elijah, and I love him as much, if not more. Differently. We've built something together."

Grayson smiled. "I know you have. The love you two have for each other is pretty rare."

"I'm sorry about Dylan. I mean it."

Grayson hugged her, sighing. "We all have our wounds. This one is mine. One day, maybe it won't hurt so much. Right now, it reminds me that once I was truly loved."

Wren watched him but had nothing to say to that. They grabbed food from the cafeteria and brought it back to the room. Tse was glued to the television and Elijah had dozed off with him in his arms. Wren gently helped Tse get down and gave him a piece of pizza from the cafeteria. It didn't look too appetizing but Tse took a bite and grinned. Pizza was pizza to kids. Elijah had a tray of diabetic food next to his bed, untouched. When Wren peered at it, she couldn't blame him. She wasn't even sure what it was. She picked at her salad and gazed at Elijah. His color was better. She worried about his kidneys but knew they'd cross that bridge when they got to it.

• • • •

Grayson took Tse after he ate and led him to the bed. "We gotta go, little man. Give your dad a hug."

Tse climbed up and hugged Elijah, who stirred, putting his arms around Tse tightly. "I'll be home soon, okay?"

Tse nodded sadly. He kissed Elijah on the cheek and climbed down, taking Grayson's hand. He hugged Wren on their way out and Grayson's eyes met hers. He'd be back the next day for initial testing for a kidney match. They were both getting tested, hoping one of them would be a match. Anna would keep Tse with her at the farm. Wren stood up and hugged Tse close to her. Then she wrapped her arms around Grayson.

"I love you," she said honestly.

He grinned, cocking his head. "I love you, too, Wren."

After they left, Wren climbed in bed with Elijah and pressed herself to him. He slid his arm under her and drew her tightly against him. She peered up at him and let her eyes lock on his. He watched her, neither wanting to break the gaze. A nurse came in to check his blood pressure and they let their eyes drop. Wren, concerned about him not eating, touched the food tray next to him.

"You have to eat. Not eating is kinda what got you into this mess."

Elijah snickered with a touch of bitterness. "Genetics is what got me into this mess, but you're right. This is just disgusting. Nothing fresh. I want food from the earth."

"Make do for now. We'll be home soon."

Elijah pulled the tray over and winced as he ate bites of the hospital food. Wren laughed, being reminded of a kid holding their nose and choking down food at the dinner table. Elijah gagged and pushed the food away.

"How do they expect people to get healthier if this is the shit they give them in the hospital? " he asked, disgusted.

She couldn't blame him, she probably wouldn't eat it in the same situation. She texted Grayson a quick message to bring food from the farm for Elijah and settled back in, tucked in next to Elijah. After a bit, he got up to use the bathroom and she observed him move across the floor carefully. He'd lost weight and his drawstring pants hung loosely on his hips. He closed the door and she held her breath, expecting something bad to happen. He came back out and raised an eyebrow.

"What's the look?" he asked.

"Nothing."

He sat on the bed and ran his hand through her hair, the IV tape on his hand catching single strands of her hair. "You're so beautiful, Wren. I'm glad you're here."

Wren watched him and put her hand on his waist. "You didn't give me much choice, now did you?"

He chuckled, shaking his head. "So, that's how I get you to stay home, try to drop dead?"

"Not funny. You scared the hell out of me. Out of all of us. I couldn't live without you, Elijah."

Elijah slid back into the bed and gathered her in his arms. "You could. You proved that, but I don't want you to. I want to walk hand in hand with you around our farm until we're too old to walk. Then we can rock on the porch."

Wren pictured them old and smiled. It would be a long time until either of them wasn't able to walk anymore. Then the thought about his kidneys crossed her mind and the smile froze on her face. Elijah frowned.

"What are you thinking about, Wren?"

• • • •

"Your kidneys."

Elijah sighed and Wren knew he was stressed, as well. "Let's face what we can and see what happens. Hopefully, they recover... if not, fingers crossed I have options. Can we just be together tonight and let that rest?"

Wren bobbed her head and laid her head on his shoulder. They could stop worrying for one night. About kidneys and fires and all of that. They watched old television shows until they were too tired to keep their eyes open. Wren went to move to the cot the nurses had set up. Elijah stopped her.

"Can you sleep here with me tonight? I like feeling you close."

"Hospital rules. Apparently, I could fall out of the bed and crack my head open, or kick you off the bed or something," Wren replied.

"I'll take my chances. Make them say something. Please, Wren? I need to feel you next to me to sleep. I promise I'll keep my hands to myself," he joked.

"Please don't," Wren replied and slid her hand under the sheet and down his pants, resting it on his thigh. She made sure not to get too close to his genitals but felt him get hard anyway.

"Wren-"

"That's all. I just want to rest my hand there. I won't go any further."

Elijah gazed at her and breathed out slowly. "Damnit. Even so."

Wren giggled, moving her hand farther down his leg to reduce the sensation. He shook his head and shifted slightly to allow himself to let the blood move away from the area. He slid his hand under her shirt over her breast. It was warm and made a pulse between her legs. Now, she understood. He winked and kissed her gently.

"Fair is fair," he said mischievously.

Wren wanted him but knew they'd gone as far as the hospital bed allowed. She grinned and put her free hand in his hair, twisting her fingers until the hair was snug in them. She tugged a little, meeting his eyes.

"Fair is fair."

Chapter Twenty-Two

Wren wasn't a match. Grayson was a partial match but low. The doctor explained it was more likely for people to find matches in their own racial and family pools. Because of this, Elijah would stand his best chance of a strong match with someone of Native American descent, however, since Grayson was a partial match he'd be considered *if* the time came and Elijah needed a kidney. Grayson took it all in stride and shrugged.

"I'm not going anywhere anytime soon," he replied with a glint of humor Wren wasn't used to seeing from him.

Ultimately, the hope was that Elijah's kidneys would repair and get back to full functioning on their own, but the doctor said it was good to be prepared if not. If he did need a kidney transplant the lifelong complications with type one diabetes were a risk. Wren found these days she was praying more and more to a god she didn't think existed. It didn't sit right with her and she was conflicted about what to believe but figured she'd take her chances. Grayson found her in the dark, wood-paneled, hospital chapel one morning and slid in next to her on the bench.

"Hey, mind some company?" he asked.

"Not at all, not even sure I belong here," Wren replied.

Grayson sighed, peering around. "If you think about it, it is just a man-made room and it can be whatever you want it to be."

"Do you? I mean, are you a God believer?" Wren asked curiously.

"I don't know. Do I believe this isn't all there is? Yeah. Do I believe in a white-robed guy in the sky? No. I think we like to put a familiar stamp on things to make it more palatable. I believe it's more cosmic than we can understand but try not to overthink it, you know?"

Wren nodded. She didn't though. Most of her life she didn't consider religion. A couple of times as a child she went with her neighbors to their church, but it felt foreign, slightly scary. The preacher waving his hands and talking about people having the devil inside of them, made her imagine a tiny, cartoon devil living in her stomach, which freaked her out. As she got older, she resented the pushy Christian teens, who told her everything she was doing was wrong in their pious manner. When Gabe died, she knew for sure God didn't exist. Sometimes when she was fighting fires, she'd get this overwhelming sense of not being alone but never chalked it up to a higher power.

"I don't know what to believe," she finally admitted.

"That's the thing though, isn't it? Belief? It's played to be so concrete. A list of rules and mindsets. I like to think my cells have a knowledge my brain can't comprehend. They know where they came from and are made of, but keep it a secret," Grayson explained, then laughed. "I like not knowing, honestly. I think the word belief has become so misconstrued. I prefer trust. I trust I have a soul. Where it goes when I die? I have no clue. I like the imagery of it turning into macrocosm. Just breaking down and joining all of the other souls into one large existence. All this separation doesn't work for me."

Wren liked that thought. She eyed Grayson and realized what Dylan must have seen in him. He was so honest and genuine, not worried about what the world thought of him. She reached out and took his hand. It was warm and rough from working on the farm. Holding his hand made her feel like Dylan was there. He smiled at her and squeezed her hand. They were family. Here and wherever they went after. A microcosm.

Elijah was sleeping when she got back to the room. He seemed almost fragile and she held her breath as she came up next to him. His color was better today. She watched him, raising her hand to touch his face, then paused. She didn't want to wake him. She let her hand drop and mentally sketched his profile in her brain. His full mouth and long, defined nose. His straight, black eyebrows and the half-moons his black lashes made against his lower lids. His long, thick hair which was almost black but had hints of brown from working in the sun. It was spread out on the pillow behind him, giving him an almost sealike aura. On the outside, he was perfect to Wren. Stunning. On the inside, his body was in a battle against itself.

Wren thought about what Grayson said about his cells having the secret to eternity and wondered if Elijah's cells knew how this would all play out. Instead of talking to a higher power, she focused inward. She thought about Elijah's cells and asked them to help. To strengthen, to become an army to fight for him.

• • • •

She could picture them as entities and imagined them as powerful beings, lighting up and growing stronger. For whatever reason, this brought her more comfort than sitting in a chapel, staring at a piece of wood in the shape of a letter.

Elijah shifted and the sheet over him slid down, exposing his bare, smooth chest. Wren placed her hand on his heart and sent all the energy she had in her, through her hand into him. Elijah didn't move, but his eyes opened and he watched her. She focused on the feeling of energy, coursing down her arm from her body and into him through their skin contact. It was like the cells between them were coming together and activating. She kept her hand in place, sensing a vibration passing between them she couldn't explain. Like a cosmic transplant was taking place. After a few minutes, the heat between her skin and his began to cool and she understood whatever she was doing had been done. She drew her hand away, smiling sheepishly. It was the first time she understood she wasn't alone in the cosmos. Something was out there guiding her. Just not anything she'd ever been told about in her life.

Elijah met her eyes and nodded with understanding. He reached out, lacing his fingers through hers. "Thank you."

"I'm not sure what that was. I just felt it," Wren explained, feeling vulnerable.

"I know. There is a lot in this world we've been taught to forget, to bury. Our connection, our power erased so we can be controlled."

"Elijah, do you believe in God? Like any sort of higher power?"

Elijah pulled her towards him and she crawled up next to him. He met her eyes and chewed his lip. "Not God like white men have perpetuated for centuries. Not the angry, judging being who expects submission to be worthy. This has been used against natives for hundreds of years. Not only natives on this soil, native tribes everywhere. Our customs and beliefs, crushed for almighty Christianity. I believe I'm part of the greater whole. The plants, the water, the animals, even the fire and wind. God isn't a who or a single entity, it's in everything. So, yes and no. I believe in a higher power, sort of. More of an equal power. Something greater we're all part of. Something we can draw from to help the world around us. Like you did just now. Does that make sense?"

Wren nodded. More than anything ever had. Grayson and Elijah were saying the same thing in different ways. There was no guy in the sky looking down and judging them or choosing to selectively help some and not others. There was a greater presence which was in all of them, giving them the ability to come together to change things, help one another. Church was about behavior control. She didn't need to sit in a row and be controlled to access the power she had in her. Elijah rubbed her shoulder and kissed her forehead.

"Will you do that again at some point? The healing you did with your hands and your body? I felt a vibration running through my cells when you did."

Wren slid her arm around his waist and bobbed her head. "I can. I don't know how I did it or really where it came from."

"You don't need to. You need to trust in yourself. It will come," Elijah murmured into her hair.

Trust. It was the key she didn't know she'd been holding. Let her guard down, connect, and it came. She had power in her. This realization made her almost giddy. Elijah was right, there was a reason this had been taught away, forced out of people. It would be hard to control the masses if they understood they had the power

189

• • • •

in them all along, and coming together made it impenetrable. It's why crimes against humanity were committed over the centuries. Torture, taking away children, isolation, locking people up, systematic brainwashing, poverty were all tools used to keep people from coming together and breaking down the system of oppression. If people were constantly in survival mode, they couldn't tap into their own power. Then present them with another controlled option of religion, of hope, and the final nail was in the coffin.

Grayson came in, ready to head back to the farm. He met Wren's eyes and smiled broadly, his face breaking into a beautiful map of lines. He came over and hugged both of them tightly.

"If they don't let you out tomorrow, I'll bring Tse by. I know he is missing you both."

"Thanks, Gray," Elijah said, calling him by a nickname he'd started calling him at the farm, and grasped his hand. "You've been a brother to me."

Grayson turned slightly red, nodding. "Same, Elijah. I hope you both know you saved me as much as I'm helping you. After Dylan died, had Wren not called and kept calling, not sure I'd still be here."

Wren frowned. "Don't say that."

"It's okay, Wren. You did and I am. That's all that matters. Now, come home," Grayson teased.

A little while later, Wren put her hand on Elijah's chest again, afraid the feeling wouldn't come to her but almost immediately she felt the same vibration coursing through her body into his. He closed his eyes and tuned in to the energy. She slid her hands down over each kidney and imagined a light carrying the energy into them, saturating them. Like before, after a few minutes she felt her hand get cooler and the feeling subside. She kissed Elijah on the mouth as he slid his hand into her hair and held her there. She felt his tongue lightly graze her lips and a different type of energy passed between them. It was all energy.

She wanted him badly but wouldn't risk his healing or getting caught. The night as they lay together, she slid her hand down between his legs and let her hands feel him. He instantly became engorged as she stroked him gently. He rolled towards her and sighed. He wanted her too much to fight her, and she steadily increased pressure until he groaned and came. She went to the bathroom to grab a washcloth, wetting it with warm water. She slipped back into the bed and used the washcloth to clean him up. He kissed her and the blood rushed between her legs. She tried to ignore it when she felt him slide his hand under her skirt. He pulled her underwear away and pushed her legs apart. He let his fingers explore and she moaned softly. His hand was hot and rough, which felt incredible against the tender flesh between her legs. When he slipped his fingers inside of her, flashes of color exploded in her brain and she pressed his hand tightly between her legs. He moved his fingers steadily until she climaxed. She cried out, clinging to him. He gently eased his fingers out and wrapped his arms tightly around her.

"I fucking love you so much, Wren."

Wren rested her cheek against his neck and nodded. "I love you, Elijah."

The room was dark and they'd gotten away with their act. Elijah ran his fingers gently down her spine, resting his head against hers. She didn't move to the cot and didn't wake up until morning, wrapped up in the arms of the man she hoped to grow old with.

• • • •

The next morning, Elijah was taken for tests that would hopefully let him go home. If his kidneys showed improvement, he could continue to rest and heal in his own bed. If they didn't, the doctor wanted to give it another couple of days to see and discuss future prognosis. A possible eventual kidney transplant if one or both of the kidneys failed. Even with a transplant she explained, the risk existed of it not either taking or if it did, not lasting more than ten to twenty years. Before his test was scheduled Wren used her hands to send energy into him. She pictured calling on the cosmos to help and used both hands, feeling tingling in them as she placed them on his skin. It was like praying with her cells.

When they brought him back, he asked her if she wanted to take a walk in the halls. He was tired of being in bed and needed to stretch. They wandered down the halls, taking the elevator to a small courtyard at the bottom which was surrounded by the building. Elijah was able to clip his IV bag with a strap the nurse gave him over his chest and held Wren's hand. It almost seemed normal. The courtyard was quiet, filled with flowers and small trees planted in pots. A little bird was hopping along the ground, then fluttered into a tree. Elijah chuckled and Wren glanced at him. He pointed at the bird, who was now watching them.

"It's a wren."

Wren peered closer at the little brown and white speckled bird as it cocked its head at her. Its black eyes blinked at her and then it flew off, making Wren laugh out of surprise. "Maybe it's a good sign."

"It is. I know your name is actually Gretchen, however, you were always meant to be Wren. Innocent enough on the outside, but hiding a tough and fierce interior. Wrens are tenacious little birds," Elijah joked.

Wren grinned at him. "Have to keep you on your toes."

Elijah slipped his arm around her and drew her to him, meeting her eyes. "That you do. More than anyone ever has."

They wandered back up to the room and the doctor met them at the door, waving a folder. She led them in and shut the door.

"We got the results of your tests back. Honestly, you keep surprising me. Your kidneys look good. Still a little sluggish but the damage and inflammation we were seeing have calmed down. It seems they're repairing themselves more than we'd thought possible. You can go home today. You'll need to come back every few days for follow-up tests, but at this point, you're safe to go home. I just don't understand how it turned around so quickly."

Wren and Elijah had their suspicions.

Chapter Twenty-Three

"I want you to adopt Tse. I know we've talked about it before, but I want to make it official as soon as possible," Elijah said on the ride home. He didn't say it like a question. "I need to know if something were to happen to me, and with my grandmother getting older, he'd have a safe, loving home."

Wren gripped the steering wheel, peering out the windshield. He wasn't taking into account she'd lose her mind if she lost him. She wouldn't be fit to take care of herself, much less a child. She glanced over at him, his eyes were locked on her face. "Elijah, I love Tse, but do you think I'd be the best person for him?"

"Wren, you *are* his mother. I have no doubt you'd be the best person for him. You can't take who you were as a girl and think that's who you are now. You've fought for all of us and are bonded with Tse. You, Grayson, and my grandmother are the only people he knows. The people he depends on. He needs you, Wren. You're his family."

"I know, but if I lost you, Elijah, I think I'd just fall off the earth."

"You wouldn't. Not if you had Tse. You're stronger than you give yourself credit for. Parenthood isn't some magical knowledge bestowed when a child is born. It's not giving up on that child. You can be human, you can hurt. Please, Wren. He needs you, regardless if I'm there or not. We talked about adopting kids."

"We did but that was before all of this. When I was driving to the hospital that night and thought you might die, I fell apart. I can't do this without you," Wren said quietly.

Elijah reached out, taking her hand. "We're both here and that's good. I plan to be here until I'm gray. You love Tse, adopt him not because I might not be, but because we're family, us three. Okay?"

Wren nodded. He was right. She couldn't plan her life on fears or what might happen but focus on what they had now. "Okay."

Elijah leaned in and kissed her cheek, trying not to distract her driving. Wren met his eyes and touched his face.

"You have to promise me, though, you'll do everything to stay here. No excuses, no reasons why you were too busy to take care of your health. I don't care how busy we get, that comes first. Got it?"

"I promise. I fucked up, Wren. I know that. It opened my eyes to losing my mother as a child, and I don't want to do that to Tse. To you. Diabetes comes first, I know. I have everything I've

• • • •

ever wanted in my life now and don't want to lose it. I need you to help me through. Remind me, use your hands on me."

"I will, however, you also need to teach me about your diabetes. I have general knowledge, but that night I didn't know what to do. I checked your blood and gave you a shot of insulin, but I didn't know when, or if, you could have more or anything I should be doing."

Elijah smiled. "You did well. I might not have made it had you not given me the insulin. But we'll go through the process, what to look for and how to handle it. I appreciate you caring about me enough to want to learn."

"Care about you? You're my breath. Your body is my body and your health is my health."

Elijah's face went serious and he tipped his head. "Wow. Thanks, Wren."

By the time they got home, Tse was already in the driveway waiting and ran to meet the car. Wren didn't even make it halfway down before Tse was in front of them, jumping up and down. Elijah got out of the car and grabbed him in a huge bear hug, swinging him around. Wren wanted to tell him to be careful, but she knew this was better for Elijah than almost anything at the hospital. Tse's hair was past his shoulders and he grinned, flinging his head back, letting it fly like a cape behind him. Yeah, she wanted to make him officially her son.

Elijah and Tse walked back down the drive and Wren followed slowly behind in the car. Grayson came out of the house and waved, wiping his hands on a dishtowel, followed by Anna who grasped Elijah tightly and kissed his cheek. He was her son. Even though she was his grandmother, she'd raised him as her own. Wren parked the car and climbed out, gathering their bags, and

• • • •

took them into the house. She could smell dinner cooking and her stomach growled. Hospital food was bland and almost inedible, so eating a home-cooked meal was all the welcome home she needed at the moment.

She set the bags in the room and took a deep breath. Their bed. No more cramming into a twin-sized bed with rails. Elijah followed, pausing at the door.

"I didn't think I'd be coming home."

Wren whipped around and met his eyes. He'd never let on how bad it was, or that he was afraid for his life. Now, seeing him in the doorway she realized he didn't think he'd survive. She practically ran to him and wrapped her arms around his waist, letting tears fall. She'd almost lost him. He rested his head on hers, she could feel he was crying, as well. All of the strength and courage it took at the hospital crumbled away, and they stood in the rawness of how close it came to never seeing each other again.

Elijah led her to the bathroom and shut the door behind them, turning on the shower. He undressed and she followed. They climbed under the stream of hot water and held onto each other for dear life. Wren scrubbed his hair and he did the same for her. They washed each other's bodies. Once they were rinsed let their hands explore each other, followed by kisses. Wren stared at the body of the man she'd committed to for life, wanting to consume every inch of him.

They were interrupted by a soft knock at the door. "Daddy, are you in there?"

They drew apart, laughing silently. Elijah responded, "Yeah, Tse. I'll be out in a minute, just needed to grab a shower."

"Okay," Tse's voice replied and they heard him move back down the hall.

• • • •

Elijah kissed Wren deeply and pulled her tightly against him. "Later, we're finishing this."

Wren was breathless and slid her hand across his buttocks. "Of that, I have no doubt."

They stepped out and toweled off, eyeing each other hungrily. But first family and dinner. Anna had gone all out and cooked a spread fit for a holiday. In a way, Wren supposed it was. Coming Home Day. Except for Tse, none of them knew if it would happen. Wren saw Anna pull Elijah aside and admonish him for being careless, for not tracking his meds and eating. He nodded, his ears turning red. They sat down and Elijah grasped Wren's hand under the table, squeezing gently. She peered at him and he met her eyes with a sense of sadness. He was lucky to be there. She squeezed his hand back and smiled.

"You're here, that's all that matters," she whispered in his ear.

Elijah carefully chose diabetic-friendly foods and ate slowly. He was thrilled to have real food after the slop they served him in the hospital, outside of the smuggled-in vegetables Grayson brought in. Elijah knew he needed to slow down and consider every bite. He'd checked his blood sugar before eating and would check it a bit after. There was no room for mistakes. After dinner, he read books with Tse in the living room as Grayson and Wren cleaned up since Anna had cooked. Wren couldn't imagine Grayson ever leaving and turned to him.

"Would you stay if we gave you a piece of the land? I mean I know you aren't planning to leave, now, but in the future. Would it be enough to have your own land here to keep you around?"

Grayson chuckled as he sealed green beans in a container. "I'm not planning on leaving. This is my home, you're my family."

• • • •

"But what if you met someone? And they lived away from here?"

"Dylan was the love of my life. I'm not looking to meet anyone."

"Neither was I when I met Elijah, but see where we are?"

Grayson sighed. "I can't think that far ahead, however, theoretically if I met someone and fell in love, they'd have to want to be a farmer, you know? This is my home. So, the real question is if I met a guy and fell in love, would they be welcome here?"

"Grayson! Of course. You, your man, and all your children," Wren teased.

"All my children? Now, you're really going out there," Grayson replied, laughing.

"Point is, you're part of this and we will do whatever it takes to keep you here."

"That means a lot."

"Grayson, you offered to give up part of your body for Elijah. To share your cells, I think that says it all."

"My cells are your cells," Grayson said and cracked up.

"Mi células están tu células," Wren replied, surprising herself by recalling her high school Spanish class. This sent them into fits of laughter.

"We should put that on a sign above the door," Grayson blurted out, holding his sides.

Elijah walked in and stared at them. Wren waved her hand, not being able to get words out. For the first time, she saw Dylan's personality in Grayson and it made her happy. She wiped tears from her eyes, standing straight up. Little bubbles of laughter kept popping out of her and Grayson rinsed his face in the sink to try and stop. He wiped it off, but couldn't make eye contact with her

• • • •

without it starting all over again. He shook his head, slipping out of the kitchen to compose himself. Wren took a deep breath and let it out.

"That got out of hand quick," she said between tiny snorts.

Elijah helped her put food away and asked if she wanted to go for a walk. They took a trail off the back of the house and meandered while the sun began to set. They headed back before dark, joining the rest of the family in the living room. Tse was playing checkers with Grayson and Anna was reading in a side chair. Both knew all they could have lost and sat on the couch, watching Grayson let Tse win at checkers with some pretty loose rules. Elijah took Tse to his room after and read him a story. Wren could hear them whispering to each other as small giggles escaped from Tse. She didn't think Elijah knew Tse was the one who found him unconscious in the hallway. It was a conversation they'd need to have.

Elijah came back in and met her eyes at the doorway. He was ready for bed. Grayson had excused himself and Anna headed to her room around that time. Elijah raised his eyebrows and stuck his hand out. They couldn't wait any longer. Wren took his hand and they went to their room, shutting and locking the door behind them. They quickly disrobed and moved to the bed.

Wren pushed Elijah back, kissing him hard on the mouth. She needed to take charge to remind both of them that he was living not just for himself. Once he was back against the pillows she straddled him, continuing to kiss him forcefully. He grasped her buttocks and slid his hands up her back. She guided him in and moved her hips with a mix between a dance and an attack. He cupped her breasts, running his thumbs over her nipples. Even though she was taking charge, she was along for the ride, her body responding to him. He leaned up, wound his arms around her waist, and buried his face between her breasts as they moved in sync. Wren tangled her fingers in his hair tightly and moaned as she felt waves wash over her. Elijah released at the same time and whispered her name into her chest. He rested back, pulling Wren with him, and held her on his chest.

"I'm sorry," he said softly.

"I know."

They lay together like this until sleep came crawling in. Wren slipped down next to Elijah and ran her fingers over his cheekbone.

"Flesh and blood. I never knew what it meant. It's not about genetics, it's about love. Anyone you love can be your flesh and blood."

Elijah met her eyes. "You are mine."

Wren smiled to herself. It had been the missing piece. Not feeling like she belonged because she didn't understand what it meant. Anyone could be family, anyone could be flesh and blood because that's just what they were made of. Flesh, blood, cells.

"Mi células están tu células," she repeated, without humor this time.

She could see Elijah translating it in his head and he smiled at her. "My cells are your cells?"

Wren bobbed her head. Elijah ran his fingers over hers and nodded.

"Mi células están tu células."

· · · ·

Chapter Twenty-Four

By winter the farm was healing, as was Elijah. The crops planted later yielded a good harvest and the land grant came through. While it wasn't much, it allowed them to purchase seeds for the crops they lost, repair the barn, and offer Grayson a small stipend for his hard work. Wren wasn't able to go back to firefighting as her hands and strength were needed on that farm. Not to mention, the promise she made to stay by his side. After almost losing Elijah, the whole cycle of farming made more sense to her. She wasn't just sticking a plant in the ground. She was part of its life cycle, her cells helping its cells grow and thrive.

Rob came out one day with his children to give Lindsay a child-free day. The boys and Tse immediately ran off to play and Rob held his ten-month-old daughter in his arms. It was mid-December and she was bundled in a mint green jacket with her little, blue-gray eyes peering out. She was the spitting image of Rob, minus the tattoos and years of hard work. Rob spread a blanket out on the ground for her with some toys, and she immediately tried crawling away. He laughed and sat down with her, blocking her exits. Wren joined him on the blanket.

"I'm so glad you came out! Sorry I never came back," Wren said apologetically.

Rob shook his head. "You had way more to deal with. I'm glad Elijah is doing well. What's the long-term prognosis?"

"He's good for now. His kidneys recovered and he's being extremely regimented about his diabetes. But it's like fighting wildfires. We never know when something is forming underneath and need to be diligent. He goes to the doctor regularly and added in a functional medicine doctor, as well."

"What's that?"

"A doctor that combines traditional treatments with other alternatives. They're always researching and looking for treatments that not only help but don't hurt. So, it doesn't conflict with his standard treatment but offers additional support. Like, a regular doctor treats the diabetes but the functional medicine practice treats all of Elijah, sees how all systems come into play. They treat him and not just his disease. I don't know if I'm explaining that right."

"I think I get it. Interesting. Is it helping?"

"We think so. He is on a strict clean diet and has been able to regulate his blood sugar so that he doesn't take insulin as often. He could probably explain it better."

"What kind of diet?"

"Fresh vegetables, mostly plant-based proteins. Some eggs and goat milk cheese from our animals here. Pretty much like

• • • •

people probably ate before grocery stores," Wren replied, laughing. They truly were living off the land.

"Nice. You're like pioneers," Rob said as he snagged Hayden before she slipped around him. She squawked and threw her toy.

"Once we move to solar and wind power, we may be able to get completely off the grid. We already have windmills to pull water into cisterns for the animals. It's all about money at this point. We're converting a little at a time."

"Oh, that reminds me! I have something for you," Rob pulled a battered envelope out of his pocket and handed it to her. "We'd collected up for you when Elijah went into the hospital. It's not a ton but might help. Sorry, I didn't get it to you sooner, but between the fires and school, I've been stretched thin."

Wren took the envelope, feeling emotional. It didn't matter how much was in there, simply the fact that they did this for her family meant the world to her. Hayden crawled to her and climbed in her lap, chewing on a plastic horse, drooling. Wren wrapped her arm around Hayden, liking the weight of her small body in her lap.

"Thank you, Rob. That was incredibly kind."

Rob shrugged. "We take care of our own."

"So, how is school going?"

"Good! Really digging it. I'm taking electrician courses but branched out into solar, as well. The world is changing, gotta keep up with the times."

"Well, if you need practice..." Wren teased.

Rob laughed, then nodded. "Seriously though, whatever help you need out here. I'm loving what you're doing. Wish I'd thought of it. I'm done with firefighting at least on a full-time basis.

• • • •

I've been thinking about selling the house and buying some land. Just not the suburban lifestyle type of person, you know?"

"What about Lindsay? What does she want?"

"Me home at night. She is willing to go anywhere to make that happen. How do you like living out here?"

Wren gazed around at their farm and watched the boys chasing each other in one of the fields. "It's heaven. I wish we had more friends closer, but at least Grayson lives out here now and with Anna and Tse, it's a nice little family."

Rob nodded and grinned like he had a secret. "I noticed when I was driving in, there's another farm for sale up the road. On the way in, the drive before yours. I stopped by and it's a lot smaller but the house looks decent. You know anything about it?"

Wren thought about it and seemed to recall seeing an old man who lived there. He was hunched over and would wave as she passed. She always felt sad for him because he never had visitors. Maybe he'd moved into town? Or died? That was the thing about farming, most kids growing up in it wanted no part and moved to towns and cities when they grew up. There were a lot of old farms sitting untended while corporate farms took over.

"I don't. There was an old guy there but to be honest, we've been so busy I rarely leave the farm. Grayson has been running our products into town to sell. I'm not sure how big it is."

"Listing says about fifteen acres. I'm not looking to start a big farm. More like grow stuff for my family and get out of town."

"We'd love to have you as neighbors! I think the land borders ours on the west end. Tse would be beside himself having kids his age to play with," Wren replied, shifting Hayden to her other leg. Hayden wound her fingers in Wren's hair and leaned back against her, trying to fight off inevitable sleep.

• • • •

"I already called the realtor. Lindsay and I are coming out tomorrow to check it out."

"Wow! Okay, well don't say anything to Tse, he'd be disappointed if it didn't happen. Hell, now so would I."

"I won't, not to our boys, either. We'd still have to sell the house but the market is booming in town, so I have no doubt that could happen quickly. The sale of the house would pretty much pay for the farm or at least a good chunk down. Hey, you want me to take Hayden? Looks like she is out."

Wren peered down at the now sleeping baby and shook her head. It felt nice. She never thought she'd feel that way, but it didn't feel unnatural. Elijah came in from the field and shook Rob's hand.

"Good to see you, man. How's it going?"

"Great, was just talking to Wren about looking at the farm next to yours tomorrow. It's for sale," Rob replied.

"Is it? Nice! It would be good to have some younger neighbors out here. Everyone is pretty much aging out. School for the kids is tough out here, though. They closed up the smaller schoolhouses and the kids are bussed into the nearest town, which is like an hour's ride each way. We homeschool Tse because of it."

Rob thought about that and watched his rowdy boys jumping off a fence rail. "Yeah, that's something to consider. Lindsay might lose her mind."

Wren laughed at that. It was a shift to have children around all day, but since Tse had unlimited areas to run and play, it had calmed him down quite a bit. But with them, there were four adults to one child, and with Rob working, it would leave Lindsay by herself with three. Wren didn't know if she could do it, but Lindsay seemed to have a better grip on motherhood. The children listened when she gave them the eye.

・・・・

"Why don't you come by tomorrow for dinner after you look at the place and we can all talk? Might help to share our experience," Wren offered. "The boys can stay here tonight and have a sleepover with Tse. You can pick them up then and we can share anything we know."

"You want me to leave the boys here? You're one brave woman," Rob said and pointed to them trying to run along the top of the wooden fence line.

"Sure, Elijah and Grayson can wrangle them if needed. Right, Elijah?" Wren squinted up at him and he side-eyed her.

"Yeah, I think we can handle it. We'll put them to work if we have to."

Rob called the boys over to tell them they were staying the night, which resulted in screams of joy and the three boys took off behind the barn. He gathered up Hayden and loaded her in the car. He turned and hugged Wren tightly as she realized he was officially the friend she'd had the longest. She was glad he was getting out of firefighting. She wanted him to be around. He and Elijah hugged briefly, then shook hands. She didn't want to get her hopes up, but it would be amazing to have them as neighbors.

After Rob left, Elijah and Wren took a walk. Elijah held her hand and gently rubbed his thumb across her skin.

"I saw you holding the baby. She seemed to like you," he said quietly.

"Yeah, it was weird but I kind of liked it. I know holding a baby isn't having a baby, however, it has got me to thinking."

"About?"

"About not being so dead-set against having a child. I didn't want to tell you before, but while you were in the hospital, I received word my petition was turned down. They told me I could

207

reapply yearly, but by then Tse will be so much older. If Rob were to move out, maybe we could work out a homeschool swap to give Lindsay a break some days and Tse kids his age to be around. Maybe we each could take all of the boys twice a week or something."

Elijah bobbed his head in thought. "That might work. So are you saying you might want to have a child?"

"I might."

Elijah stopped to face her. "I support whatever you want, but I'd like that if you decide it's something you want."

Wren appreciated his understanding she had to ultimately make the decision. They walked back to the house just as the boys ran across in front of them, playing some type of pirate game. They told them to stick close to the house and headed in to prepare dinner. Anna had a head start and was watching the boys out of the window, smiling. She turned to them when they came in.

"It's so nice to see Tse playing with other children. It's good for him," she said, gesturing out the window. Tse was laughing with his head back and mouth wide open.

"Well, hopefully, they'll become our neighbors," Elijah replied and stepped in to help Anna cut vegetables.

"Oh?"

"They're looking at the farm next door tomorrow," Wren explained.

Anna beamed. "That would be lovely! The land belongs to the children, they should be out here."

Once dinner was ready, they called the boys in and insisted they wash up. Wren could hear them giggling in the bathroom and dreaded what kind of mess they were making. She checked their hands before they sat down and left the bathroom for later.

Grayson came in and washed his hands, coming out shaking his head.

"It looks like a tornado came through there," he joked, tipping his head at the boys. "After dinner, you're helping me clean up in there, got it?"

The boys nodded in unison, their eyes wide in awe over Grayson.

"Thanks, Gray," Elijah said, chuckling.

After dinner, they had the boys help clear the table and wash the dishes. Then Grayson took them to clean the bathroom. Wren would've never guessed Grayson would be the one to get them in line. After that, they followed him around like puppies, asking for things to do. He got them ready for bed and told them stories until they settled. Once he was sure they weren't going to start trouble, he came back out and joined Elijah and Wren on the porch.

"You have a way with kids," Elijah said with appreciation.

"I've always wanted children, but the system makes it tough. Even being gay in a marriage is harder to adopt or find a surrogate. Being a single, gay man makes it pretty much impossible. There's always this underlying suggestion that I must be a pervert to want children."

Wren winced. "That's so stupid. There are kids who need homes and parents who want them. I was turned down because almost ten years ago I was arrested for heroin. Which I haven't used since."

"Oh, I'm sorry, Wren," Grayson replied genuinely. They were in the same boat for different reasons. "I hope one day to be able to have children but not counting on it."

• • • •

"Well, Gray, we may be having a lot more around here soon. Rob is looking at the farm next to us tomorrow."

"Really? That would be awesome. Starting our own little community out here."

"Now, you can't leave," Wren insisted.

Grayson grinned. "Actually, I wanted to talk to you about that."

Wren felt a knot in her stomach. "You can't leave."

"I'm not. I'd like to make this more permanent. Once you asked if I had land, would I stay? I'd like to buy some land from you to build a proper house. I think it's time for me to commit. I mean, if you want me."

"Want you? Gray, you're my brother," Elijah said firmly. "We'll gift you land for all you've done. What are you thinking?"

"I'd like a couple of acres and I insist on paying."

"Four acres? And I insist you don't."

Grayson met Elijah's eyes and knew he was going to lose this battle. "Four acres is more than generous, and I'll pay you somehow."

"You already do. Without you, this farm wouldn't be where it is now."

Wren interjected. "As I said before, this is your home, your land, and your family. That goes for anyone you chose to spend your life with."

"All my children, right?" Grayson teased.

Wren busted out laughing. "Yes, *all* your children."

Chapter Twenty-Five

W ren wiped the sweat from her brow and leaned against the moving truck. Grayson and Rob carried a couch into the house, then came back out to check the truck. Rob stepped up into it and came back out, waving his hands in the air.

"I think that was the last of it!" he said happily and jumped down.

Wren glanced up and saw Tse peering out an upper window with Rob's oldest boy, Drew. They were making faces and cracking up. Elijah came out after dropping off a box in the kitchen and wound his hair in a quick bun. Wren admired her husband's muscular, lean body. He caught her eye, grinning. Since she'd had the IUD removed, they'd taken any chance they could to be alone. It had only been a couple of months but she liked the trying part, either way. Rob and Lindsay had agreed no matter what, they wanted to raise their children on land and bought the farm next to

• • • •

Wren and Elijah. It took a couple of months, so they could sell their home and allow Rob to get his electrician's certificate. Now that he was licensed, the calls for help didn't stop coming in. He took those while he focused on learning as much as he could about installing solar panels.

Lindsay came out holding Hayden's hand as she learned to walk. It was like watching a drunk being guided home from the bar. A step, wavering, foot down, almost falling, then another step. Over and over. If Lindsay tried to pick her up to give her back a break, Hayden would screech and kick to get back down. Then she'd throw herself back forcefully, making it almost impossible for Lindsay to keep her grip. Rob saw Lindsay losing patience and stepped in to take over. Lindsay rubbed her back and sighed.

"Last one, Rob. I swear it."

Rob laughed, then kissed her on the cheek. "I know, honey. This one has worn us both out."

Hayden dragged Rob along at her drunken pace and Lindsay headed back in to start unpacking. The youngest boy, Seth, bolted past them and ran inside with a pile of rocks in his hands. Rob watched him and shook his head, not even bothering to ask why. Grayson swept out the moving truck and closed it up.

"You want me to ride with you back, Rob?" he asked.

"Sure, I wouldn't mind the company, that way we can take Hayden with us so Lindsay can unpack. We can pick up some take-out food to bring back."

They loaded Hayden in her seat and climbed into the truck. Hayden gazed out the window, kicking her feet. Rob ran in to let Lindsay know and Wren followed to check on Tse. From the sounds of maniacal laughter coming from up the stairs, he was fine. She glanced out the window and saw Elijah checking his blood

• • • •

sugar. He was frowning and her stomach dropped. He pulled out a syringe, gave himself a shot of insulin, and stared off pensively. Lindsay came around the corner carrying a couple of candlesticks.

"Thanks for all of your help today. Moving sucks and having all of you here made it a lot easier."

"For sure. Hey, is it okay if Tse hangs out for a bit? We need to run home but will be back by the time Rob brings food."

"For sure. He is keeping the boys entertained and out of my hair anyway," Lindsay replied and set the candlesticks on the mantle.

Wren went out to Elijah, who looked at her like nothing was wrong. She sighed and put her hand on his arm. "I saw you from the window. What's going on?"

Elijah's face fell. "Probably nothing. I have been overdoing it, I think. Just a little stressed."

"Come on, let's walk home and talk about it, okay?" Wren took his hand and they cut across the field that joined the two farms.

Wren was worried but knew she needed to be the calm one. He'd been working hard lately. He and Grayson had built two long greenhouses for seedlings, and he'd been helping Grayson with building his house. Plus, staying up at night reading about soil composition and the best crops to pair together. It was all part of running a farm and while Elijah was in great physical shape, any small variation could mess up his internal balance. He was still healing from before. While he could outwork most people, he probably shouldn't be.

When they got home, Wren led him to the bedroom and told him to lie down. She unbuttoned his shirt and put her hands on him. This time to lend to his healing. She closed her eyes and relaxed, imagining her cells activating and pulling energy from all around. She mentally directed the energy through her and into him. She opened her eyes and could see Elijah letting tension out of his body. Her hands felt hot and tingly, almost uncomfortable, but as she moved them around across his skin it was like releasing pent-up energy. After a time, her hands started to feel cool and she gently lifted them off of him. Elijah was fast asleep, breathing easily. She climbed in next to him and matched her breathing to his.

Knowing he needed to eat and check his blood sugar again, she woke him after a bit by kissing him softly. His hand slid around her waist and opened his eyes.

"Hey."

"Hey. Do you want to go back over to eat there or we can make something here?"

"I probably need to eat here. I need to be careful, right now."

"Alright, I'll let Grayson know to bring Tse back after they're done eating. You check your blood sugar and I can whip us up something," Wren offered.

Elijah sat up, his hair creating a veil around his face. He pushed his hair back and sighed. "It gets old. Always trying to find the balance inside of me. Being dependent on a needle to survive."

Wren sat beside him and braided his hair. "I know. You're doing good, Elijah. You need to pace yourself. You have us. We're all a team. Maybe we should hold off trying to have a baby for a while?"

Elijah met her eyes and for a second his eyes looked haunted. "I don't always want my condition to dictate everything we do."

• • • •

"It's not your condition. If you see it as something external, then you're always fighting it. It's part of you, whether or not you want it to be. Part of your body. It's less something you control, more something you adapt to. We can wait. I need you here with me, Elijah."

"The thing is, Wren, it's not going away. As you said, it's part of me. If we put life on hold because of my diabetes, we put life on hold forever. I want to keep trying. I'll pace myself better, let others help me. We may need to hire this summer."

"Then let's hire. Grayson's cabin will be empty so we can offer that, plus meals and a small stipend. Maybe more, depending on how things go."

Elijah leaned against Wren and smiled. "Okay, let's eat."

Anna was reading in the living room and glanced up when they came through. She gave them a small wave, then went back to her book. Wren could see she was enjoying some alone time and left her be. They headed to the kitchen and made a quick but healthy meal. Later, when Elijah checked his blood sugar, it was back to a safe level. There'd never be a time he wouldn't have to maintain the balance and Wren wanted to make sure they took the steps to grow old together.

Later, Grayson dropped off Tse and stopped in for a few minutes. Wren could see he was beat, too, and decided the next day needed to be a rest day for everyone. They'd all been pushing hard to get the farm up and running, but it wouldn't do any good if they were all too exhausted to keep it going.

"Hey, let's just take it easy tomorrow. Maybe cook out, have a fire. Listen to some music?" she suggested. "We can invite Rob's family over and anyone else who'd come on short notice. We haven't had a chill day in a very long time."

• • • •

Elijah nodded, knowing what she was doing, "Fair enough. I could use the rest."

"I think Rob said Lindsay's cousin was coming tomorrow to help them unpack, too," Grayson said.

"The more the merrier, but let's make this a potluck. I don't want Anna bending over backward cooking for anyone. Same as always, anyone is free to bring tents and stay, but it is going to get cold at night," Wren said.

After a few calls to invite friends, Wren couldn't fight her exhaustion and headed to bed. She could hear Elijah and Grayson talking in the living room for a bit before she dozed off. Elijah came in later and climbed in next to her, yawning. She rolled over and placed her arm around him.

"No more late nights. You have to rest and I know you'll be up with the sun."

Elijah laughed. "You know me well."

"Eight hours, mister."

"Okay, starting tomorrow, eight hours."

Wren was up at the crack of dawn and Elijah was still sleeping. In the hopes to keep him asleep, she slipped out, closing the door behind her. Anna was up making coffee and poured Wren a cup.

"I'm worried about him," she said to Wren.

"I am too. I told him no more late nights and to let other people help."

"His mother, my daughter, was so stubborn. You tell her to go left, she'd go right. She was that way with her diabetes. She'd never listen and ate all the wrong foods. I kept at her but she shrugged it off. Elijah was just little. Such a sweet, bright boy. A lot like Tse, but quieter. Elijah always watched everything. You could

• • • •

see his brain ticking away, analyzing. She died at home, wouldn't even go to the hospital when it got bad. I begged her but she wouldn't listen. By the time the ambulance came, it was too late. Elijah was maybe eight years old. He'd cried when they took her away. He thinks he's being different because he eats well and takes his meds, but he pushes himself too hard. Always trying to make things okay for everyone. He's going to leave that little boy fatherless if he keeps this up."

Anna's voice was full of frustration and she wasn't wrong. Stress can do as much damage to the body as not eating well. Maybe more. He was still that little boy losing everything, seeing his mother's body being taken away. Wren set her mind to something and waited for him to wake up. She spoke to Grayson about it and he agreed to back her up. By the time Elijah got up, she had a plan and let him eat his breakfast before she confronted him. Once he was done, she slid a piece of paper and pen across to him. He looked at her, confused. She met his eyes hard.

"Write my obituary."

"What? Wren-"

"Write what you'd say today if I died. How you feel about me, who I was."

"I can't do that," Elijah said painfully.

"You have to. I'm going to die one day, so write it."

"Wren, don't say that. You're here."

"Fine, then write your mother's. Say what it was like to be a little boy watching them take her away. How it felt to be abandoned like that."

The suffering that crossed Elijah's face was almost too much for Wren to bear, but she dug her fingers into her leg and stood strong. Elijah met her eyes with a form of horror at the things

217

• • • •

she was saying. "Why are you saying this, Wren? Why are you bringing up my mother?"

"Did you know that Tse was the one who found you unconscious in the hallway?"

Elijah's face went pale and he shook his head. "I didn't know that."

"He was terrified and cried out for you. What if it had been just you and him and you died?"

Elijah didn't answer at first, then stumbled over his words. "I'm eating right and watching my levels. I'm doing everything I can to be here, Wren. To be for Tse."

"Are you though? Elijah, you're so busy making sure everything is done, you don't realize you have people just as willing to do those things. I think you're still dealing with your mother's death in front of you. Trying to fix everything. Let us help. Grayson is willing to run the farm, for now, so you can do some research and apply for grants. Maybe so we can get more equipment to help with the manual work. Hire people. We need your brain more than we need your muscles. You can't work more than half the day in the fields. Then half the time of you doing the back end work. I'll work half the day with Grayson, so he's not alone."

Elijah rubbed his nose and looked away. She'd struck a chord in him, she knew it was time for the final push.

"I want you to think about that little boy seeing his mother die, and how she chose to be stubborn over her own child. You didn't deserve that, it wasn't your fault. You deserved a mother who did everything in her power to take care of her child and herself. It wasn't your job to take care of her. It was your job to be a child, like Tse. Elijah, I need you to let go and forgive yourself for

• • • •

whatever you think you did or didn't do to lose your mother. For Tse. For any children we will have. But mostly for that boy. For you."

Elijah met her eyes and she saw that little boy. Frightened and alone. She grasped his hand and squeezed it, guiding him out of the dark. Elijah closed his eyes and went back, fear and pain crossing his face. He held Wren's hand tightly and stood up, pulling her close to him as he faced his childhood. They stood in the middle of the kitchen, holding on to each other as he resolved the past and recognized the anger and distress he'd been carrying for years. Wren could physically feel his body let go as he freed the child he'd been, from the chains he never deserved.

Chapter Twenty-Six

F or being such short notice, the gathering was of epic proportions. Grayson and Rob marked off a path between both farms. By midday, at least forty people had come between the two homes. Elijah used the Mule to show people around. Though it was unplanned, large amounts of their produce and products were sold to friends. Lindsay's cousin, who'd come to help them set up the house, came over and Wren wondered why she assumed the cousin was a girl. Instead, a tall, lanky guy trailed behind Lindsay as she walked over. He appeared to be in his late twenties and had golden-brown hair and dark, mocha eyes. His mouth seemed too big for his face but somehow it worked. When he smiled his whole face became part of the smile. He looked nothing like Lindsay. Next to him was a little girl about five years old and she clung tightly to his hand, obviously his daughter. Wren glanced around for a wife or girlfriend but didn't see one.

• • • •

"Wren! I'd like you to meet my cousin Evan. This is his daughter Memory."

Evan reached his hand out and Wren took it. He met her eyes and smiled, making her like him immediately. She peered down at Memory, who had white-blond hair but the same dark eyes as her father. She slipped behind Evan's legs and put her head down.

"Sorry, she's shy. She'll warm up, eventually," Evan explained. "Nice to meet you. This place is amazing!"

"Thank you. We try. How long are you here for?" Wren asked casually.

"As long as Rob and Linds will have me. Kind of in a transitional phase, right now."

"What he means is he's living with us currently. Him and Memory," Lindsay told Wren in a side conversation when Evan went to get Memory something to drink.

"Oh? I thought he was just here to help unpack?"

"Long story. He and Memory's mother split. She was pretty devastated and needed some time for herself. So, he brought Memory here to be around other kids and work some things out. Some pretty big things."

"It'll be nice to have another kid around for sure," Wren replied sympathetically. She guessed this might have been sprung on Lindsay and Rob recently.

"It will. Our house is full for sure, now! Rob has been really good about it, but you know Rob. Not much phases him."

Wren laughed, that was an understatement. She'd never seen Rob so much as raise his voice. He rolled with everything. He was currently walking his daughter down the driveway. Lindsay went to help and Wren headed over to introduce Grayson to Evan since it looked like Evan would be around for a while. She waved Grayson over and saw as his eyes sized Evan up.

"Hey, this is Lindsay's cousin Evan and his daughter Memory. They're going to be staying with Rob and Lindsay for a bit," Wren said as Grayson made his way over.

Grayson shook Evan's hand and their eyes met for a moment before Grayson glanced down at Memory. "Hey there. How old are you?"

Memory poked her head out and smiled shyly. "Five."

"Five? Wow, you're a big girl then, huh?"

She giggled and nodded. Grayson kneeled down to her, putting his hand out. "Can I tell you something?"

Memory took his hand, watching him.

"My hair was like yours when I was five. White as snow. Doesn't look like that now does it?"

She shook her head.

"You want to take a walk? We have some new chicks that hatched, do you want to see?"

Memory's eyes lit up and she bobbed her head ecstatically. Grayson peered up at Evan. "Is that okay? It's just over there by the barn."

"Sure. Memory, Daddy's going to be right here, okay?"

Once Grayson and Memory headed to see the new baby chicks, Evan turned to Wren with his mouth hanging open. "Wow, that has never happened. She's never taken to anyone like that."

"Grayson has a way with kids. They really like him. He's so open and genuine, everyone likes him," Wren said and laughed.

Evan gazed at Grayson walking to the barn with his daughter, then he murmured, "I can see that."

Wren's eyes followed Evan's and she glanced back at him. His eyes were still on Grayson. Lindsay said he and Memory's mother had split and he had some big things to work out, now she wondered what those things were. There was no denying the way he was watching Grayson. She excused herself and went to help Anna bring food to the tables. When she came out, she saw Echo had arrived and ran to hug her. Echo laughed and squeezed her back.

"Thank you for having us out! Did I tell you I got married?" Echo asked slyly.

"Married! No, you did not. Details?"

"We ran off and did it. Woke up one morning and we decided it was the day. Just us and the kids. Now, we're going to be adding another to the fold."

"Wait. You're pregnant, too?"

"I am. Crazy, right? It's a good thing we came to help your crew with that fire. That's how I met Mike."

"I remember you two dancing together that night we had the cookout."

"Yes! He asked me to dance and the rest is history. I wanted to rip his clothes off that night."

"Echo!"

They busted out laughing. Wren recalled the look on Echo's face that night and she wasn't exaggerating. Mike glanced over, grinning slightly. Echo blew him a kiss and he pretended to catch it.

"So, where do you live now?"

"We're renting right now in town. He's gone a lot fighting fires, so I'm going to school and keeping an eye on the kids when we have them for visits," Echo said.

"School? Like college?"

"Yep, nursing."

"Echo, that's awesome. I can see you as a nurse."

They chatted for a bit when Wren saw Elijah come up and she wanted to hold him for a minute. She came up behind him, sliding her arms around his chest. He put his arms on hers and leaned into her.

"Hey."

"Hey," Wren whispered. "You're the best thing that ever happened to me. I just wanted you to know that."

Elijah turned and smiled at her. "What brought that on?"

"I don't know. Maybe seeing all of our friends gathered at our home, something we built together. We never would've met if not for the wildfires, but out of that came all of this. It makes me want to pinch myself."

Elijah gazed around at all of their friends and family talking and eating, then nodded. "It's the way things are supposed to be. Land and community. Society has pulled so far away from it, but we're fortunate."

"We are. I think we should do this monthly. Just have an open farm day and whoever wants to come can."

"I like that idea. Maybe we can convince more people to buy the farms and land around here."

"That would be amazing. Bring children back to the land," Wren said wistfully.

"I love you, Wren. You're the perfect person for me."

Wren grinned at her beautiful husband and ran her fingers through his almost waist-length black hair. "Same."

Later, she saw Grayson and Evan talking while Memory kept bringing them small rocks from the driveway. They each had a pile in their hands and were laughing about it. They chatted easily and from the way Grayson was waving his hands around, she could tell he was explaining what they did at the farm. Evan was listening intently and nodding his head, his eyes never leaving Grayson's face. Grayson met his eyes a few times and Wren swore she read something pass between them. Grayson eyed her and she could tell he needed to talk to her. She called him over as if she needed something and he used that to step away. He walked over to her.

"Thanks, Wren. I needed to get away for a moment."

"Everything okay?" Wren asked, concerned.

"Yeah, nothing like that. It was just intense... I needed to regroup."

"Intense how?"

"Evan's a nice guy and his daughter is the bee's knees but the connection there is eerily strong," Grayson said quietly.

"I'm not sure I understand. Connection to Evan?"

"To both of them. It's like I've already known them if that makes sense. Like in another lifetime or something."

"Oh. Maybe you have."

"Maybe. Anyway, I needed to step back, so thanks."

"Of course. You know Lindsay said he and Memory's mother split up. It sounds like it was his decision because he had some things to work out. Not sure what those things are, but so you know the backstory."

Grayson nodded, watching Evan for a moment before turning back to Wren. "Oh, he's gay."

"Did he tell you that?" Wren asked, surprised.

"He didn't have to. He may not have come to grips with it yet, but he's totally gay."

Wren stood there flabbergasted. Grayson was usually not so blunt, but he clearly saw something in Evan that Evan probably hadn't come to grips with yet in himself. Evan glanced at them and blushed. He must have sensed they were talking about him. He stared at Grayson for a moment and shifted his focus back to Memory. Grayson watched them, then sighed.

"So, now what?"

"Now what, what?" Wren asked back.

"I'm not going to deny I find him attractive, but I don't think either of us is ready to cross that bridge. He just broke up with his long-time girlfriend and child's mother, and I'm still grieving Dylan."

"You know, Grayson, maybe just be friends?"

Grayson started to laugh and met her eyes, his gray eyes twinkling. "That's a novel concept, huh?"

Wren gave him a little shove and for a moment felt like Dylan was there with them. "I think he could use a friend, right now. If something comes out of it, you won't need to question it. It will be there."

"You're right. Friends is good. Besides, he might be another good set of hands around here we could use. And Memory is awesome!"

"You have a knack with her. Evan said she doesn't open up to anyone like she did with you."

"Really? Aw. She reminds me of me as a kid. I was painfully shy, too."

Wren could picture it. Little Grayson with his blond hair and gray eyes peering out from around things. It made her chuckle. She reached out and rubbed his head.

"I love you, Grayson. You're one of a kind."

• • • •

He flushed, beaming. "Thanks, Wren."

He grinned at her, then took his leave. He was going back in. He headed towards Evan and Memory. Memory ran up to him, wrapping her arms around his legs. Evan smiled both at his daughter and Grayson. Grayson picked Memory up and slung her on his shoulders as he walked up to Evan. The connection was immediate and Wren could see them laughing and talking. Friends was a good start.

She just wasn't sure how long they could hold off being more.

....

Chapter Twenty-Seven

B y the time summer rolled around, Grayson's house was built. He'd chosen to build it as an Earthship home, using old tires as the inner walls. They were covered in a stucco-type finish, giving the home a natural extension from the earth. He used colorful bottles to make decorative windows and created a rainwater cistern system, diverting water from washing dishes and bathing to flush toilets. The home used backup propane for heating and cooking, as well as specifically placed windows and vents for natural heating and cooling. Once Evan saw what he was doing, he jumped in and helped Grayson finish the building. It was an impressive feat and the local paper did a spread on his home once it was complete.

They installed solar panels to run small appliances and the home itself seemed luxurious, straight out of a magazine. It had an open floor plan, allowing the rooms and air to flow into one

• • • •

another. A small guest room was built on one side and the master on the other with sliding opaque glass walls, which could be closed off or left open for airflow. It was a masterpiece. The part which blew Wren's mind was that Grayson did it almost completely free, having bartered for materials, scavenged, and repurposed what he could find. It was amazing how many people had stuff sitting in sheds and garages they were willing to offload if someone would just come pick it up. He saved everything they paid him, which wasn't much, for the solar panels and Rob helped him install them.

The home was placed on the other side of the field, giving them all privacy. While Wren missed him being right by the house, she knew he needed his space, especially since they all worked together and ate most meals around the same table. He built his own chicken coop, though his chickens also free-ranged during the day, and a small area to bring goats and a burro in at night. With Rob on the other side, they'd started a community, allowing their children to have a place to call their own. Evan helped out on the farm a few days a week and Memory joined the other children to play, which helped her come out of her shell. She was close in age to Rob and Lindsay's boy Seth. Tse was the oldest with Drew a year younger, Seth and Memory a few years younger than that. Hayden brought up the rear at a year and a half old. It was a nice spread.

Summer was super busy all around. Wren and Lindsay took turns either watching the kids or running the farmstand by the road. They'd added bee houses and were quickly adding honey to their product line. They now had various fruits, vegetables, eggs, goat milk products, honey, Anna's breads and pastries, and pottery from a shop Rob had set up in an old barn on his property. Wren had no idea he did pottery until he brought food over in some one night for a potluck. He blushed, admitting it was how he

• • • •

de-stressed and found time alone. She made him promise to teach her. Since then, she'd been going a night a week after work to learn. She wasn't good but was coming along. Rob was amazing, adding etchings, colors, and designs she couldn't wrap her brain around. He made a beautiful, decorative egg, but when Wren tried hers it came out looking like a cat turd. They laughed until they cried.

Grayson took all the children a day a week, letting Wren and Lindsay focus elsewhere. It was hands down the children's favorite day of the week. Sometimes they stayed and explored on the farm, other times Grayson loaded them up and took them on an adventure. Evan tagged along these days, helping keep track of the five children. Wren noticed Grayson and Evan were becoming closer as friends but hadn't seen any hint of anything more blooming.

Echo and Mike came out for dinner about midsummer and she looked like she was about to burst, even though she had a couple of months left in her pregnancy. Joe came along at Wren's request as he'd not made some of their monthly gatherings. She noticed he seemed frailer and this concerned her. She pulled him aside.

"You doing okay, Joe?"

"Oh, you know. Getting older. Not what I used to be."

"Are you in good health?"

"Nothing outside of that. Arthritis has gotten worse. I'm okay, Wren. Thanks for asking. Work is taking its toll. My body can't keep up."

Wren knew in addition to firefighting, Joe did plumbing to make ends meet. He was good at it, but his knees were wearing down and it caused him a lot of pain. She thought about

• • • •

something and went to find Elijah. He was helping Anna in the kitchen and she touched his arm. He turned and smiled.

"Hey, beautiful," he said, leaning in to kiss her.

"Hey. I had an idea I wanted to run by you."

"Shoot."

"Grayson's old cabin is sitting empty and it's really only enough space for one person. Can we offer it to Joe? He could help run the farm stand, which would free me up to help you on the farm. I'd love to have him around and it would give the kids a grandfather figure."

Elijah considered this, then grinned. "Yeah. I think that would be good. Have you asked him?"

"No, I wanted to talk to you first. Make sure you thought it would work. I mean, he may not even want it, but I'd like to ask. Honestly, I'd like you to ask him as a sense of community and bringing it together here."

Anna cleared her throat. "I can talk to him. I've known Joe for a long time. Back in the day, I dated his older brother. I remember when he was a small boy, running around getting in the way."

Elijah hugged her tightly. "Grandma! Are you telling me you dated someone other than Grandpa? Oh, the scandal."

"Hush, child," Anna teased and slapped him on the arm. "I'll go talk to him."

She stepped out and Wren saw her talking to Joe in the driveway. They wandered down the drive, her arm laced in his. They were about ten years in age difference with Anna being older, however, Wren could see how it didn't matter. They'd grown up together and shared a lot of the same memories. They were old friends. Joe was leaning his head close to hers as they walked, chuckling and nodding. Hopefully, Anna could convince him to move out to the farm.

Echo came in and sat in a chair and rubbed her back. "I don't know how women do this more than once! This is it for me."

Wren laughed. "We'll see. I see you with six or seven."

Echo's eyes got wide. "Perish the thought! I mean, technically this is number three, even though we only get Maddie and Nate on weekends, alternating holidays, and a month in the summer. It's still a lot. What about you? Are you planning on having any?"

Wren glanced at Elijah and turned red. It wasn't like they weren't trying. Elijah nodded. "We're working on it."

"Well, that's the fun part, am I right?" Echo said, winking.

Wren turned even redder, then snorted. "You're incorrigible."

Mike and Rob came in talking up a storm and Echo raised a brow. "Uh-oh, shop talk?"

"New shop talk more like it," Rob replied and hugged her. "Trying to convince Mike to come work with me. My electrician's business is taking off and Evan is over here more than at our place, so I could use some help. Branching out in solar, as well; I have enough work to keep me busy twenty-four-seven."

"Really? Are you thinking about it, Mike?" Echo asked, running her hands over her large belly.

"Do you want me to?" Mike asked carefully. He knew who called the shots.

"I mean, if it kept you home at night, then of course. But it's a far commute."

"Yeah, we talked about that, as well," Rob said. "I have about fifteen acres and I'm no farmer. I was thinking about selling off some of it if you're interested. There is no house but the land is there."

"I guess let's talk about it. I'm not opposed, however, I know nothing about making the land living-ready. It would need what? A well, a driveway, a house, of course, electricity, what else?" Echo asked.

"The driveway would be covered because the piece I'm looking to sell used to have cattle on it. There is a road, a windmill with water, and it's already pretty cleared. We could do it under the table, just have you lease-to-own from us for the land. Of course, you'd cover anything you added to it. As far as electricity... well, I think we have that covered."

"I was thinking maybe getting one of those log house kits or something like that?" Mike added.

Echo shifted in her seat and motioned for him to rub her lower back for her. He came over and pressed his fingers in, causing her to breathe out deeply. She rested her head in her hands. "It sounds good in theory, and I'd love to live out here. Harass Wren on the regular. You'd need to talk to your ex-wife about the kids' visitation and make sure our bills would be covered. Let's chart it out and see."

Mike laughed. "My Echo, the ultimate planner."

He kissed the back of her neck and stood up straight. Anna and Joe came in, followed by Evan and Grayson. Lindsay was still chasing Hayden around the yard and Rob went out to help wrangle their fearless daughter. By the time everyone was corralled for dinner, the house was alive with laughter and chatter. They added the leaves to the table and set up another table for the children in the living room. The house was small and full. Grayson and Evan joined the children to make room, but mostly because they enjoyed their company. Wren could hear Grayson making funny voices at them, followed by peels of laughter. He should've been a teacher.

During dinner, Anna announced Joe had agreed to move into Grayson's old cabin, which made Echo bite her lip. If Joe moved there, her community was shifting to the farm. She met Mike's eyes and nodded. They'd make it work. Mike leaned in to say something to Rob and he smiled. They agreed to lease the land first until Mike made sure the work was there to buy it. Mike would commute until Echo had the baby; by then they'd be able to have a house on the land and work out the details.

After dinner, they walked out to the farmstand to show off their goods. Echo was mesmerized by the pottery. She pulled out her phone and showed Rob pictures of beadwork she did and he was equally impressed. Wren told her she should get some into the farmstand. They got a lot of locals for the produce but were seeing an increase in tourists that also stopped in for local wares. Lindsay had started sewing coasters and potholders to sell in the farmstand, as well. Everything was flying off the shelves, so they were planning on expanding it to be half indoors and half out so it could continue over the winter months. The more non-perishable items they could carry, the more they could support themselves year-round.

Wren and Elijah headed back to the house, so he could check his blood sugar, leaving the rest chatting at the farmstand. He pulled out his kit and Wren took it from his hands.

"Can I do it? I want to help."

Elijah nodded and stuck his finger out. Wren's hand shook as she gave him the finger prick and watched the blood well up. She held his finger over the meter and let the blood drip in. He waited for the results and sighed. He was doing a lot better, but at the end of the day his sugar tended to spike.

"Do you want to give me the shot of insulin?"

Wren chewed her lip. The last time she had was the night he almost died. She bobbed her head and took the syringe from him. She filled it, then tapped the air bubbles out. She cleaned and pinched the skin on his upper arm and stuck the needle in, letting go of the skin as she depressed the plunger. She went to draw the needle out and he stopped her.

"It's better if you leave in for about five to ten seconds, then pull it out."

"Okay, sorry."

"No, you're doing good."

She withdrew the needle and met his eyes. "That okay?"

"Perfect. Thanks, Wren. It was kind of romantic, you know?"

She did. There was an intimacy of taking care of another person. She leaned in and kissed him, holding the back of his neck with her hand. He made her breathless.

"You think we have a minute before everyone comes back?" she asked huskily.

He glanced out the window and saw everyone was still at the farmstand. He nodded and practically dragged her to the bedroom. They stripped off their clothes and took each other fiercely, trying to consume one another. Wren tangled her hands in his hair and pressed herself as far to him as she could as he drove himself into her. When they were spent, they quickly dressed as they heard voices drawing closer. Wren laughed and met his eyes, the secret between making them feel like high schoolers behind the bleachers. Damn, she fucking loved every ounce of him. He drew her close and breathed in deeply. They kissed and checked themselves in the mirror before stepping out. Wren could see it written all over their faces and shook her head helplessly.

She placed her hand on her belly and felt a weird sensation. Somehow this time she felt something was happening inside of her. Cells were connecting.

Chapter Twenty-Eight

I t all would have been idyllic had they not heard the news. Had they been able to come together without knowing their absence might have changed things. One by one, they left wildland firefighting for a chance at a better life, to be there for their families. It was the right decision but for everyone who left, not every spot was filled. The more experienced got tired of the endless cycles of fires and low pay, leaving for greener fields. More inexperienced firefighters and prison program workers rose quickly without the knowledge and instinct to take the lead. This caused a breakdown in the smaller crews, creating more injuries and fires to spread further before being extinguished. The reality was higher pay wasn't offered to keep the seasoned firefighters, better conditions and updated equipment weren't in the discussions. Longer hours, more prison workers, begging for more volunteers were on the mouths and minds of the powers that be.

• • • •

They can't say they didn't see it coming, those powers. They just didn't care. When a group of prison workers led by a green twenty-one-year-old supervisor got surrounded in a canyon by jumping embers setting their exits on fire, the grim reality of piss-poor planning and cut budgets came to light. The crew desperately radioed for help. Winds were too high to send in helicopters. Other crews in the area rushed to get there in time and fight the fire from the other side to make a path. A construction worker drove his bulldozer in to try and clear the way. A lot of heroes rose to the occasion, but they were all too late. By the time anyone got through, all they found were the bodies of the thirteen men. Twelve prisoners and a kid who did his best, considering the circumstances.

The news got a hold of the story and it made national news, shedding doubt on the validity of the prison firefighter program, state funding, and climate change. In the end, nothing changed. It made for great headlines and a lot of finger-pointing, but ultimately no one cared. Some families of the prisoners tried to sue the state but lost due to the fact all of them had signed waivers, stating they understood the dangers and were volunteering to be part of the program. Volunteering to have some small chance of a life and career on the outside. To not be shut out by society as worthless, or worse, dangerous. A chance to redeem themselves, often for crimes that were truly struggles of a failing society.

Most were young, not much older than their crew leader. A lot of people brushed it off. *If they hadn't committed crimes. If they weren't thugs. If they'd been good people.* It went on and on, a justification to not see them as who they were, to assuage themselves of any guilt. That the men were human beings, trying to undo their past and the wrongs not only they did but were done to them. Young men with children and families. Young men ready to face a wildfire to reclaim their lives. Young men, who in their dying breaths, came to the reality that no matter what they did, society had set a bar so high, they couldn't reach it.

Wren and Rob cried together over the loss. While the others had been wildland firefighters, only the two of them had come to it through the prison system. They didn't know any of the men, but they didn't have to. The men were them. When they saw the pictures in the paper, Wren touched them with the sadness they were fighting for the same chance she'd found. She was still a criminal and heroin addict in the eyes of society, but she'd found a community that accepted her for her scars and determination. As long as she was on the farm, and didn't have to fill out paperwork asking about her history, she was just Wren. The girl she'd been long before heroin had both opened a door and slammed it in her face.

It was early September when the men lost their lives. Fires were raging in multiple states and calls went out for assistance. None of them took it. Wren still felt the draw in her veins but was quick to recognize that like heroin, it was an addiction with no end. Rob stayed focused on his business, which now had Mike on full-time. Even so, they were still working six days a week. Echo was very close to having her baby and was staying on the reservation with her mother while their log cabin was being completed. Joe was too old; his knees were bad. Elijah and Wren were working long hours on the farm. They were in a field with the goats when he turned to her.

"Are you thinking about it?"

"I am," she replied.

"Not about going though, right?"

• • • •

"Of course not. I mean, of course, and of course not. Part of me will always be out there, but I'm not stupid enough to put my life on the line when they refuse to protect the firefighters. Not after what they did to those men... boys, really."

Elijah sighed and leaned on his pitchfork, peering over the field. "Their lives had no value. Not in, not out. I don't know what we're going to do. The fires are only getting worse. I know what we're doing here matters and makes a difference, but we're only one farm."

"Maybe you need to teach people, go around to other farms, show them how we're successfully doing this. Both financially and for the land."

"Maybe. We'd need more help here."

"What about working with post-release inmates? Have them come out and train in regenerative agriculture and work with us."

"With the kids around?"

"I mean, they'd be heavily supervised, but also they'd be people like Rob and me. No violent criminals or ones who have any sort of history we weren't comfortable with. We could put up a few cabins like Joe's and have them come out for say a month or so. Learn the system, work the land, teach them about how to get land, and do it themselves. I bet we could get funding for it. Start a non-profit."

Elijah's eyes lit up. "I wonder if we could get everyone else on board and look at using more of the land. Maybe Rob and Mike could add in training in electrical and solar. It would give us more bodies for help and give them options for work training. Let me make some calls tomorrow. It's supposed to rain starting tonight,

• • • •

so if we can finish up here we can stay in tomorrow and do office work."

Wren felt giddy with the new idea and got back to work on the row she was on. They were aerating the soil and the rain would be welcome in more ways than one. By the end of the day, she was tired and ravenous. Lindsay came over and waved at her.

"Hey, I'm driving into town for some groceries, you want to ride along?"

Wren looked at her soiled embedded hands and shrugged. "Sure, why not? I need to grab a couple of things. Elijah, are you okay if I head in with Lindsay? You need anything?"

"No, I think we're good. Lindsay, is Rob home? I wanted to run an idea by him. Wren, you want to fill her in?"

Lindsay looked between them and nodded. "Yeah, he's on kid duty."

"Let me go wash my hands and grab my bag," Wren said and ran to the house. When she came out, Lindsay had brought her car around and was waiting. Wren climbed in. "So, Elijah and I had an idea that may help us with extra hands on the farm but also post-release inmates like Rob and me."

Lindsay's eyebrows went up as she cocked her head. "Nice. I'm all ears."

Wren ran through their idea, including having Rob and Mike on board with training as Lindsay listened quietly. Of course, all of them wanted to make sure anyone around the children would be safe but knowing Rob and Wren helped the cause. Lindsay waited for Wren to finish and breathed out.

"I mean, as a mother I have my concerns, but as the wife of someone who has succeeded because of that type of program, I'm on board. Where would the cabins be? Who'd be in charge? How would we vet these people? I have a lot of questions but I think it would be good for us all to sit down and hash it out. I think it's a great idea, though."

"It's supposed to rain tomorrow, so why don't we plan to get together and have dinner and talk about it? Elijah and I are going to look at non-profit status for the farm and should know more then about the process."

They got to the grocery store and grabbed their reusable bags. When they walked in Wren headed for the bulk section to buy anything they couldn't grow or make on the farm. As she passed the deli, the smell of rotisserie chicken cooking hit her nostrils and a wave of extreme nausea came over her. She swallowed hard and tried to breathe through her mouth but couldn't keep it down. She ran outside, vomited into the bushes, and took shallow breaths. They didn't eat meat anymore, but this was beyond that. The smell was overpowering and even remembering made her gag again. She didn't know if she could go back into the store and sat on a bench.

When Lindsay came out she eyed Wren, seeing her sitting with empty bags. "Hey, you didn't buy anything?"

"I couldn't. The smell of that chicken made me sick."

"Sick how?"

Wren motioned to the bushes and cocked her head. "Gagging in the bushes."

"Oh. You want me to grab some things for you?"

"If you wouldn't mind. I need a couple of pounds of rice, garbanzos, pintos, navy beans, and buckwheat."

"Sure, I can grab that for you." Lindsay took her bags and headed back in.

● ● ● ●

By the time she came out, Wren felt better and thanked her profusely. Lindsay handed a small bag. "I think you might also need this."

Wren peered in, confused, and saw a pregnancy test. Her eyes met Lindsay's. Lindsay nodded. "For me it was coffee. Poor Rob isn't allowed to make coffee anywhere near me for the first couple of months."

Wren clutched the bag and felt beads of sweat break out on her forehead. She'd already wondered but had pushed it off, not ready to know either way. Lindsay dropped her off at the farm and Elijah helped her carry their bags in. She didn't say anything to him, giving Lindsay the eye not to either. Lindsay smiled and winked. They unloaded the bags and Wren made an excuse to go to the bathroom with the test in her pocket. She followed the directions and cleaned the bathroom to expel nervous energy while she waited.

When the time was up she picked up the test, checking the box. The second line was light, but it was there. One dark blue line, one light blue line, which was becoming increasingly darker as she stared at it. Whether or not she wanted to have a child, she was going to. There was no going back. She was afraid to leave the bathroom, but having only one bathroom for four people, it wouldn't be long until someone else needed it. She took the test, stuck it in her pocket, and opened the door. No one was around, so she headed outside for fresh air to think. Part of her was excited, part of her was terrified.

She started down the driveway, attempting to clear her mind. She was pregnant. Even though women had done it forever and her friends and neighbors either had been or were, it felt foreign. The concept. She worried her years of heroin use would somehow affect it but had researched before even trying. Tears ran down her cheeks and she didn't know why. Joy? Sadness? She landed on confusion and made it to the end of the drive before turning back. She wanted this, yet also felt invaded in some way. Not resentful, but put upon maybe. She walked back to the house, loving the way it stood against the landscape behind it. She saw Elijah come out to the porch looking for her and waved at him. This was his reality, too. Her body but both of their futures. He stepped off the porch and began moving towards her. By the time he reached her, he could see she'd been crying, and worry crossed his face.

"Wren, what is it? Did something happen? Are you okay?"

She put her hand on his arm and nodded. "I'm okay. Sort of. I have something to show you."

Elijah peered around, his knitted brows as he grasped her hand tensely. She used her other hand to pull out the pregnancy test, handing it to him. He peered at it and met her eyes.

"Does this mean what I think it means?"

"It does. I'm pregnant."

Elijah's eyes grew large, glistening. Now, they were both crying. He hugged her tightly and sighed. "We can do this. You and me together. We can do anything."

Wren laughed and wiped her nose with her hand. She didn't doubt Elijah's abilities. "I'm leaning on you on this. I have no clue what I'm doing."

"Neither did I as a young single father with Tse, but I did alright."

"You did more than alright. He's the best."

"Well, hopefully, the adoption paperwork is finalized soon to make it official."

Wren nodded. "He's mine, anyway."

"He is. We all know it."

"Should we wait to tell him?"

"It's up to you. I'm terrible at secrets, just so you know," Elijah admitted.

"Okay, we can let the cat out of the bag. I can't keep a secret either."

They walked back to the house, sitting Anna and Tse down first. Tse would be eleven by the time the baby was born but he had friends now, so he was excited about helping take care of the baby. Anna smiled and touched Wren's hand, knowing now all of her great-grandchildren would have a dedicated mother. Word spread fast and by the end of the evening, everyone knew their news with the help of Tse.

A week later, they were given a date to go before the judge to finalize Wren adopting Tse. His birth mother never even responded.

Chapter Twenty-Nine

T wins. Wren cried all the way home. Having one baby was stressful enough. She was still struggling with that idea when an early ultrasound showed two little forms with heartbeats. She'd gone alone for the checkup as the farm was hopping. Echo had her baby, a boy, which took Mike out of rotation, so it was all hands on deck for the rest of them. It was just a regular three-month check-up, but Wren was measuring larger than she should be for as far along as she was. The doctor thought she heard two heartbeats; they squeezed her in for an ultrasound to be sure. And sure they were. Wren burst into tears and the doctor gave her a moment to compose herself before explaining the risks and how delivery would differ. Wren sat numbly, nodding.

When she got home, she saw Elijah working with Grayson, fixing a tractor in the barn. She tried to decide exactly how she'd break the news. Some people would be over the moon with the idea of twins but Wren wasn't. She'd been unsure about having a child of her own to begin with and the universe laughed in her face. Elijah saw her drive in and raised his hand in a wave. She watched him, taking a deep breath. She pushed the door open and walked slowly to the barn. Grayson turned, smiling.

"Hey, Wren. How'd the visit go?" he asked genuinely.

She shook her head, causing alarm to cross Elijah's face. He put his tool down and came over to her. "What did they say?"

Wren handed him the ultrasound picture and he frowned at it. The image was just gray shadows and unclear to an untrained eye. Wren pointed at one of the blobs and the heart.

"That's a heartbeat."

Elijah tried to understand what he was looking at. Wren moved her hand to the other heart.

"And that's a heartbeat."

Elijah pushed his black hair out of his face and shook his head. "I don't understand."

"Two heartbeats. Two babies."

The silence filling the barn was palpable. Wren had already had to drive home to let it soak in her brain. Elijah was going through the same shock she'd had when she was first told. Grayson's eyes were big, but he stayed quiet. Elijah stared at the picture and back at Wren, then back at the picture. It was almost comical. His dark eyes met hers, attempting to read her thoughts. She shrugged.

"It is what it is," she said flatly.

Elijah could see she was on the verge of crying and wrapped his arms around her. "Hey, it's going to be okay. We have a lot of help around here. It's a bit of a shocker, I'll admit, but I think our babies will have more hands to hold them than we can fathom. We may have to fight to get them back."

Wren nodded into his chest, knowing he was right. Grayson cleared his throat.

"I, for one, am going to be wanting to be a big part of their lives," he said quietly.

Wren turned and smiled at Grayson. "Uncle Gray. Trust me, you will be."

Elijah turned her face to his and brushed a strand of red hair off her cheek. He smiled, his black brows lifting slightly. "Healthy otherwise?"

"Yes, the babies and I are right on course. I have to go more often, they'll determine if I need to be doing anything differently as I go along. Because of the distance and higher risk, the doctor said she may want to set an induction date rather than waiting for them to come on their own. Right now, everything is fine, though."

"Whatever we need to do. I want to start going to the appointments, Wren. I want to be hands-on," Elijah replied. "I'm making Gray the foreman with the new groups coming in and can step back more into an office supervisory role some days."

After filing non-profit status, they'd reached out to offer an on-site program to post-release inmates and already had a group of six coming out. The program was six weeks long and would offer them help on the farm, in trade for training in regenerative agriculture, machine repair, and electrical and solar basics, as well as room and board. At the end of the program, the trainees would be given a certificate and a small stipend. If they seemed to catch on and wanted to stay longer, there was an option to help build their own cabin to do so.

• • • •

They'd received a grant which would cover materials cost and feeding the trainees, but paying them if they stayed on would come out of the farm's budget, so they were only looking for those committed to the goals. The rest they'd offer references to and try to help find them job placement if needed. They'd already spoken to the local college to come out during the training period to talk about courses in trades such as mechanical, plumbing, and electrical to help the trainees determine a path. A local chef agreed to come teach culinary skills, as well.

The goal was to give the trainees the best chance possible to develop the skills and confidence to work their way back into society. Elijah was spearheading the communications between the prisons, colleges, and businesses allowing him to step back from some of the manual labor on the farm. During the day, the trainees would work the farm with Grayson, and after dinner, classes were set up with different agencies for education and networking. The demand for the program well outweighed the ability they had to take no more than six at a time.

The four farms met once a week to discuss the non-profit and how to move forward with the demand. Being the four families and farms they called the non-profit Four Directions, representing all stages of life, the different directions and paths each can take. Echo would teach beadwork and painting, Mike solar installation and benefits, Rob electrical and pottery, Grayson animal care and how they can be used in regenerative agriculture, Joe basic plumbing, Elijah how to take care of the soil through multi-crop planting and covering topsoil, and Wren would cover wildland firefighting including risks and mitigation. Then various speakers and teachers would cycle through for single classes to give the trainees a broad range of options. The six weeks would be full. The first group was due right after the new year and the cabins would be ready to go by then. Just four walls, a wood stove, a table with two chairs, and two beds per. Very basic as the trainees wouldn't be in there except to sleep and sometimes eat. The goal was to integrate them as much as possible into the community. Make them part of the family.

Elijah took her hand and turned to Grayson. "Hey Gray, you good for now? I need to take my wife for a walk."

Grayson grinned and waved his socket wrench in the air. "I got this, Elijah. Congrats, Wren. Those babies are going to be beautiful."

Wren smiled, trying to be excited but her gut wasn't there. She let Elijah lead her out of the barn and through the field. Chickens scurried out of their way, squawking as they came near. Elijah led her down an embankment to the small creek running through the property. He slipped his arm around her waist, pulling her close.

"One day, I'll bring our children here and let them play in the water. Let them understand the beauty and all the earth has to offer. I'm a good father, Wren. My children, my wife are everything to me. When Tse was born and Mandy walked out, I was scared. I mean, really scared. Tse was so little and fragile. And helpless. I was afraid I'd break him, but when I held him it all made sense. He was mine and our bodies made sense together. He fit right into the crook of my arm. Like you do," Elijah paused and winked. "When something is yours, it just connects. The love you feel makes the strength come."

"I have no doubt you will be an amazing father, Elijah. It's me I'm worried about."

•   •   •   •

"Why? You're a great mother to Tse. I mean, he calls you Mom, now, and you two couldn't be any more mother and son than you are."

"Yeah, but he was almost nine by the time I became part of his life. Not a baby. And certainly not two."

"If you can love a child who didn't come from you, why would you doubt you could love one, or two, who did?"

"Mandy didn't," Wren reasoned.

Elijah's face flinched and he breathed out heavily. "You're not Mandy. She liked the idea of sleeping with a Navajo. She told me that, but I was too young and naive to understand she never loved me. It was a challenge to her parents and white upbringing. I was how she chose to rebel. Except getting pregnant and having Tse became way too real for her. Then she ran off with an African American guy. It was always about her daddy issues and never about love. You're all above love, Wren. That's what drove you to Gabe, then to me and Tse. Never doubt that."

Wren watched the water flow over the rocks, creating a sparkling array of light. She loved Elijah and Tse more than anything she ever had in her life. Even Gabe. She'd loved Gabe but they were both so broken it was a desperate love. Clinging on to each other to not drown. With Elijah it was secure. She could be halfway around the world from him and know her love was as strong. She glanced at him and looked at his profile. His hair hit his waist now and he had it loose, letting the wind blow it gently. He was the epitome of a strong Native American man, but that's not what drew her to him. It was his commitment to everything in his life. His son, the land, his people, himself. Now, her and their babies. Their babies. She put her hand over her womb and pictured the little heartbeats fluttering away inside of her. She did feel love for them. Scared as hell, but love.

Elijah met her eyes and smiled. "You're everything beautiful in this world, Wren. I wake up every day and look at you, not believing you're mine. Your hair is fire, your skin the snow, your eyes the crest of the waves in the oceans, your freckles the map of the world. Your voice is the songs of the birds. I can't wait to hear you sing to our babies. When you came into my life, it was like you were the earth and sky personified. The reality that we made children together blows my mind, and I can't wait to meet them."

Wren blushed and buried her face in his chest. Elijah kissed her head and she peered up at him. She ran her finger down his long, straight nose and across his full lips. They were complete opposites and she couldn't imagine what their children would even look like. Elijah kissed her, making her stomach flutter. She wrapped a tendril of his black hair around her finger and slid her hand around the small of his back. Heat rose between them and Wren peered around for a soft place to lie. She spied a mossy spot near the creek, guiding him to it. They kneeled in the moss and she unbuttoned his shirt, sliding her hands across his smooth chest. She pulled off her shirt, letting him caress her tender breasts. Her nipples reacted immediately and she slid her underwear off from under her skirt.

Elijah removed his pants and Wren reached down to touch him, his hardness making her want him even more. Their eyes met and she nodded. She wanted him, now. He carefully moved inside of her, following her lead. The more slowly he drew in and out of her, the more it drove her crazy and she bit his shoulder as she felt ecstasy wash over her. Elijah released right after and placed his head against her shoulder, bracing his weight on his elbows. His breath was ragged and she felt the sweat running down his back. He shifted to lay next to her in the moss.

"The things you do to me, Gretchen," he teased, using her birth name.

Wren rested on her side with her head on her hand, propped with her elbow. "You started it."

"Did I?"

"You kissed me."

"Mmmm. I did, didn't I? You're just so beautiful here by the creek. Like a forest nymph. I was warned about women like you."

"Were you, then? Why didn't you listen?"

Elijah rolled over and slid his hand over her buttocks. "This is why. Who wouldn't chase an angel if they could?"

Wren grinned. "Who wouldn't bed the sun if they could?"

"The sun, huh? I haven't ever been called that," Elijah replied.

Wren rested her head on his chest and listened to his heart's steady beat. "You are to me."

They lay listening to the water gurgling by them until they knew someone might come looking for them. They dressed and walked hand in hand back to the farm. Lindsay was talking to Grayson by the barn doors and his face was stone. Wren cocked her head and met his eyes as they walked up. Lindsay put her head down as she left.

"Gray? Everything okay?" Wren asked.

Grayson shook his head, trying to keep his mouth in a straight line. "Evan left."

"What do you mean?" Wren replied. She'd seen how close Evan and Grayson had become, almost inseparable. Grayson had

• • • •

bonded with Memory, as well. Grayson blinked rapidly and bit his lip.

"He went back to Memory's mother. They're going to try to make it work."

"But he's obviously gay."

"I know that, you know that, and even he knows that. But I guess he's willing to sacrifice who he is, who we were becoming, to make a pretend happy family," Grayson answered bitterly.

"I'm sorry, Gray," Wren whispered.

"Me too, Wren. Me fucking, too."

Chapter Thirty

G rayson threw himself into responsibilities on the farm and worked with the first batch of trainees that came on board.

For being so soft-spoken, he immediately took control of the group, first having them build a structure to eat meals and meet in. It was no shoddy building, either. He made sure they braced it and laid a strong foundation. By the time it was done, it was more sound than the barn. He also showed them how to safely use the wood stoves in their cabins and how to build a fire that would last. This group had four men and two women. They were attentive and eager to learn whatever he had to teach them. One of the women made eyes at Grayson, to which he was completely oblivious. He gave strict orders, working side by side with them. Wren watched him and knew it was Evan's loss. The thin, shy boy who'd come to the farm was now a strapping man with a fire in him. Wren was in awe of the man he became.

• • • •

Her mind drifted to Dylan and sadness washed over her. He should be here and part of this. He and Grayson. She could see him, cutting up while he worked, his light brown eyes twinkling. Her mind shifted to the day he died and she couldn't hold back the tears that came up. Pregnancy had made her more sensitive, but there would never be a time she didn't miss Dylan. Or Gabe. Two of her best friends. Grayson came over to see if she had anything particular for the trainees to focus on. He saw the tears in her eyes and cocked his head.

"Hey, Wren, you okay?"

Wren nodded, then rubbed her nose. "I was just thinking about Dylan. About how he should be here."

Grayson laughed, shaking his head. "We'd never get anything done. He'd be cracking jokes and pulling pranks."

That he would. Wren sighed. "I really miss him, Grayson. Life isn't fair."

"No, it's not. I miss him, too. I grew up with him in a way, you know? We met as teens and got in so much trouble. I guess I wanted to have more, and he was still wanting to explore and try things out. I was stupid. He worked hard and I was feeling left behind. He always loved me. I knew that. The nights got lonely and I overreacted. We were finding our way back to each other when..." His voice trailed off and he cleared his throat emotionally. "Now, I'm used to being alone and probably always will be."

"Maybe Evan wasn't ready. Obviously, it was new to him and maybe he was scared," Wren reasoned.

"I know he was, and I don't fault him for that. I fault him for not talking to me. For just leaving. I was close to him and Memory, then they simply disappeared out of my life. Like Dylan."

• • • •

"Aw, Gray. I'm sorry. I know that hurts. Maybe he'll come back."

"Maybe I don't want him to. I'm not a landing place."

"Fair. I love you so much and hate that you're going through this."

Grayson met her eyes. "You're my family. My sister. At least I have all of this. I can't keep losing things, you know? My heart can only take so much."

"I know."

Grayson dug at the dirt with his foot. He was hurting. He was so much more sensitive than he let on. He looked at the trainees who were waiting for his guidance. "Okay, so where do you want them?"

"Elijah said something about the south field. Maybe ask him."

"Oh yeah, we need to weed that. On it." Grayson paused and watched her. "I love you too, Wren."

He placed his hand briefly on her belly and headed to take the trainees out to the south field. She quietly cursed Evan and his rashness. But she knew he was just a kid, too, who was confused and trying to do best by his daughter. As she watched Grayson head off, she sent him energy to be strong. Elijah came in with a load from the supply store and she walked over to him when he got out, wrapping her arms around him tightly. He chuckled and rubbed her back.

"What's that about?"

"Thank you for not giving up on me. On us. For being my friend and standing by me.

"It goes both ways. You saved me, Wren."

She peered up at him. "I guess we both needed each other."

"That we did. How are the trainees doing?" Elijah asked.

"Great! Gray took them out to the south field to weed it. He's really taken charge."

"He has. I'm glad he is here. I don't know what we'd do without him."

"I wish Evan could've seen that."

Elijah sighed. "Good things don't come easy. What is meant to be will be. Had we both not suffered loss, we would never have found each other."

"True." Wren helped unload the supplies and hoped there was an Elijah out there for Grayson.

At her next visit, they did another ultrasound and said it appeared like the babies were both girls. Elijah was there and his eyes got wide. Two girls. That would keep him on his toes. They were healthy and progressing normally. Wren was over four months along but looked six. On the ride home, Wren yawned and planned to take a nap as soon as she got home. Elijah rubbed her leg as he drove. He glanced at her.

"Two girls. If they're anything like you, I'm in for it," he teased.

"Ha, if they're anything like *you*, you're in for it. We're both stubborn."

He laughed and bobbed his head. "Basically, we better prepare ourselves."

They announced the genders at dinner and Tse wrinkled his nose. As a preteen boy, the idea of two little sisters was probably less than exciting. Wren knew he'd adore them and poked him.

"Do you have any ideas for names?"

Tse glanced at her, shrugging. "No. Where are they going to sleep?"

Wren met Elijah's eyes. They'd planned on the babies being in the study off their room for a bit but they'd quickly outgrow that small space. Anna spoke up, surprising them all.

"They can have my room. Joe and I are going to share the cabin."

Elijah's mouth dropped open and he stared at Joe, who grinned sheepishly.

"We can get married if that would make you more comfortable," he said and touched Anna's hand.

"That's not necessary, Joe. I just had no idea," Elijah replied.

"Anna wanted to keep it under wraps, she felt you had enough to deal with."

Anna nodded and shrugged. "It's all good and well. We'll fit in there and I can still use the rest of the house, but now the babies will have their own room."

Wren chuckled to herself. Even the old people were getting busy. Elijah read her chuckle and nudged her with his foot under the table. She met his eyes, trying not to crack up. A smile played at the corner of his mouth and he shook his head.

"Thanks, Grandma."

Anna grinned at Joe, raising her eyebrows suggestively. Elijah blushed and looked away. Wren bit her lip to stop the laughter from coming out. She focused her attention back on Tse.

"Think about names for your little sisters."

"Chocolate and Puppyface," he answered.

"Tse, how about real names? No rush, think about it, okay?"

"Okay, Mom," he replied and pushed his food around his plate.

The adoption had been finalized the week before and they'd had a party, but for Tse not much had changed. He already called Wren Mom and his name stayed the same, but for Wren hearing him say it now had such beautiful weight. Like a river stone, she could turn over in her hand. She was his mother, and now would be the mother of two daughters, as well.

Grayson ate with the trainees and afterward he sent them to set up their spaces. Some had families and tacked up pictures of children and significant others. Each cabin had a homemade quilt they could take with them when they left, to make their space personal. Echo had worked with the senior center on the reservation to have them made. Wren saw Grayson heading to his house and called out to him. He turned and waved. She felt like a pumpkin but made her way out to him, lacing her arm in his.

"We're having two girls," she told him breathlessly.

He grinned and put his hand on her belly. "I had a feeling. I could picture it in my head. Do you have names yet?"

"No, we asked Tse if had any input and you can only imagine what an eleven-year-old boy had to say."

Grayson chuckled. "I won't venture to guess, but I assume you aren't going with his first choice?"

"No! I'm not calling my daughters Chocolate and Puppyface."

Grayson cracked up and shook his head. "Actually, less disgusting than I was expecting."

They strolled towards his house and he invited her in. It was warm inside, despite being the middle of winter and the front room of plants was lush and green. He offered her tea and they sat

• • • •

by the woodstove. Grayson was the complete package and Wren worried them having had him move out there, may have stunted his chances of finding love and family. Reading her mind, he leaned back, eyeing her with his stormy, gray eyes.

"I'm happy here, Wren. We all put so much into finding the love of our lives, we forget to appreciate the people and life around us. I love my home, I love you and Elijah, and your children. Sure, I'd love children of my own, but it's not the end all be all for me. I get lonely sometimes, however, most times I'm at peace. I get to work the land and be surrounded by the most amazing community. When I was with Dylan, I ate most meals alone and spent my days and nights pretty much by myself. Now, I can look in any direction and see my loved ones. If and when the right one comes along, they'll have to be willing to share this with me. This life. You all. It is enough, anything else would be a bonus. You have to believe that."

She did. Grayson was never one to make things different than they were, and she could see in him a sense of self she'd struggled to find in herself. A confidence and security. She smiled and sipped her tea. "I believe everyone comes into our lives for a reason, Gray. I'm glad you came into mine."

He leaned forward and brushed a curl out of her eyes. "However you believe our souls are, I believe we have crossed paths before. Dylan made sure we did again."

The intimacy they shared was something Wren couldn't understand. Like a brother and sister, but ones who'd lived many lives together. She saw the same between him and Elijah. Maybe he was right, maybe their paths had crossed before. She didn't know friendship could feel like this. More than family. She finished her tea and stood up, stretching her back.

"These two, I swear. I'm already running out of room."

Grayson rose and walked her to the door. They embraced and she could feel it again. The connection of cells. They didn't need to share blood to be related. They shared a connection on a different level.

The walk home was peaceful, the stars shining bright in the winter sky. Elijah was rocking on the porch and squeezed her hand tightly when she came up. "You get our boy home safely?"

"I did. We had tea and talked. I think he's okay."

"He is. Gray is one of the most in-tune people I've ever met," Elijah agreed. "He is one of the special ones that can pass between the cosmos and the earth."

Wren liked that idea. Grayson did have an almost otherworldly way about him. Maybe that's why children and animals immediately gravitated toward him. She yawned as she rocked. It wouldn't be long now before their arms would be full and their time not their own. She felt movement inside of her and placed her hand on her belly. She hoped somehow she could give the girls and Tse the support and guidance she'd so desperately needed as a child. It wasn't that her parents weren't around, they just didn't know how to reach her. She was quiet and her grades were good, so they never questioned. Meanwhile, she was trapped in her own hell of loneliness and self-loathing. She didn't want her children feeling that way. She stood up and kissed Elijah's cheek.

"I'm going to say goodnight to Tse."

"Okay, I'll be there soon."

She found Tse in his room and sat with him. He was reading a comic book, pausing when she reached out and pushed his hair out of his face.

"Tse, you're my son and my first child. I want you to know

• • • •

I'd do anything for you, fight anyone to protect you. You're everything to me. I know life can be hard, but I want you to know you can always talk to me. About anything. I want you to. If you don't, you know I'll harass you until you do, right?"

Tse laughed and nodded. "I know, Mom. I will."

"Promise?"

"I promise."

Chapter Thirty-One

Wren drove the Mule out to the west side, closer to Rob and Lindsay's end of the property. At almost eight months pregnant, walking that far was out of the question and she needed to bring lunch to Grayson and the trainees. They were on their third round of trainees, and the program had been such a huge success, they'd added four more cabins and hired three previous trainees. Rob had hired two, also, and the majority of the rest were able to either continue on with trade school or other jobs after they received their certificate. The farms had been given an award and featured in a documentary about reducing recidivism. Other farms had reached out about the program, as between a shortage in farm help and trade skills, the program was generating a lot of interest.

Wren parked the Mule and watched the team working on planting. Grayson was explaining the importance of planting multiple crops, not only for the farm but how it helped the carbon in the soil. He caught her eye, grinning. She motioned to the coolers and he paused, letting the group know it was time for lunch. They headed for the Mule as Wren stepped aside with Grayson.

"Thanks, Wren! The fields are looking good. We're going to switch to mitigation for the afternoon to clear the land around the fields in case of fire."

"At least we've had more rain this year. Hopefully, it doesn't come anywhere near us."

Grayson nodded and peered towards Rob and Lindsay's house off in the distance. All of a sudden, his face went pale and Wren followed his gaze. A familiar tall figure was walking from the house across the fields towards them. Evan. He must have come for a visit. But why was he coming out to where they were? Where Grayson was? Wren felt like a protective mother seeing Evan approach. She stood between him and Grayson, waiting. Evan had his eyes down and when he lifted them she could see he was embarrassed. He came within about ten feet of them and stopped. He stared at Grayson, who was frozen in place, his shoulders tensed and his mouth set in a tight line.

"Can we talk, Grayson?" Evan asked, his voice tight with pain.

"About?" Grayson replied, his voice hard and quiet.

"I'm sorry I just left like that. That was unfair, I want to apologize."

"Fine, apology accepted. Are we good?"

Wren felt her eyes grow wide and glanced at the ground. She'd known Grayson a couple of years and never heard him speak like that. He didn't need her to protect him. She moved towards the team, watching quietly. Evan shifted uncomfortably, peering at the group, then back to Grayson.

"I don't think we are. Look, Grayson, I had things to work out. Things about me. Things for Memory."

At the mention of her name, Wren could see Grayson's veneer crack a little. He loved that little girl and missed her. He took a deep breath, letting it out. "How is Memory?"

"Not great since her mother and I split up again. She still asks about you."

"You split *again*? How much are you going to put that little girl through for your own selfish needs?" Grayson practically yelled it, causing some of the team to stare over in shock.

Evan turned beet red and shook his head. "I get it. I was fucking wrong, okay? I shouldn't have gone back. I was attempting to keep her family together. I thought I was doing the right thing."

"Yeah? How did that work out for you?" Grayson spat.

Evan sighed, dropping his shoulders. "Not great. I didn't feel anything and we ended up fighting all of the time. I began sleeping on the couch and asked her how we should handle parenting rights for Memory. She agreed to let me take her here, said she couldn't mother her because it reminded her of what I did to her. We're trying to work out visitation, but she isn't pushing too hard. Rob hired me on, and we're living there again. Grayson, I couldn't get you out of my mind."

Grayson put his hand up and laughed bitterly. "Don't. Don't do that. You don't get to yo-yo back and forth because you can't commit. Be a father to your daughter, get your shit together. Leave me out of it."

Evan's face fell. He didn't have any rights there and turned to head back to the house. Wren gave him a small wave as he started back. She saw him pause to watch Grayson. Wren could see on Grayson's face, he felt something for Evan and was putting up a wall to protect himself. He spun, striding in the opposite direction to put as much space between him and Evan. Evan sighed and left. The team finished up, so Grayson took them out to the property line to clear the land, creating a buffer in case of wildfire.

Later that evening, Lindsay brought Memory over and Wren's heart ached when she saw the little girl run full speed into Grayson's arms. He scooped her up and hugged her tightly as Evan watched from a distance. They both loved Memory and she'd suffered enough already. Memory patted Grayson's face and giggled as she told him some secret. Grayson laughed, swinging her around. His eyes caught Evan's, for a moment they found common ground. He set Memory down, taking her hand. She tried to pull him toward Evan but he held back. She stared up, confused, and tried again. Grayson kneeled and hugged her, telling her he needed to go. She watched him sadly and took Lindsay's hand. They walked back to Evan as Grayson disappeared into the barn.

A couple of weeks later, Wren was in the barn talking to Grayson when Evan came to the door. He paused and cleared his throat. Grayson turned and saw him, then went back to loading hay on the Mule. Evan didn't budge.

"Grayson, we can't keep doing this," his voice was firm but pleading. "You were one of my closest friends, and I know we were both feeling something more before I blew it. I can only apologize so much, but please for Memory, for me, can you just talk to me?"

Grayson flinched and walked past Evan out of the barn. Evan looked at Wren and she put her hands up helplessly. He turned, heading out of the barn. Wren followed and saw him catch

• • • •

up to Grayson in the driveway. He touched Grayson's arm and Grayson turned with fire in his eyes.

"Do you know what you put me through? You were the first person I felt anything for since Dylan, and you ripped that away from me! You took my trust and crushed it. I didn't want to let you in but I did, and you made a mockery of it. Of my feelings for you," Grayson was between rage and heartbreak.

"I didn't know you felt that way. I was confused about myself and was starting to fall for you. It scared me. I didn't know you felt the same," Evan blurted out, flustered.

"How could you have not known, Evan? We started to cross that line. Memory was like my child."

"I thought I was making it up, pushing for something I didn't even comprehend. I wanted to be more but was afraid you didn't feel the same. I was ashamed for what I recognized in myself."

"I fucking laid myself on the line for you. Opened my heart and bared my soul to you. About Dylan. About everything," Grayson replied with so much pain in his voice Wren took a step forward towards them.

She stopped when she saw Evan get on his knees at Grayson's feet. "Please, Gray, forgive me. I never stopped thinking about you. About us, what we could have been. I love you. Just give me a chance."

Grayson looked towards the sky while tears streamed down his face and he bit his lower lip. If he let Evan in, he risked another heartbreak. If he turned him away, they'd be stuck in the orbit around each other, both wanting more. Evan didn't move, his eyes on Grayson. Grayson took a step back and turned to walk away. Wren's heart clenched and she wanted to tell him to stop.

• • • •

Evan got to his feet and he watched as Grayson moved away from him. Grayson had his head down and paused, wiping his face with a bandana. He put his head up and came around, walking swiftly back to Evan. He got to Evan, put his hands on either side of Evan's face, then kissed him deeply. Evan pulled back and met his eyes. They stared at each other for a moment before Evan leaned in, kissing him back.

Wren stared in amazement, feeling like a voyeur when hot liquid rushed down her leg making a puddle in the dirt. She gasped and looked down, knowing what it was. It was too early. She still had weeks until her due date. She shoved her skirt between her legs and yelled. "Gray, get Elijah! My water just broke!"

Grayson glanced at her, then nodded as he bolted for the farmstand where Elijah had last gone. By the time he and Elijah made it back down the drive, contractions had started and Wren was in a panic on the phone with the doctor. She needed to get to the hospital as soon as possible. Elijah helped her into the truck and they sped toward the hospital. They made it to the emergency room where the doctor met them at the door. They quickly moved Wren to a room and hooked her up to see what was going on. The babies were breech and one had a dangerously low heart rate. The safest option was a c-section. Wren began to freak out at that news. They were going to cut her open. She dug her fingers into Elijah's arm and he met her eyes.

"It's going to be okay. They know what they're doing. I'll be there with you," he assured her.

"Elijah, I'm scared."

"I am, too."

Somehow him saying this made her feel better. She wasn't being unreasonable. They brought her back to surgery prep and gave her an epidural. Before they started, Elijah was brought in dressed in head-to-toe covering and he grasped her hand. The doctor started talking through what they were doing and while Wren felt pressure and shifting, she didn't feel any pain. Her lower body was separated from what she could see and Elijah kept his focus on her face. The doctor lifted up their first daughter and showed her to them over the curtain before handing her off to the nurse, reaching in to pull the next baby out. Once the next baby was out, they showed her to them, as well, and handed her off. The doctor focused on Wren, while the nurses tended to the babies who both cried out. The nurses wheeled both babies to either side of Wren, so she could see her daughters while the doctor closed her up. It was surreal not knowing what was going on with half of her body while staring into the face of her beautiful babies. Elijah whispered to each of them and grinned at Wren.

Once the doctor finished, Wren was wheeled to a recovery room and the babies were taken to the nursery. Elijah didn't know which way to go when Wren grabbed his hand. "You go with our girls, don't take your eyes off of them," she insisted.

Wren fell asleep in recovery, waking up a few hours later sore and unable to move much. She groaned, looking around. She was still in the recovery room and tried to sit up. Pain shot through her and she lay back, exasperated. How could she take care of two babies if she couldn't even sit up? A nurse came in to check on her.

"We're about to move you to a private room. Your husband can stay, and you can have the babies in with you as much as you'd like. They're beautiful, healthy little girls."

Wren nodded, pushing down a wave of nausea. She lifted her shirt and saw a nasty wound above her pubic line where the babies had been taken out. Her stomach had a weird sponge-like

• • • •

texture and she put her shirt back down. The nurse left and came back with a wheelchair.

"Your room is ready. Your legs may feel weak from the epidural, but I'll be here to help."

Wren sat up again, trying to ignore the pain, and swung her feet over the edge of the bed. The nurse put her arm under her and helped to guide her to the wheelchair. They went down a couple of halls and came to a room at the end of one. The nurse pushed open the door to Elijah standing with a baby in his arms. He saw Wren and put the baby in the bassinet. He helped Wren into the bed, kissing her forehead.

"I missed you," he whispered.

Wren felt torn and broken. She began to cry and Elijah sat on the bed with her. He put his arm around her, comforting her while she cried. When she felt the tears come to an end, she leaned against him. "I feel ugly and disgusting. I hurt everywhere and I have a huge gash on my stomach."

"You are gorgeous. Never doubt that. That is your battle scar. You brought two amazing little beings into the world. You're a warrior."

Wren wiped her nose and chuckled, not feeling much better about it. "So, what does that make the babies?"

"I don't know, but they terrify me," Elijah confessed.

He handed her a baby and he held the other. They looked almost exactly alike, except one had deep reddish-brown hair and the other's was black. Fraternal twins. Other than that, they both looked like two matching wrinkled old ladies.

Except to Elijah and Wren, they were the most beautiful babies ever.

Chapter Thirty-Two

T he girls' tests came back healthy for type 1 diabetes, however, the doctor reminded them it often didn't show until a few years later. They stood a higher than normal chance of developing diabetes since their father had it before age eleven. The estimate was a one in eight or nine chance. They, like Tse, would need to be watched and tested if they showed signs. On the last day at the hospital, they still had not settled on names and had Tse come help. He peered at his sisters and shook his head.

"They look like grumpy dolls," he replied. Maybe asking an eleven-year-old boy to pick names for girls wasn't a good idea. He stuck his finger in the redheaded one's hand and she clamped down on it, making him laugh. "This one is like Grandma. She's strong."

Wren leaned in. "So, do you like the name Anna?"

Tse shook his head. "No, that's an old lady's name."

Wren had an idea and winked at Elijah. "Okay, what about Elianna?"

Tse grinned and nodded. "We could call her Ellie."

They had one name. Tse wandered off, absolutely done with the conversation. Elijah rubbed the black-haired baby's toes and stared at Wren.

"I have an idea for this one."

Wren raised her eyebrows and waited. Elijah bounced the baby, then met Wren's eyes. "What about Gabriella?"

Wren caught her breath. "Elijah, that's like Gabe."

"I know. That's why I suggested it. It goes well with Elianna and I think it's good to honor those who helped define our path."

"That's one way to put it. Gabe helped define my path but not always in a good way."

"He did. You both dealt with addiction but he taught you to love and appreciate yourself. He was an important part of your past. If Elianna is named after my grandmother, I think it's fitting that this one should be Gabriella."

"Elianna. Elijah and Anna actually."

Elijah thought about it, then grinned. "Even better."

"So, are we set? Red-haired Elianna and black-haired Gabriella?"

"We still need middle names," Elijah pointed out and Wren groaned.

"Elianna Dylan and Gabriella Gray?" Wren suggested.

"Perfect, let's get it on paper before we change our minds," Elijah teased.

They finalized the birth paperwork and had names for their girls. Tse insisted on calling them Ellie and Ella which Wren knew would get to be a tongue twister all too soon. She stuck with their full first names. Elijah had switched out the truck for the car when he picked up Tse, even so, the kids were crammed in the back with the two car seats. It was time to move to a bigger vehicle. Tse sat between the seats and rotated between each baby sister. The babies fell asleep and by the time they were home, Tse was ready to play with kids his own age. He took off to play with Seth and Drew. Grayson met them at their car with Memory in tow. When she heard there were not one, but two, baby girls she was beside herself with excitement. He unloaded Gabriella while Elijah got Elianna out. Grayson smiled down at them and showed Memory, who cupped her hand over her mouth in amazement.

"Do they have names yet?" Grayson asked, not taking his eyes off their tiny faces.

"The one you're holding is Gabriella Gray and the one Elijah has is Elianna Dylan," Wren said, knowing he might be taken aback.

Grayson stopped and stared at them. His ears turned red, tears pricked his eyes. "Are you serious? You named them after me and Dylan?"

"Is that okay? It's their middle names," Wren replied, feeling maybe she should've asked.

Grayson nodded and peered down at Gabriella Gray. He came around and smiled at Elianna Dylan. "Thanks. I can't tell you what this means to me."

"It means to you, what you mean to us, Gray," Elijah said, his voice low with emotion. "Let's get them in. I know Wren is moving slow, so if you want to help me get them changed and settled, I'd appreciate it."

"Of course! Memory, you want to help me change the baby?"

She nodded enthusiastically and followed him in, hopping back and forth from one foot to the other. After the babies were changed, Memory sat on the couch and took turns holding each one, her eyes glistening with joy. Wren was happy to be home and let Elijah take care of her. The doctor told her it would take six weeks to heal which sounded like an eternity. Elijah brought her tea, leaning in to kiss her.

"I'd never have guessed the day I saw you sitting on the table reading, we'd be sitting in our home with two baby girls and a community of friends and family surrounding us."

"You didn't even want to give me the time of day," Wren reminded him.

"Oh, I wanted to, but you scared me," Elijah teased.

"You intimidated *me*! Now, I can't imagine you not being here. You need to be here, Elijah. For me, for our children."

Elijah knelt by her and took her hand. "I am. You give me a reason to fight."

Wren watched his eyes and remembered Gabe's. He hadn't been strong enough to fight for her. Or her for him. No one had fought for Elijah. His mother gave up, his father was never around, and Mandy walked out. It had been just him. It had been just her. Now, it was them and their family. Wren leaned in close to his face.

"I live for you."

Elijah knew what she meant. People always said *I would die for you* but living for someone was as hard, sometimes harder. He met her eyes. "I live for you."

Grayson cleared his throat and handed them a package. "Evan and I got you a gift. Memory helped paint the flowers."

• • • •

Elijah unwrapped the package and Wren laughed, her eyes twinkling at Grayson. It was a sign that read *Mi células están tu células.*

"You remembered!" she exclaimed.

Grayson tapped his head. "Steel trap."

Elijah grinned and held the sign up. "This is going above our door. Thanks, Gray. I love the flowers, Memory, they're beautiful. I'll thank Evan when he gets home."

Memory nodded, not looking up from Elianna. She was enamored. Elianna grunted and squirmed, letting Wren know she was hungry. Wren took her and put her to her breast not long before Gabriella started to fuss. Elijah grabbed a bottle to feed her. They agreed to rotate the babies on the breast to give Wren the chance to heal and allow Elijah time to bond with his daughters. He opened his shirt, laying Gabriella against his chest as he fed her. Next time would be Elianna. Wren fed Elianna, burped her, and tried to fight off sleep. Grayson saw her yawning and came over to take the baby.

"Go rest. I'll take care of her. Evan is going to meet me here and we can do baby duty for a bit."

"Gray, you're a godsend. You definitely have a little helper," Wren said and motioned to Memory who was peering over Elijah's shoulder, watching him feed Gabriella.

They heard a knock at the door and Evan poked his head in. "Hey, reporting for duty!"

Elijah handed him Gabriella and helped Wren up. Anna and Joe came in and all of a sudden the babies had more hands to hold them than imaginable. Anna offered to cook and Elijah guided Wren to the bedroom. They reclined in the bed and she checked the surgery incision. It was healing but still had large, ugly staples holding her together. She covered it back up and closed her eyes. It would heal. The girls were worth it. Elijah slid his hand over her, snuggling in close. She sighed and wondered where her sadness was coming from.

Over the next few weeks, even though Wren was totally in love with her daughters, she felt disconnected and empty at times. The whole community came forward and helped with the babies, but she still felt an underlying drain she couldn't put her finger on. At her six-week check-up, she talked to the nurse who said it was likely postpartum depression. She assured Wren in most cases it passed on its own but to talk with the doctor about it.

The doctor took the time to explain how hormone shifts, exhaustion, and the build-up could create a big letdown. While she was justified in what she felt, it wasn't uncommon. Wren opened up about her past drug addiction, how she often found herself pulled down by life. The doctor gave her a referral for a therapist, reminding her life wasn't always easy and it was okay to struggle. Wren slipped the paper in her bag and headed out. As a child, she'd had bouts of the blues, but this was something she couldn't shake.

A week later, Wren called the number on the paper and made an appointment. She knew in order to be there for her children, she had to face what was holding her back inside. Elijah was supportive and went with her to the appointment, though he waited in the lobby while she met with the therapist. The therapist went through her history and asked her questions about stress and how she dealt with changes in her life. Wren talked about Gabe and being bullied as a child. She said she didn't know why it was all surfacing again. The therapist set down her pen and gazed at Wren.

"It's not surfacing. You just aren't trying to bury it. You have used drugs, prison, and jobs to not allow yourself to stop and face what you went through. Having your children can bring up natural postpartum depression but with that, it sounds like these other issues piggybacked their way to the top. You've been through a lot and don't have to be strong all of the time. I'm guessing when someone is hurting, you're the first to jump in and be there for them? It's time to do that for yourself. You can only take care of others if you take care of yourself. Over the next week, before we meet again, journal your memories and how you felt. Instead of trying to bury the feelings, let's work through them."

Wren felt wired and drained after the session. Elijah met her in the lobby and held her hand.

"You hungry? We can grab lunch while Grayson and Evan have the kids."

Wren almost said no, worrying about the kids, then remembered what the therapist said about taking care of herself. "Yeah, that sounds nice."

When they got home, nothing had burned down, each Evan and Grayson had a baby in a carrier and were taking a walk with Memory between them. It was a quaint family scene and Wren almost didn't want to disturb them, but her milk had come in and she needed relief. They gathered the babies and sat on the porch to feed them. Evan and Grayson held hands and walked across the field towards Grayson's house with Memory running ahead of them. If taking care of babies hadn't scared Evan off, hopefully, nothing would.

Wren wrote in her journal before bed, recalling her earliest memories of feeling isolated and bullied. She thought about that little girl and a fierce protectiveness rose in her, thinking about her own children. She transferred that feeling to that little redheaded girl in her mind and somehow it helped in fighting for herself. Each

• • • •

of them slept with a baby on their side and took turns feeding them in the night. In the early morning hours, Joe and Anna slipped in and took the babies to let them catch up on sleep.

When Wren woke up, she was alone and felt somewhat rested. She showered and peered at the scar which was starting to fade into a red line. She slipped on a sundress, feeling pretty for the first time in a while. Elijah made eyes at her when she came into the kitchen, moving Elianna to his other arm as he reached out to draw her close.

"You look like sunshine today, Gretchen," he murmured. She'd never liked her name, but when he said it, she did.

Joe was rocking Gabriella on his knees and grinned down at her. "These girls are so striking. This one with her wavy, black hair and soulful eyes. That one with her rich, red hair and impish smile. She's going to give you trouble, I think."

"That's the thing about redheads," Elijah joked. "They come at you all sweet and cool, then erupt into fire."

Wren smirked at him and kissed him hard on the mouth. "Better watch yourself."

"Or what?" Elijah challenged.

"Or you will feel my heat."

Chapter Thirty-Three

The first time Elianna laughed was in the kitchen. Echo had brought her baby boy, Kai, over. He was a brute of a boy, throwing everything he could find. Grayson, not one to miss out on hanging with the babies, came over to visit. He was holding four-month-old Elianna and making faces at her when she laughed. Gabriella, who was being held by Echo, heard her sister laugh and bubbled up a chuckle in response. Anna spun around from the counter to see who'd made the babies laugh and stared at Echo with her eagle eye. Echo shook her head, pointing at Grayson who was utterly confused.

Wren, delighted to hear her daughters' laugh, stared at Anna. "Okay, what gives?"

"The person that makes a baby laugh for the first time has to throw an A'wee Chi'deedloh party for the family," Anna explained. "It's a ceremony welcoming the child from the spirit world to the physical world. The first laugh completes that transition."

Elijah had come to the door and nodded. "Anna held one for Tse. It's a big deal in Navajo tradition."

Grayson held Elianna up, grinning at her. "I'd be honored."

"I guess since technically I was holding Gabriella when she first laughed, I'll help Grayson plan it," Echo offered.

"Did you have one for Kai?" Wren asked, not remembering a party of that type.

"We did, but since my mother made him laugh she threw it on the reservation. It's big. You wouldn't miss it. I think we had over a hundred people at Kai's ceremony."

Grayson sat down next to Echo and began asking questions. As soon as he realized he was in over his head, he handed Elianna off to Elijah and grabbed a pad of paper and pencil off the counter to take notes. Echo laughed and assured him she'd guide him and take care of the important details. Wren listened in, trying to gather information as well since it was all unfamiliar to her. She wanted her daughters to grow up with traditions from both sides and realized she'd not made an effort to learn much about Navajo culture. Anna was steeping in it and Elijah wound it into everyday things, but she'd not dug deeper to understand the importance of what she saw.

Culture wasn't something her family had. They did the normal American holidays, and whatever was taught in school or on television. She knew her family had German and Scottish ancestry, but that was about the extent of it. There were no special ceremonies or traditions which expressed any defined culture to them. Elijah and Anna often spoke words in Navajo to Tse and now the babies, but she'd always felt like an observer. That somehow asking questions might be considered insensitive. Now, she understood to help guide her children, she needed to become aware and immerse herself in their culture. She'd also ask her mother if she knew of anything specific she could teach the babies about her own.

When the girls were born, they called her brother and mother to announce their arrival. While they were excited, they made no mention of coming out to meet the babies, or Elijah, for that matter. Geoff again mentioned her coming to see them, but she could see the effort would always have to be on her end. So, she sent pictures and updates and was grateful when she heard back from them. Family was different on her side. Not like Elijah's. His family was multigenerational and inclusive. She knew he struggled, too, having lost both of his parents and having no siblings, but others had stepped in and filled those roles. Joe was like a father, Anna his mother. Echo acted like a sister. Wren learned when she stepped out of the expectations of her family, it meant she was on her own. It was partly her fault for running away, but it still hurt. Regardless of the reasons, she'd been alone.

Until she met Gabe and later Elijah. Through them, she learned family could be anyone and didn't have rigid borders. Gabe was her first love and Elijah wanted to learn about him, to include his memory in their family. They opened their hearts and doors to others, bringing Grayson in as a brother. Then he brought Evan and Memory in to be his family, making them part of Elijah's and Wren's extended family. Wren wanted to explain this to her brother and mother but knew they wouldn't understand. To them, family was blood.

To Wren, family was love.

•   •   •   •

Echo was laughing and waving her hands around, trying to explain something to Grayson as Wren watched with humor and appreciation. This was family. Elijah met her eye and gestured his head towards the door. Wren gathered Gabriella and followed Elijah, holding Elianna, outside. Wren smiled at her little girls and they smiled back toothless. Their skin was golden and each peered out with dark brown, little eyes. Elianna was surrounded by a halo of auburn curls and Gabriella's black curls blew in the wind. They were so much alike, yet had their own personalities and looks. Wren glanced at Elijah.

"I want to learn more about Navajo culture. I want the children to grow up knowing who they are and what they connect to. I know Tse is a native name, but the girls' names aren't. Does that bother you?"

Elijah chuckled and shook his head. "Their names are who they are. It doesn't matter where they come from. Each of them has a name that ties them to their ancestors and family. That's all that matters. As far as traditions, I'd like them to grow up knowing Navajo ways. What about your culture?"

"My culture? Unless you're talking about fast food and strip malls, I don't really have one. My parents didn't teach us anything. I didn't even learn the last name Meyer was German until high school when a teacher pointed it out. I'll ask my mother, but I'm pretty sure that will be a dead end."

"So, we make our own, too. I do believe it is important for children to understand where they come from and their place in the world, but it has less to do with genetics and more to do with an understanding of being human, living on this earth. Respecting what is given to us and our part in taking care of it."

• • • •

That Wren could agree with. She stared out over the farm and saw they were already teaching the next generation. She could see Tse and Drew running out in the field behind them, aware the world they were growing up in would be one where they were there to coexist with their environment, not conquer it. They were fortunate in that way. The world outside of the farm was burning in more ways than one. The farm was a sanctuary and their community a welcoming respite from the realities outside its borders.

She saw it in the trainees who came through. They came in jaded and tired. Within days, their faces relaxed and they found rejuvenation in the soil. As the farm helped to heal the earth, the soil was helping to heal those who touched it. None wanted to leave but part of their teaching was to go out into the world and bring this knowledge.

Gabriella wiggled in Wren's arms impatiently. They'd been standing still too long. She eyed Elijah and he nodded. They stepped off the porch and wandered into the field where they saw Drew and Tse playing. Tse came running by them laughing and yelling, which made the babies laugh all over again. Tse stopped when he heard it and doubled back, tickling their toes.

"Hey, Ellie and Ella." He leaned in close and made faces at them, making them giggle. Tse's eyes lit up and he ran off, his long hair whipping behind him.

"See? Their names make sense. Ellie and Ella," Elijah said and chuckled. "No matter what we'd named them, Tse would've renamed them, anyway."

"In a way, now they both are named after you," Wren agreed. "Elijah, Ellie, and Ella."

Elijah kissed his daughters, grinning. "Was my plan all along."

Wren knew he was joking but acted aghast anyway. "Sly fox."

"We'd better head back, I think this one needs a changing," Elijah replied, wrinkling his nose.

Wren caught the wind and nodded. She most definitely did. By the time they got back to the kitchen, it was full and everyone was chiming in on the Baby Laugh ceremony party. It sounded like it was going to be huge. Thankfully, they had a farm. Wren suggested they invite the families of the current and past trainees, too, so they could partake in the festivities. She and Elijah stepped through and over Memory entertaining Kai on the floor. He was laughing hysterically as she showed him different colored blocks.

They took the girls to their room across from Tse's. After a change, feeding, and another change, the girls were sleepy and happy to curl up together in their crib. Eventually, they'd have their own beds, but for now they only really slept when next to each other. Gabriella turned her head, somehow managing to get Elianna's thumb in her mouth, and began sucking. Wren laughed and rubbed each curly head. Elijah came up behind her, slipping his arms around Wren's waist.

"I'm glad they got your curly hair," he murmured into her own mess of twists and turns.

"Luckily, theirs is a little less. I cried every time I had to brush mine as a little girl. So many knots."

"Mmm... I like it, though."

"Well, at least they got something from me," Wren teased.

"Oh, just wait. I have a feeling they'll look more like you as they get older. I heard freckles don't appear until about two years old," Elijah replied.

Wren groaned and ran her hand over Elijah's unblemished arm. "I hope not. I was teased terribly about my freckles."

"Fools. Those are the map of the world," Elijah whispered. "Besides, who is going to tease them out here?"

That was true. They'd formed a community where differences were embraced and not frowned upon. All the children had their own looks and none of them thought anything of it. Wren leaned back against Elijah, feeling the heat from his body through the back of her shirt. She turned and faced him. His dark eyes beckoned to her and she ran a finger against his smooth, black brows. Beauty was in the differences. He kissed her gently and her body immediately responded to him. Beauty was in how it all fit together.

They slipped across the living room, hearing the chatter in the kitchen, and into their room. They closed and locked the door behind them, stripping off their clothes and climbing under the sheets to explore each other's bodies. Elijah ran his hands down her pale, freckled body and sighed, admiring her curves. His eyes met hers and a smile turned up at the corners of his mouth. Wren traced his high cheekbones and stared into his deep, almond-shaped eyes, moving herself into the slopes of his body. Beauty was in the connection between them.

Beauty was in the soul.

Chapter Thirty-Four

T he morning of the ceremony, Wren was woken up by the sounds of the girls in their crib. She slipped out of bed and when Elijah stirred, she leaned in to kiss him.

"No, I'll get them. You sleep. It's going to be a long day," she whispered.

Elijah opened an eye. "Are you sure?"

She'd heard him get up in the night with them and smiled. "My turn."

The girls were kicking when she got in and she quickly changed them in the crib. She unbuttoned her nightgown and scooped them up, moving to a rocking recliner next to the crib. She situated one on each breast, rocking gently. Normally, someone would feed one while she breastfed the other, but she'd gotten the hang of feeding them both at once. Elijah had bottle-fed them overnight to let her get some sleep. Once they were done, she rested one on her lap while she patted the other, then switched them. She didn't notice Elijah had been observing from the doorway until she put the babies side by side in her lap and sang to them. As she was singing, he came in and kneeled beside her, gathering Elianna in his arms. He sat on the floor and rocked her in his arms as he listened to Wren sing.

"Wow," Elijah said as she finished the song. "Your voice is mesmerizing. Why don't you sing more often?"

Wren blushed. "Nerves, I suppose. It's easy with the babies because it settles them and they just listen."

"I can see why. It's so beautiful, Wren. You should sing more."

"I'm sure with the girls I will."

"Sing for me sometimes. My mother used to, her voice wasn't as pretty as yours, but it used to comfort me," Elijah said as he rubbed Gabriella's cheek.

It was the first motherly thing Elijah had said his mother had done. Wren nudged him with her toe.

"Tell me about her. Your mother?"

Elijah gazed off thinking and leaned back against the crib leg. "She was beautiful. Funny... always made me laugh as a kid. Sometimes she was more like a big sister than a mom, but she had me young, maybe that's why. She wasn't a bad mom, just not like the others. She didn't fuss over me and wasn't overprotective but she talked to me. Asked me questions, told me about the land and our history. She was committed to life on the reservation, even when it was detrimental to us. To her. She didn't trust white people and warned me to be careful around them. That they were opportunistic and selfish. I believed her until I was a teenager and started sneaking off the reservation into town. There I met some white kids and they were fun to hang out with. I did get called names and made fun of about my hair. Not from them, from random strangers. My mother died when I was little, but I could see why she felt the way she did. I was spit on once. Tripped. Guys tried to start fights with me. Refused service at some places. Accused of stealing. It was hard and made me bitter. Then I met Mandy and she was all over me. I liked the attention and didn't see her ulterior motives. Anyway, we know how that turned out. My mother was everything to me when I was little. Even though she could have been more attentive and motherly, she did instill in me a pride in who I am. I miss her and wish she could have met her grandchildren."

Wren chewed her lip and ran her hand across his head and down his hair. "I'm sorry, Elijah. You deserved better."

"So do you. Your mother is alive and won't come to see them."

"Sad but true. But she wasn't all that motherly, either. She never talked to me like a person. I was just her child and she treated me as such. We all had our allotted roles and filled them to the expectation laid out."

"Ouch. That's rough."

"It was. I had to unlearn that. I want our kids to know they can talk to me wherever, whenever, and about anything," Wren replied.

"I hear you talk to Tse. He knows, and these two little imps will too."

The party was in a few hours, so they ate a leisurely breakfast and got ready. Elijah stunned Wren when he came out wearing jeans and a purple, button-down shirt, fastened with a beaded and silver belt at the waist. His hair was twisted into a bun.

He wore a turquoise bolo around his neck and a headband sewn with beads in an eagle design. She stared with her mouth open, wondering how long it would take to undress him. Echo had gifted her a multi-tiered, colorful skirt she wore with boots and an off-the-shoulder blouse. Her hair was loose and she'd controlled the curls with water and oil, giving them definition. Elijah eyed her appreciatively and slipped a turquoise necklace around her neck. It had three little carved birds, separated by silver beads. On either side of the birds, were two larger birds facing in as if to protect the smaller ones.

"Elijah! This is beautiful. Where did you get it?" Wren asked, running her fingers over the cool stone.

"I had it made on the reservation. It represents our family."

"I love it, thank you."

He slid his hands around her waist and winked. "You can thank me later."

Wren felt the heat rising in her. "So, I get two gifts, then?"

Elijah laughed and let her go. "Let me make sure Tse is actually getting dressed."

The children were dressed in their finest. Tse a miniature version of Elijah, and the girls in colorful dresses. As they made their way out, Wren was astonished at how many people had come. People from the reservation, firefighters, neighbors, and some she didn't even recognize. Anna and Joe said a blessing in Navajo and presented the girls to the crowd. Regardless if everyone understood what was going on, cheers went up as the girls were lifted into the air. Elianna laughed and Gabriella cried. The girls were presented with gifts ranging from traditional turquoise and silver to modern toys and clothes.

$$\bullet \ \bullet \ \bullet \ \bullet$$

After the ceremony, the party commenced and Wren hardly saw her daughters as they were being passed around and fawned over. Grayson being the dutiful uncle watched them like a hawk and stepped in to have them changed, fed, or given a break. Wren noticed he and Evan had drawn even closer, hardly leaving each other's side. Memory slipped up a few times, calling Grayson Daddy, and wasn't corrected. Wren thought she noticed Evan and Memory had moved over to Grayson's house.

Later as the crowds ate and played music, Wren found Grayson and pulled him aside. "Hey, Gray. Thanks for helping with the babies. It gave us a chance to mingle."

"My nieces won't be out of sight today. I promise. You and Elijah need time to celebrate, too."

Wren reached out, brushing Grayson's hair out of his eyes. "I saw you and Evan earlier. Seems like you have found a good place?"

Grayson blushed. "We have. I love him and Memory. He told me he realized as soon as he left, I was the love of his life and he'd messed up. He wants to get married."

"Oh! Are you going to?"

"Probably. I told him we needed to live together and make sure before putting Memory through all of that. They moved in last week. She loves her room with sliding doors. Wren, it's like she was always my child. I can't explain it."

"Yes, you can. We've all crossed paths before, remember? Our cells are connected. What about her mother?"

"She is fine with monthly visits. She's a good person, who was handed an unexpected twist. She loves Evan and probably always will. Memory is a connection to that part she struggles with, but she loves Memory. She feels we're more stable to raise her."

• • • •

"That's thoughtful of her. To make sure Memory has a good home."

"It is. I can't fault her, I love Evan, too. He broke my heart when he left, so I got a taste of what she was going through. I want her to be more involved, to be part of the family."

Grayson had the biggest heart and Wren was touched by his generosity when he didn't have to be. She hugged him close and kissed his cheek. "I'm so grateful you came into our lives."

Grayson grinned and turned away, not wanting the attention. "Go on, Wren, find Elijah and spend some time together. I'll keep an eye on the Els."

Wren laughed. The Els. Ella and Ellie. Elianna and Gabriella. "Technically that includes Elijah, but I have him covered. Do you know where he went?"

Grayson pointed over the field towards the woods and a rock outcropping that looked over the land. Wren nodded and headed in that direction. Across the field, she could still hear music playing and sang to herself. When she got to the outcropping, she saw Elijah with his back to her. He was performing a smudging ceremony, waving smoke out over the land. She watched quietly as she heard him reciting something in Navajo with his eyes closed. His face appeared pained but relaxed as he set the smudge down into a bowl. He opened his eyes, though Wren could see he was still far off. His shoulders released and he breathed out as his eyes came into focus.

He hadn't noticed Wren, so she walked up slowly behind him and sang to him. It was a Gaelic song she'd heard once as a girl at a festival and it made her cry. She didn't know what the words meant exactly but she'd learned the song anyway, feeling it spoke to her. She'd found a recording and listened to it hundreds of times until she had it memorized. She hadn't sung it since life before heroin and was surprised she remembered the words. It flowed out of her, along with tears as she embraced the girl who believed in the beauty of the world. Elijah didn't turn and listened to her voice carry over the rocks and trees. She came behind him just as she finished, sliding her arms around him. He rested his head back onto hers and let out a long, gentle breath.

"My Wren. That was beautiful. What language was it?"

"Gaelic. It's about seals who are actually people and come out of the water to shed their seal skin sometimes. I learned it as a teen and haven't sung it since. Definitely not since..." she trailed off. He knew and turned to hold her.

"Thank you for coming to find me," he whispered. "I was trying to send a message of sorts."

"What kind of message?"

"To protect our family. To set my mother free. I worry about the girls having diabetes and was asking my ancestors, including my mother, to watch over them. To protect them from this disease. Wren, I don't want them burdened with this. I don't want them to have to suffer like I did. I think Tse is safe now but they are at risk, because of me." His voice was pained and frustrated.

"Elijah, we're doing everything we can to make sure they stay healthy. You have controlled this since recognizing you matter. Hopefully, neither of them does but *if* it happens, at least they have a father who takes care of himself and can show them how to do the same. We're growing old together and will watch all of our children grow into strong, aware adults. I feel that in my body, in my cells. I can see us with our long, gray hair, rocking on the porch as our grandchildren and great-grandchildren play on the farm."

• • • •

Elijah smiled and kissed her forehead. "I like that."

Wren stepped forward onto the outcropping and closed her eyes. She thanked Gabe for being in her life, teaching her that she mattered. She pictured him laughing with his shaggy, brown hair falling over one eye, as the other sparkled with joy. She envisioned holding him, then letting him go. His image slowly joined the sky and disappeared. She knew he was always a part of her but didn't need to keep him to herself anymore. He was a part of everything.

Wren smiled and let her breath out as she felt a weight lift off of her shoulders. They were both free now. She felt something brush her arm and opened her eyes, half expecting to see Gabe standing there. She met Elijah's eyes and he smiled warmly at her, understanding her in a way no one ever had. He glanced out over the land and took her hand firmly in his. His voice was clear when he spoke, turning her back towards the farm, to the land and community they vowed to protect.

"It's time to go."

• • • •

Epilogue

Five years after the first trainees had joined the Four Directions farm, the cooperative closed on a hundred-acre land deal, allowing the non-profit to establish a permanent camp for post-release inmates to learn a variety of skills, ranging from agriculture to cooking to the arts and everything in between. The farmstand got a second location on the new land and twenty-four cabins were erected, as were classroom buildings. Over the years, previous trainees had moved up and helped run the farm. This was to be their arm to run. Grayson would continue to run the original farm with other graduated trainees who chose to stay on. Elijah and Wren successfully secured ongoing funding and worked with the prisons on establishing other programs around the nation.

Rob and Lindsay welcomed yet another boy into their brood and Lindsay joked maybe having Rob home at night wasn't

••••

such a good thing. Rob got a vasectomy after that, having dropped the ball after Hayden was born. His business was booming and regularly brought on help from the program. He'd made Mike co-owner and as promised, Echo only had Kai to raise. At six years old, he was more than a handful. His siblings visited often and that gave her more than enough child time. She finished her nursing degree and was hired almost instantly at the local hospital. She also taught classes to the trainees.

Grayson and Evan agreed to get married when it seemed the only option to be able to adopt was to be legally married. They'd lived together for years and it was simply a piece of paper, but they had a small ceremony because Memory wanted to be a flower girl. Memory's mother eventually married and came around to being more involved in Memory's life. Grayson and Evan adopted a three-year-old girl from China and kept her name Liling, calling her Lily as a nickname. She was shy but followed Memory around in awe.

As Elijah had suggested, both Elianna and Gabriella developed freckles after age two. Just sprinkled on their arms and over the bridge of their noses, but with their long, wild, curly hair and flashing, dark brown eyes, they were a striking pair. Elianna's hair turned a brighter red in the summer and Gabriella's dark brown hair got streaks of auburn in the sun. Gabriella was diagnosed with diabetes type one at age four. So far, Elianna showed no signs. Elijah taught Gabriella how to test her blood and give herself shots, though he and Wren still did that for her. The whole family ate the way Elijah and Gabriella needed to eat to stay healthy, and never questioned this was a family requirement.

Wren watched Tse, her son, from the kitchen window and smiled. He was sixteen and so much like Elijah sometimes she had to do a double-take. His hair was a shade lighter and when he turned his eyes to her, she could see the copper in them, but he had his father's stance and jawline. At times, Wren forgot she hadn't birthed him because they were so close. He saw her watching and waved with a broad grin. She raised her hand, feeling a pang in her heart. He'd talked about leaving the farm to go to college to study engineering. As much as she wanted him to chase his dreams, she couldn't imagine not seeing him every day. Out of the corner of her eyes, she saw two little figures run towards Tse and he scooped them up in each arm, running around with them giggling in his arms. The twins. The Els. Even though he was unimpressed with them at first, now he was their go-to. At least she had him on the farm a couple more years. He set them down and they clung to his neck so he couldn't stand back up. He kneeled down and gathered them close, pointing at bugs in the soil.

Elijah came in, set his tools on the counter, and muttered. "That damn tractor."

"Just get a new one."

"You know I can't. If it can be fixed, I need to fix it."

"I know. Always the fixer," Wren replied. She stared at the kids from the window and sighed. "I want him to stay."

"Maybe he will. He has to figure things out on his own. You need to let him fly the nest, Wren."

He said Wren with emphasis and she threw a dishtowel at him. "I get it."

She'd come a long way over the years. Not only from prison and heroin but going to therapy helped her resolve her feelings of inadequacy. She knew to be the parent the kids needed, she couldn't be stuck on repeat. She wished her parents and Elijah's had seen that, as well. Regardless, they as parents were breaking the cycle. Their children wouldn't have to feel alone with nowhere to turn. The door swung open and Tse came through with Ellie and Ella clinging to his legs. Elijah pried one off and Tse pried the other off. Wren set a snack on the table to distract them and picked leaves out of their crazy, winding hair. She turned to Tse.

"Hey, Grayson asked if you could help this evening with goats. He is moving them to the south pasture."

"Sure, Mom. Moving the goats will be like dealing with these two wild hooligans," Tse replied, popping a piece of apple into his mouth.

"Hooligans," Elianna repeated and snickered.

"Hoooooooooooooooligans," Gabriella chimed in, shaking her head back and forth, which sent bits of leaves and branches to the floor.

Elijah combed out the twins' tangled hair with his fingers and wound them into traditional Navajo buns, tying them off the yarn. This made them look more presentable but their shrieks of laughter said otherwise. Elijah met her eyes and grinned.

"We should've known that with the two of us this is what we'd get."

Wren wrapped her arms around him, breathing in his scent. With him, she always belonged.

"I wouldn't have it any other way."

Resources

- **Regenerative Agriculture/Conservation-**
  - kisstheground.com
  - nrdc.org/resources/regenerative-agriculture
  - nrcs.usda.gov/wps/portal/nrcs/main/national /programs/
  - greenamerica.org/native-growers-decolonize-r egenerative-agriculture
  - nfu.org/2020/10/12/the-indigenous-origins-of-regenerative-agriculture/
- **Diabetes**
  - diabetes.org
  - diabeteseducator.org/living-with-diabetes/pe er-support
  - angelfood.org/programs-and-pilots/native-am erican-diabetes-project-
- **Prison wildland firefighters**
  - washingtonpost.com/outlook/prison-firefight er-california-exploit/2021/10/15/3310eccc-2 c61-11ec-8ef6-3ca8fe943a92_story.html
  - firerescue1.com/inmate-firefighters/articles/a rizona-to-train-700-inmates-as-wildland-firefi ghters-ikFUy25EIJVr9Q7s/
  - denverpost.com/2021/11/20/colorado-priso n-firefighters-pay/

Acknowledgements

~Thank you first and foremost to our Indigenous people who were forced from their land, yet have continued to teach us how to live with the earth and its species. During my time in NW Nebraska, I had the privilege of learning about Indigenous culture and while I'm no expert, I'm humbled enough to respect and open my mind to what it has to offer. Their ways can save the earth.

~Thank you to all of those prison wildland firefighters who without your service I believe we wouldn't have been able to fight these massive fires, continuing to ravage our land.

~To *all* wildland firefighters, your bravery is noticed and appreciated. To leave your loved ones and walk into the mouth of hell is beyond courageous. You are heroes, but first, you are humans and my gratitude is not enough.

~For all those who've lost their lives fighting wildfires... what can I say? I am sorry. I'm in awe of your dedication and courage. I hope somewhere you are being celebrated for who you are and what you gave to the rest of us. For the families left behind, I see you.

~To Theda. You saw a broken mother and reached out. Thank you.

Made in the USA
Columbia, SC
05 April 2023

14396209R00181